Introductio

Healer of My Heart by Pamela Griffin
Fearing for her life, Seona is smuggled [illegible] her cousin's message and her brooch. In America, she finds a haven with Colin Campbell's warmhearted cousin. But before Seona can tell Colin why she fled Scotland, another shipload of immigrants arrives with men who know part of her story. Can Colin make the colony see the truth? Or will their chance at love turn to dust before it's given a chance to truly flourish?

Printed on My Heart by Laurie Alice Eakes
Now a spinster of twenty-four, Fiona sails to America to find the sister she hasn't heard from in years and to retrieve an heirloom brooch so all will be as it was in the past back home. But for Fiona, the New World holds more than the brooch, if she can learn to set aside foolish superstitions and to trust God. . .and the heart of Owain Cardew.

Sugarplum Hearts by Gina Welborn
When Scottish broker Finley Sinclair bargains he can sell Seren Cardew's entire stock of candy for triple the selling price, she thinks he's out of his newly-immigrated mind. But Seren is desperate to make a go of her fledgling business. With little funds left after selling a treasured family heirloom, Seren knows Finley's proposal is what's needed to save her dream. But on the way, he might steal her stock. . .and her heart.

Heart's Inheritance by Jennifer Hudson Taylor
Niall Cameron arrives in North Carolina to claim his inheritance, but Brynna Sinclair, the local tartan weaver, thwarts his ideas of innovation in order to preserve the town's traditions. Brynna isn't sure she can trust newcomer Niall. Then Niall risks his safety to track down her great-grandmother's stolen brooch, and Brynna worries she's put too much emphasis on the wrong things in life.

HIGHLAND CROSSINGS

HIGHLAND CROSSINGS

FOUR-IN-ONE COLLECTION

LAURIE ALICE EAKES, PAMELA GRIFFIN,
JENNIFER HUDSON TAYLOR,
& GINA WELBORN

Print ISBN 978-1-61626-644-8

eBook Editions:
Adobe Digital Edition (.epub) 978-1-60742-766-7
Kindle and MobiPocket Edition (.prc) 978-1-60742-767-4

All scripture quotations are taken from the King James Version of the Bible.

This book is a work of fiction. Names, characters, places, and incidents are either products of the author's imagination or used fictitiously. Any similarity to actual people, organizations, and/or events is purely coincidental.

Cover design: Kirk DouPonce, DogEared Design

Published by Barbour Publishing, Inc., P.O. Box 719, Uhrichsville, Ohio 44683, www.barbourbooks.com

Our mission is to publish and distribute inspirational products offering exceptional value and biblical encouragement to the masses.

Printed in the United States of America.

HEALER OF MY HEART

by Pamela Griffin

Dedication

Thanks and dedication: A huge thank-you to Theo, Gina, and Mom for all of your wonderful help in critiquing this story. Your help is so appreciated. And to my Lord and Savior, the one true Healer of my heart, who binds all the deep wounds in my soul with the balm of His love, as always with every story I write, I write for You.

He healeth the broken in heart,
and bindeth up their wounds.
PSALM 147:3

Chapter 1

Scotland, in the year of our Lord, 1739

"Be there no other way?" Seona whispered fearfully, holding back. "I canna do this!"

The vibrant gloaming had long faded into the dark of an ink-blue sky, swathing the three cousins in nighttime's shadows. Not another soul moved along the wharf.

The subdued rays of the moon drifting from beyond a cloud caught the sudden moisture in Murdag's eyes. "If ye stay, they might burn you. You know it. I know it. 'Tis the sole way to escape such an evil end!"

Seona clutched her cousin's arm in anxious regret and wished to forget the horror that had brought about this moment. Wished to forget the shocking discovery that led to her flight on foot, from the landlord's lofty home high on the moors to her cousin's thatched cottage over an hour distant, near the waterfront. Murdag had listened to Seona's frantic greeting for aid, spoken not a word to her family gathered inside, and grabbed Seona's arm, hurrying her to a ship leaving for the Carolinas at daybreak. The same ship on which Murdag's brother was a crew member.

"I'm not what they accuse me of being," Seona insisted, hopeful that at last her defense would be heard. "I fear God as much as anyone in Scotland." Still, she could not relinquish her complete trust for protection to the Almighty. Given her history, she felt she could not be blamed for her lack of faith. Nonetheless, she held a reverential fear of the Lord.

"We know the truth, Seona," Murdag's brother Alec assured. "If we didna believe your innocence, I wouldna be risking my neck to help you escape."

"I dinnae wish to burden you, Alec. If your captain discovers what ye've done in smuggling me aboard and ye lose your place as a sailor, I'll find no peace."

"And if ye dinnae leave on this ship, *they will find you* and you'll have no mercy!" Murdag insisted.

"I agree. 'Tis the only way. I would gladly risk my service here, even holed in the brig, than have you risk your neck!" He clasped Seona's shoulder, giving it a reassuring pat, before dropping his hand away. "Ye maun be careful not to be seen till those bound for the colony come up for air. Mingle with them, go below when they do, and 'tis likely ye'll not be discovered. For tonight, hide yourself well. Midship is the companionway—stairs that lead below. . ."

Seona nodded at her cousin's instructions. A temporary shadow blocked out the lantern shining on the deck and caught her startled attention. She inhaled a nervous breath as her eyes made out the form of a man standing at the rail high above yet close enough to see his face. Hidden in shadow on the wharf below, she doubted he could see her but defensively took a step backward, closer between crates that stood ready for loading. Thankfully the man gazed ahead and not in their direction, as if his mind were intent on some grave matter.

The glow of the lantern cast his face in a striking study of golden light and black shadow. His firm jaw and trim, upright bearing suggested strength and authority. His clothes appeared finer in cut and quality than the homespun of the common folk.

"Be that the captain?" Seona whispered to Alec.

Her cousin swung his attention to the man at the rail. "Nay. 'Tis Colin Campbell, an agent for the migration and friend of the captain. You would be wise to steer clear of him, lass. 'Tis doubtful he remembers every face among the immigrants he persuaded to join his colony to know yours doesna belong, but you'd be wise not to take the risk. Be it curse or blessing, you stand out in a crowd. And he is a learned man, as shrewd as they come."

Seona gravely nodded at Alec's warning, her eyes never straying from the tall, unmoving form of the agent.

"Once he leaves, you must board," Alec whispered. "The crates are stacked close enough for you to reach the rail and climb over."

Seona lifted her eyes to the wooden boxes stacked precariously near the hull. She could well imagine herself misjudging distance in the dark and falling to the wharf—not a death by fire, but a death all the same.

Murdag grabbed her arm and pulled Seona from her grim forebodings, deeper between crates and away from Alec. Murdag fiddled with the brooch that fastened her plaid. Since her mother passed on, Seona could not remember seeing Murdag without it. Now she unfastened the silver, bejeweled pin belonging to her mother's side of the family and pressed it into Seona's hand.

"Find Rory when you reach the new land. Tell him I changed my mind, to wait for me. Give him this as a sign that I'll come to him soon, once Fiona fares better."

Despite her worry, Seona faintly smiled, happy for Murdag that she'd made the decision to join her childhood sweetheart. "Then I *shall* see you again." Seona slipped the pin into her pouch hanging at her side and clutched Murdag's hands. "I'll hold fast to that truth to sustain me through the voyage."

Murdag tearfully nodded and clutched Seona's hands harder. "Fare thee well, cousin. May the Lord go with you to this new land and stay by your side as you maun cleave to His. Dinnae let the vain superstitions of foolish men hinder you, but always stay true to your heart and ye will prosper."

Seona squirmed inwardly, feeling that God had long ago abandoned her, but returned the farewell with a sincere heart. "May He do the same for you, Murdag, dear cousin. If not for you, I would be dead."

"Hush." Murdag kissed her cheek. "You'll live a long life, of that I'm certain." Her conviction didn't register in her eyes, which still held fear. But Seona clung to the hope of her cousin's words, all she had left to take with her.

" 'Tis time." Alec's whisper reached them. "Campbell's gone below. We maun be quick about this before any of the crew returns from the village."

Seona nodded and embraced her cousins in fond farewell. She then took Alec's hand as he assisted her to step to the top of the first box and up to the ship that had become her escape but could prove her snare if she wasn't careful.

Above all else, as Alec cautioned, she must stay far away from Colin Campbell.

Colin shut the ledger with the names of the immigrants and laid his quill on the small table provided. The air felt stale, the cabin close. He decided to go topside once more and take in the bracing sea air to stir his dulled mind into attentiveness. Quietly he stood.

"Colin?"

Apparently not quietly enough.

His thirteen-year-old brother stirred and sat up in the top bunk. "Where are you going?"

"Topside." He shrugged into his waistcoat. "Go back to sleep, Evan. The hour is early. 'Tis not yet daybreak."

"I hear noises."

"As you oft will on a ship this size. I expect that you hear the crew returning or the immigrants boarding."

"In the middle of the night?"

"Some will have begun to arrive for the voyage. They come from all over the land, ye ken. You must go back to sleep."

"Colin?"

He sighed. "Aye, little brother?"

"I miss *Mither*."

A dull pain gripped Colin's heart, as it often had these past weeks, since he learned that his mother and sister died of a sickness seven months before. He blinked back tears.

"'Tis just us now, laddie, and I vow always to care for you. But you're of an age that ye must be a man."

"Can I be a scholar like you? And learn books and numbers and letters?"

Colin chuckled at his sudden exuberance. "Evan, you can become whatever your mind and heart dreams ye should be. And aye, I will teach you. But for now, sleep."

As Colin left the cabin, he looked with concern at his brother's wan face against the pale sheeting, doubtful the lad should embark on such a voyage. But Colin had no recourse but to take his brother away from the wicked landlord who'd treated his family as unworthy peons and had beaten the poor lad black and blue with a cane. Upon his return to Scotland weeks ago, Colin had been livid to learn of his brother's gross mistreatment and had taken Evan back with him to the inn the very day of his return.

Moving through the companionway, Colin found that a mist had moved in, obscuring objects in the distance. No matter, he could see directly in front of him well enough and strode along the deck in search of a secluded spot. He heard a few sailors tend to their duties in these early morning hours, and a sentry spoke with two men at the gangplank. All else was relatively quiet.

From out of nowhere, a hooded shape suddenly came at Colin through the mist, with head lowered, and ran straight into his chest. The impact almost knocked the slight figure off her feet, the soft exclamation proving to Colin it was a woman.

"Did I hurt you, lass?" He put his hands to her arms to steady her. In the crystalline mist he got the impression of huge eyes, their color indeterminate. But he did not mistake the long, fiery curls of dark carnelian that escaped from beneath the plaid she used to cover herself.

She gave no answer except for a quick, agitated shake of her head. In their collision, she had lost hold of her pouch and he dropped to one knee to retrieve it for her. Herbs and vials had fallen out, and he suspected her of being a healer. Something silver and round had also rolled onto the deck and he wondered if she was a thief. The mist obscured clarity, but he got the impression of gemstones in a design from an earlier century as he picked up a brooch, wide enough to fit the circumference of his palm, just as she crouched down before him.

"Please, sir, give it back. 'Tis mine."

Her soft voice held a spark of courage now mirrored in her eyes. This close they appeared gray-green or perhaps blue. Her plaid and dark skirts were of simple weave; she certainly didn't look as if she would own such a brooch.

"This is *yours*?"

At his blatant skepticism she stiffened her shoulders and lifted her chin. "My cousin gave it to me. It has been in the family for generations."

He narrowed his eyes, taking in her plain clothing then looked back at the filigree design of the brooch. He brought it closer and noted topaz eyes staring back in the shape of a lion's head. As if sensing his continued doubt whether to turn her over to the captain, she spoke again.

"They are only paste. Of no special value to anyone, save for the sentiment such a piece would bring."

Her manner seemed overwrought, but her tone bore a steady quality that suggested she was sincere. He handed the brooch to her. Quickly she slipped it into her pouch and gathered the remainder of items spilled. He watched, his eyes intent on her face.

As an agent for the Argyll Colony, he had worked to persuade disgruntled men dissatisfied with their oppressive landlords' methods and eager for change to migrate to America but rarely had he spoken to their wives or daughters. Still, he had visited many a township and had a unique gift for recollection. Had he seen her, he would never have forgotten such a face. Oval in shape, high cheekbones, full lips, a long nose that might detract elsewhere but on her face complemented her other features, and skin the color and clarity of rich milk with lips and cheeks of rose and hair that reminded him of red-bronze fire. Even in the mist, he could discern her rare beauty, as rare as one of the gems from her brooch. He could not turn her over to the captain as a thief based on supposition alone; perhaps the piece was an heirloom. He had seen enough gemstones to doubt her claim that the jewels were paste.

"I am Colin Campbell." He picked up a vial that had rolled near his boot and slipped it inside her pouch.

"I know."

"You know?" He saw her wince after she said the words, as if she thought she shouldn't have spoken them.

"I've heard of you. You're in charge of the migration."

"Aye. But how would you know—"

"If you'll excuse me, sir"—her belongings retrieved, she moved swiftly to her feet—"I maun be going below."

"Of course." He also stood. "I imagine your family is wondering where you are."

She gave a faint smile and nod of farewell before hurrying to the companionway.

Colin watched until she disappeared. Something about the flame-haired lass with the spirit to match would not let his mind rest, and as he turned his attention to the dark, fathomless sea obscured by fog he felt that the young woman proved as much a mystery.

Chapter 2

Evan tossed and turned in the damp sheeting. "My chest hurts, Colin."

Colin pressed his hand against the boy's forehead and cheeks. If his skin were cold and clammy and not hot and dry to the touch he could attribute this sudden illness to seasickness, but he'd never known the irksome malady to bring fever. Moreover, the boy spoke thickly and hoarsely, coughing up sputum as if a sickness congested his lungs. This was more than the accursed symptoms of a restless sea. Recalling how his mother and sister died of a fever, Colin panicked.

There was no physician aboard, not among the crew, not among the immigrants; he knew that from his ledger. But there was a healer. . .

"Stay strong, laddie," he soothed, "I'll be back with help soon."

Minutes later, in the ship's hold, Colin searched the faces of people huddled together in conversation, also checking the bunks of those sleeping, but saw no one with the features of the woman who appeared out of the mist. He didn't even know her name; his description of her to those he asked earned him a curious shake of the head or a respectful, negative response—it seemed no one knew of the woman or had seen her. Such a beauty would be difficult to forget, and they were four days out to sea. Surely someone in steerage must have seen her!

Beginning to wonder if in his weariness and loneliness he dreamed the mysterious lass into being, he left the cargo hold. His mind in a muddle, he searched the passageways. A cloaked figure darted ahead as he turned a corner near the galley.

"Wait! You there."

The figure came to a swift halt, turned to look, then swung around and fled.

Both baffled by her behavior and triumphant at his discovery, Colin raced in pursuit, easily catching up to her and grabbing one arm to bring her to a swift stop. A loaf of bread fell from her plaid and to the deck. One glance told him it was the dark rye the captain favored with his meals and not the flat, unleavened *bhannag* given to the crew and the immigrants. His quick mind added up the betraying figures that led to the sum of the truth.

"So, you *are* a thief," he accused, "and a stowaway, too, I'll warrant."

She tried to wriggle away, but his hold remained firm. Her eyes grew rounder, her lashes thick smudges against pale flesh, and faint circles darkened the area beneath her eyes. Her body was strong and slender, though her face appeared thin. He wondered when she'd last eaten.

"Please, sir, I be no thief."

"That is the captain's special bread. Nor have any of the passengers seen or heard of you—explain that if you will."

Colin tightened his grip on her arm, ready to haul her down the passageway and turn her over to the captain, who likely would put her in the brig for the remainder of the voyage. One troubling matter delayed his course of action.

"Please," she entreated softly. "I was hungry. And. . ." She lowered her gaze, "I havena a farthing but will pay back whatever is owed, however ye wish t' be paid, for the bread and the voyage, in whatever way you ask. I vow I will do this."

He narrowed his eyes in deliberation. She must have misconstrued his expression, for she wrenched her arm away. Her eyes—a deep blue-green, he could see now—burned in indignation, a flush of rose coloring her wan cheeks.

"*Almost* in whatever you ask," she corrected. "I could clean for you, wash clothes, do errands, only please dinnae lock me away. I had no choice but to leave Scotland."

"Why?"

Her features grew pinched with anxiety. She shook her head, refusing to answer.

"You beg for my mercy but are unwilling to give me a reason I should extend it?"

"There—there was a man in my village, an evil man. He threatened to—I—I was in danger." Her nervous gaze fell to her shoes.

Remembering Evan's plight under the vicious cane of the brutal landlord, Colin sympathized with the girl. She was fair of face and form, and he'd seen his share of men's wickedness in his six and twenty years. He could well imagine what someone with malicious intent would attempt with such a bonny lass, and it sickened him. A surge rose within, strong and fierce as a sudden gale, to protect this girl, no more than a score of years surely, from any who would cause her harm. Surprised, he tempered the unexpected emotion, not yet willing to trust her. Though, for his brother's sake, she was all he had.

"What is your name?"

For a moment, he did not think she would give it.

"Seona." She offered nothing more.

"Tell me then, Seona, why I should believe you?"

Her eyes lifted to his, entreating him not to deal harshly with her. "I *did* stow aboard. I *did* take the bread. But I meant no harm and will pay you back. Once in America, I—I will find a way."

The fire and courage that first charged her words petered out in a quiet whisper. Her body trembled, whether from the chill, damp air or her dread to be caught and punished he wasn't certain. He couldn't help pity the lass, who seemed naught but a wee slip of a girl dealt a harsh blow of sad misfortune.

Colin made his decision. "Come with me."

He had the strangest feeling that those three words were about to alter the course of his entire existence.

Four days at sea and Seona still felt as if her legs did not belong to her. The wooden planks seemed less than solid beneath her feet as the ship steadily rocked on the ever-changing waves. Sometimes gentle, sometimes tumultuous, and the ship—always moving. She prayed not to fall as she hurried to keep up with the tall, dark-haired agent who pulled her down a narrow passageway and into another. She tried to keep fear from surfacing in her tone.

"Are ye takin' me to the captain then?"

He gave no answer but continued to pull her along in his relentless course to a destination only he knew.

She dug her worn leather soles into the planks, attempting to hold back. "Please, sir, I wish to know what you intend to do with me. Do I not have that privilege?"

He turned on her suddenly, his intense blue eyes wide with disbelief. They burned her clear to her core. "You stow away and I catch you thieving. Tell me, pray, what privilege ye feel is owing to you?"

Stung by his mockery but not knowing what else to say to plead her cause, for the full truth was sure to make him even more an enemy, Seona kept silent.

He tightened his lips in frustration, which brought into prominence a tiny round hollow on each side of his wide mouth, making him seem somehow less formidable. A strange thought, when he towered above her, his captive hold on her arm likely to bruise.

"I'm not turning you over to the captain," he said at last. "You're a healer, my brother needs your aid. If you help to make him well, I'll see that you're not brought to harm."

"Your brother is ill?" she asked, stunned by his true intent.

"Aye."

"Take me to him and I'll do what I'm able."

At her firm declaration, he looked at her in puzzlement as if he didn't understand her. He shook his head, coming to himself, and brought her through the passageway and to a cabin where a boy, frail and wan, tossed and turned on an upper cot. She could hardly reach it and without a word the man lifted the boy in strong arms and carefully laid him in the lower bunk.

One look into the child's bleary eyes and a hand to his clammy brow told her it was not the sickness of the sea that beset him. Sage leaves had helped relieve her pitching stomach but would do nothing for the boy. Hearing him wheeze then cough, she checked the glands in his neck to find them swollen and made a quick estimation of what must be done.

She turned to his brother. "I need water at a boil. A clean cloth. A vessel from which to drink, and a little wine to mix with the healing oil."

The agent nodded and hurried to the door, opening and relaying the order to someone outside. Seona realized Colin Campbell must indeed be important to issue orders and have them obeyed without question.

The next two quarters of an hour she spent devoted to her calling, thankful she'd had the foresight to replenish her supplies the day before her world caved in. The agent watched her every movement as if he did not trust her.

She met his gaze, holding up the cup. "It is the oil from flaxseed. I will give him this to drink and lay a poultice on his chest to remove the sickness from inside."

"I did not question your methods."

"Ye dinnae trust me."

"If I did not trust you, ye would not be tending my brother."

For the third time that night, he took her by surprise. His slow, quiet words made no sense. "How can ye trust, knowin' what you do about how I came to be here?"

His somber expression remained unchanged. "How can I afford to do less?"

Drawing her brows together in curious marvel, she slid her arm beneath the boy's neck and put the cup to his chapped lips. "Drink it down, laddie," she soothed. He looked at her through unquestioning blue eyes, a shade lighter than his brother's intense ones—those eyes that reminded her of the bottom of a slow flame. The elder brother's manner matched the fire's description well: steady and true but dangerous if brought too close. . .

He never ceased watching her, and she hoped she would not need to fight him off during the voyage; she was completely at his mercy. A lamb in a wolf's den? Or had she left the danger behind and found the promise of sweet pasture before her, with a shepherd to watch?

As she worked, she uttered beneath her breath a prayer for the Almighty's intervention for the boy. Once she applied a paste of herbs to his chest and drenched a cloth in hot water to rest atop his skin and release the power of the herbs to work, she wiped her hands on her skirt and looked up at his brother.

"He will recover?" His eyes now rested on the boy, and her heart gave a tiny lurch at the unexpected gentleness found there.

"His lungs will start to clear and he should sleep. Come morning, I will give him more of the healing remedy and change the poultice."

He looked at her, puzzlement again on his face. "You would have helped, regardless of what I said or did not say earlier. Is that not true?"

Wondering if he tested her, she hesitated. "I dinnae understand."

"I offered protection. The manner in which you so quickly agreed to aid Evan led me to believe you would have helped my brother even had I offered no such pledge."

Would he now withdraw his promise of provision? Her heart beat faster in dread and she phrased her answer carefully. "I was taught that each soul is precious. I am skilled to help those in need."

"You did not answer my question."

Her reply could be a snare and she might spend the rest of the voyage incarcerated, but she spoke what was in her heart. "I would have helped the lad, regardless."

He nodded as if he knew the answer before she gave it. Nervously she waited for him to act, wondering if he would now drag her to the captain or take her to the brig himself.

"You look exhausted. I'll arrange a place for you to sleep."

She blinked at him. "To sleep?"

His mouth quirked in weary amusement. "I canna imagine you prefer to slumber standing on your feet. I will make arrangements and tell the captain I need you close for Evan, away from steerage."

She gaped at him. A true cot, with no further need to seek slumber in what concealment she could find—one night piles of hemp, and later, in the hold behind crates—sounded like heaven. She could scarce believe her good fortune. "You're not turning me over to be imprisoned?"

"I said I would help you, lass. I'm a man of my word."

She watched as he left the cabin. Listening through the door he left ajar while he gave orders to a crew member for her lodging, Seona wondered what else the man Colin Campbell could claim to be. Not a sinner, surely. Nor did he seem to be a saint. But his conduct with his brother had been gentle. His eyes, when they had been calm, invited her confidence.

And for one stunned breath Seona MacKay wished to possess the daring to trust.

Nearly six weeks at sea and Colin was no closer to discovering the truth about Seona.

What manner of woman was the slight, strong-willed lass with the riotous curls of ruby flame—no more than a veritable stranger he'd entrusted with the care of his brother? A thief she had proven to be. A stowaway as well.

But *why?*

From her diligent labors to bring his brother to health, he'd seen she was gentle, caring, and kind. Twice he heard the Lord's name uttered beneath her breath in solemn prayer over Evan and knew her to be God-fearing though he could hardly call her righteous. Yet all of what he witnessed in her behavior warred with what he knew of her crimes.

She had helped others, too. When food grew scarce and sickness abounded, she treated those who sought her out after having heard of Evan's recovery.

Yet in the matter of herself, she offered nothing.

When asked, she evaded mention of her past or what had brought her to stow away, frustrating Colin. Given her reason for being aboard the *Thistle*, for the others' safety as well as her own he kept a close watch on her. He felt responsible for her welfare, perhaps in part due to his guilt at not being there for his mother and sister, and refused to let danger come to Seona. And she needed his protection. He'd seen the covetous expressions of crewmen who'd stared at the lass, and didn't like it. Not one bit.

Grimly he caught the eye of a gangly sailor barely old enough to shave. Quickly the boy looked away from Seona and went back to work, picking up coils of rope from the deck. His warning thus delivered and received, Colin approached Seona where she stood at the rail, the salty wind whipping her abundant locks into dancing tongues of fire. She stared out over the choppy sea, a perfect foil for her beauty. Currently it lay in a spread of blue-gray silk with waves tipped by white froth, and her face shimmered, damp from the spray. Her plaid she wore loosely about her shoulders, her lush, womanly curves apparent now that she no longer hid behind the covering, and the wind pressed her dress to her form. Did the lass have no common sense to realize the dangers to which she subjected herself by wandering alone on a ship teeming with roguish sailors? Strict penalties threatened those who would dare harm a woman, even attempt it, but Colin knew that did not stop some men.

Without conscious thought, he stepped up behind Seona and lifted her plaid to better cover her form. It was a pity she had no veil to hide her face.

She turned to him, clearly surprised that he'd taken such a liberty, but pulled the wrap more securely around herself. He wondered why she did not fasten it with her brooch.

"The air is cold. I do not wish you to become ill," he explained weakly, wishing now he'd kept his hands to himself.

Rather than be affronted, she smiled. A mannerism she had indulged in with frequency as the weeks passed. It always made Colin's heart jump then feel warm inside, dispelling the chill that plagued him since learning of his mother's and sister's deaths.

" 'Tis good fortune I'm a healer then."

"I dinnae wish you to require the need for your own remedies."

"I rarely do. 'Tis not often I suffer from illness of any kind."

It was the first she had voluntarily offered information about herself. Rather than expound on her need for caution and the foolhardiness of walking alone, he grabbed the morsel of opportunity she had proffered.

"How did you come to be a healer, lass?"

An instant guardedness sobered her features. "I was

taught almost from the time I was a wee bairn." Her words came stilted, as if she carefully gauged each sentence before uttering it. "My *auld-mither* taught me."

It was the first she had spoken about her grandmother, about any family at all. "She was a healer, too?"

"Aye. Until her death two years ago." Her eyes, which had been bright before, now seemed haunted.

"What about the rest of your family?" His words came gentle.

"Besides my cousins, I have no one."

"And do you plan to join a cousin in the colony?"

"You ask many questions, Mr. Campbell."

"I wish to know more about you and where you hail from."

"Why?"

Why indeed. He had asked himself the same question repeatedly these past weeks, his desire stemming from much more than anyone's need for protection.

"Is it not natural to learn more about each other as we continue our acquaintance?"

She gave a light shrug. "I'm not accustomed to speaking of myself. Nor to conversation."

How odd. She didn't seem as meek as a mouse, though her clothes and admission of having no money did prove she was as poor as one. Had his father never lost their wealth through his foolish gambling ventures, had his parents still lived, Colin knew his mother especially would disapprove of his interest in a lowborn lass who lacked the highbrow, feminine skills she'd possessed. Colin had been brought up in a life of plenty. Up until more than a decade ago, when suddenly he'd been thrust into a life of want and had become *fir-bhaile*, a common middle-class worker. Had tragedy not riddled his family, in all likelihood he never would have met Seona. For the first time he acknowledged some fragment of good had come from his misfortune though he chose not to analyze the root of his satisfaction too closely.

"You did not answer my previous question," he prodded.

"I have forgotten."

He felt her excuse a ploy, in the hope that he might drop the subject. He would not give up so easily.

"Do you have cousins in the new land?"

She hesitated, as if she would keep silent, then quietly shook her head.

"There is no one to greet you?"

The thought of her struggling by herself in a land unknown to her did not sit well with him.

"I'll manage. I've always done so before. . .this happened." She gave a little wave of her hand toward the ship.

He did not doubt her claim. She possessed a determination and courage he'd rarely seen in a woman so young, however foolhardy her idea to survive in the colony independent of others' aid. His mind began formulating a plan.

"And you, Mr. Campbell," she surprised him by saying. She rarely struck up conversation, much less concerning him. "How many voyages to the colony and back to our homeland have you taken?"

"One. I was part of the original party that sailed over three years ago to examine the area."

"Colin!"

He turned to look behind him. Evan waved his arms in greeting as he gamboled along the deck like a young fawn. His face was rosy and healthy, his eyes sparkling and vibrant. No sign of illness remained, thanks be to God and to the unerring dedication of the lass at his side.

"And here comes the reason for my decision to settle there," he mused.

"You love him very much," she acknowledged with something akin to wonder.

"Of course." He looked at her, stunned she would think otherwise. "Evan is my brother. All I have left in the world, and I am all he has."

A swarthy, old sailor stopped Evan's reckless jaunt when the lad nearly ran into him and upset the pail he carried. Ol' Jock shook his finger in Evan's guilt-reddened face in stern warning. Colin had previously cautioned his brother not to race along the deck, to avoid possible mishaps. Such reprimands proved pointless; the boy was full of pent-up energy and too excited to be so close to their destination. Every morning he ran topside to see if he could spot land before the sailor in the crow's nest did.

" 'Tis fortunate to have kith and kin t' care." Her words recaptured his attention. " 'Tis a good thing ye took him away from the man who beat him for missing a day's work when Evan was unwell. Some landlords be pure evil."

Colin detected sorrow in her tone and wondered at the cause of it. "Did you have no one to care, Seona?"

His soft question clearly startled her. From past

experience, he didn't expect her to answer and was surprised when she did speak, albeit hesitantly, as if she feared saying something she shouldn't.

"My mither died giving me birth. My father couldna stand the sight of me. 'Twas my auld-mither who took me in and raised me."

Before he could inquire further, Evan reached them.

"Did ye hear, Colin? Ol' Jock said we should be reachin' land soon!"

Colin raised his brow and crossed his arms over his chest. "That is not all that Ol' Jock had to say, I'll warrant."

Evan had the grace to look ashamed. "I'll be more careful."

Colin nodded. "See that you are."

Excitement again catching hold, the boy went into a breathless spiel of what some of the sailors told him about the colony, asking Colin question after question of what to expect, as he'd done every day since his recovery. Patiently Colin answered each one, though he couldn't help but feel disappointment at Evan's bad timing. Had Seona actually been about to confide in him, or was it wishful thinking on his part? No matter. In every aspect of his life, he was considered strong-minded, never one to surrender in a matter of great import. He would get to the truth and God help them both if she had just cause to fear discovery. For Colin realized he had come to care far more than he should for the bonny lass about whose life he knew so little.

Chapter 3

Bone weary from the voyage, Seona stood close to the rail and eyed the foreign banks of the new land where she would spend the remainder of her days. She only prayed they were full in number and no one from the colony knew her.

During the long journey, her fear had decreased since those immigrants she had met by chance on deck had not known her. And she had at last allowed herself to relax as well as could be expected, with the ever-present threats of storms at sea and starvation when food supplies dwindled. Illness had run rampant. A few had gone mad and jumped overboard. She'd done what she could with what little she had to the few who asked for her aid, but death still took the weakest of their number.

Now, faced with entering a new colony and strangers from her homeland, the threat of exposure returned. At least she *hoped* the settlers were all strangers to her.

"Seona?"

The concern in Alec's voice shook her from her dreary

musing and she turned to smile at her cousin who'd taken a risk to approach her in public. Soon he would again set sail to wherever the captain decided. She might never see him again, and she gripped his arm at the sobering thought.

"Be careful, lass," he said beneath his breath so only she could hear. "May God keep ye in His care."

She met his somber green eyes and felt he conveyed more in his warning than the moment at hand. Tears clouding her vision, she nodded her assurance. He offered a sad, parting smile, stroking the back of his fingers against her cheek, then turned away to resume his duties.

Ever since Colin Campbell uncovered her presence aboard, she and Alec kept their meetings brief and secret. Colin's eyes were as sharp as a hawk's, and while she appreciated his efforts to keep her safe from the men, he could never know Alec was her cousin. She feared if anyone discovered they were kin Alec would be blamed for helping her stow aboard. And he might then suffer the punishment Colin spared her.

In her heart she whispered a fond farewell to her cousin, asking that God abide with him wherever his travels took him next.

Days later, Seona sat next to an exuberant Evan, Colin on the other side of the boy as they took the last leg of their journey on one of several longboats that had left Wilmington a week ago to travel along the Cape Fear River—not a name that inspired the reassurances Seona craved, nor had their landing instilled ease: The *Thistle* had run aground, brought to shore by a storm. Yet all had survived their arrival.

The boy had not been the first to sight land as he'd hoped, but Alec, with the captain's permission, had allowed him to climb the netting to the crow's nest, allowing him to peer through his spyglass for Evan's first sight of his new home before the sudden squall had hit. Later, impressed with the boy's agility and eagerness to learn, the captain told Evan if he ever desired a life at sea there was a place for him as a crew member on his ship.

"Thank ye kindly, sir," the lad had replied. "But I'm going t' learn letters and numbers and books and be an agent one day, like me brother."

Seona also hoped to learn what she needed, to survive in this foreign land.

Not as mountainous as her former home, the Carolinas appeared covered with fine white sand and laden with thick forests of tall trees, among many Colin told her were long-leafed pine. He also told her that these trees burned like paper! Here there was no peat to cut in the bogs to provide fuel for their fires.

What she had seen of this new world was beautiful and wild, not as breathtaking as her rugged Highlands, which was barren in comparison with its lochs and moors. These hills here were less steep and jagged, flowing in gentle slopes. She found it odd, however, that in their week of travel along the river she'd not yet spotted one keep.

"Be there not one castle in all of Carolina?"

Colin chuckled, not unkindly. "You will find no castle in

these parts, lass. I've never gone beyond the Argyll Colony to know if any exist elsewhere. The land here is fertile, as you see from the abundance of plants. Many will choose plots of land to farm. There are cattle and sheep to herd, too, and animals for hunting and trade of pelts."

"What will you do?"

He gave an embarrassed smile. "I'm better with books than I am with soil or a gun, though I can plow, aim, and shoot well enough to keep meat on the table. When the opportunity arises, I plan to offer my services as a clerk."

"Be there wolves and bears about?" Evan asked hopefully.

Seona shuddered. "Och, why should you wish for such dreadful creatures?"

Colin smiled and tousled the boy's hair, clearly understanding his thirst for adventure. "The forest teems with wildlife. Black bears. Wildcats, snakes, lizards. Also a creature called the alligator. It swims in water but crawls on its belly on the ground. It resembles a lizard, to some extent, growing in length over the size of a man and bearing what must be a hundred teeth. I saw one with its mouth wide open once."

Evan eagerly scanned the waters, as if hoping that one of those horrible, many-toothed mammoth-like lizards would surface. Seona shivered again and Colin met her eyes over the boy's head.

"Never stray far into the forest and you should fare well," he assured. He didn't say the words, but his eyes held a promise that he also would see to her protection.

Seona never planned to step foot outside the walls of

the settlement. By nature, she wasn't a timid soul and had endured much; at nineteen she bore no cowardice. But animals far bigger than her and with mouths full of sharp teeth she preferred to keep their distance, the farther, the better. Yet the creature she most feared, the superstitious sort who walked on two legs and knew of her past, that sort she feared even a strong and respected man like Colin Campbell couldn't protect her from.

The hour of reckoning fast approached.

Seona found herself almost wishing they would return to Wilmington and head back out to sea.

Colin noticed Seona stumble and put his hand to her arm to steady her. He had no need to ask the cause. His legs also felt unsure and strange after stepping on the first solid ground in months, one that didn't pitch to and fro held up by restless waves. Their journey had ended, but grim matters awaited. First he would tend to Seona's needs, then he would help one of the men bury his good wife who had died on the journey upriver. Such a sad state of affairs; to have come so far and be so close.

Seona stumbled again. "Take my arm, if you have need," Colin urged, again feeling a rush of protection with regard to the lass. The land was so wild; what could she be thinking to have traveled so far and have no family to take care of her?

"I can manage well enough, thank you."

He tempered a sigh of frustration. "So you have proven. But there are times all men have a need to rely on others. 'Tis the way of things."

"For two years I've had no one to give me aid."

"And now you do."

She seemed about to argue the point further but he shook his head. "Take the offer in the spirit it was given, lass. I have no desire to quarrel."

She kept silent and he forced his mind to the issue at hand, of finding Isabel. After weeks of sleeping in a bunk too small for his tall frame he felt thankful that on his previous voyage, with the aid of other men, he'd foreseen the need to build a small cabin where he and Evan would reside. It was the one reason he'd not bided the coming winter in Wilmington, as many but not all of the immigrants had done. He'd also had help in crafting a large bed and acquiring a feather tick, where he could rest comfortably. With evening approaching he and Evan had their needs met. If his plan was successful, Seona would also have a place to lay her head.

The ground was rough to the weary and those not accustomed to land and a third time she stumbled. To his satisfaction, this time she took his arm. Soon they reached their new home.

"Welcome to the colony, lass."

She stood in the clearing and stared at the lofty trees. "This is it? There be only one building!"

"Aye, a postal office. Dinnae look so horrified." He chuckled. "Now that many more have come to make this their home, you will see a true settlement take shape."

"But there be no walls," she said distantly.

"None but the trunks of the forest surrounding us."

To Colin's relief, Isabel suddenly appeared through the trees. Catching sight of them, she dropped her bucket and hurried forward, her face glowing with delight.

"Evan, how you have grown, my laddie!" She exuberantly embraced the boy. Evan seemed awkward and Colin wondered if he remembered her. "Colin. . ." She smiled and held out her hands. "You look fit. The voyage was without troubles?"

"What voyage is without troubles? The Lord brought us safe passage."

She nodded. "Thanks be t' God for that!"

He returned her fierce hug, grateful to note the dark smudges were absent from beneath her eyes. "You look well, Isabel. The land agrees with you."

"Fighting off bears and other wild beasts who get close to my chickens has been something of a challenge."

He noticed the twinkle in her eye but Seona's face went ashen.

"And who is this bonny lass?" Isabel asked.

Seona eyed her warily, taking a small step back. Colin noticed but Isabel appeared not to.

Isabel's smile grew as she looked between the two of them standing side by side. "Colin, have you gone and gotten yourself wed? Aye, for certain my eyes dinnae deceive me!"

Stunned by her blunder, his face growing hot, he could only stand with mouth agape. Seona snatched her hand from his arm, her cheeks going rosy. Evan sniggered. He would be sure to give the boy a sound word later.

"I am Seona," she said when Colin failed to speak.

"I am Isabel, Colin and Evan's cousin. How long have you two—"

"We're not married," he put in hastily before his brash cousin could cause further embarrassment or irreparable harm.

"Oh?" She looked between them. "It seemed so, with that gleam in your eye and the way you two were standing so close—"

"Actually," he interrupted, remembering well his cousin's fondness for gleams in others' eyes and the meaning she construed for them, "I had hoped you might be of help, Isabel."

"How so?"

"Seona has no family. She came across the Atlantic alone—"

"Say no more." Isabel looked at Seona. "You maun stay with me. I live just a piece beyond those trees."

Incredibly Seona seemed about to refuse then hesitated as if thinking better of it. She murmured a soft thank-you and lowered her lashes.

An uncertain quiet settled among them.

"Well then." Colin awkwardly cleared his throat. "There is business to which I must attend. I leave you in good hands."

Anxiety clouded her eyes as Seona lifted them quickly his way, but the emotion disappeared as swiftly as it came and she only nodded.

He wished he knew what worried her but felt it pointless to ask. He had tried many times to invite her trust, and she was just as determined to avoid speaking of her situation.

Somehow, Colin would find a way to change all that.

Seona studied her new home in a strange dread mingled with relief.

A small cabin of logs that held a covered porch, Isabel's home looked sturdy enough, though there wasn't one rock wall to enclose it, nor, in fact, anything but trees that towered on all sides and likely held a multitude of fierce creatures. Her persistent fear of walking into a village filled with superstitious townsmen ready to do away with her vanished when she saw how remote the area was. Only one other cabin of the same ilk stood a fair distance away, and Seona squinted against the sunlight that flickered through leafy boughs, wondering who lived there.

Her curiosity was satisfied when Colin's tall, lean form moved through the open entrance. She gasped and pressed a hand to her racing heart before dropping her arm back to her side. She hoped she looked more confident than she felt. He caught sight of her and took the step down from his cabin then moved across the mossy, leaf-strewn area between them.

"Hello, Seona. Are you settling in well?"

How could his voice, just hearing him say her name, have such an effect on her senses to rob her of the power of speech? She'd heard him every day for nine weeks without such a reaction. . .not such a strong one, anyhow.

She cleared her throat. "Well enough."

"Good. I must attend to some matters. We will talk more later."

She gave a sober nod in return, realizing one of those matters was to help one of the men dig a grave for his good wife, a kind woman Seona spoke with a few times during the voyage. Seona had noticed that Colin never felt himself beneath any task, always lending aid where needed, whether it be intellectually, in solving problems that had arisen during personal conflicts between immigrants, or in manual labor, as he did now.

She watched him walk away, his stride confident. Flustered when she realized Isabel stood behind her on the porch, watching them, she directed her gaze to another area of the forest. Colin's cousin came up beside her, looking to where Seona stared.

"'Tis a good sight different than Scotland, but no longer are we beholden to the unjust landlords. Here, we carve our own life, no longer serfs but owners of the land and exempt of taxation." She turned to Seona and smiled. "'Twill be nice to have another woman about the place. I've been lonesome, since my husband and daughter passed on, coming on three years now."

Seona knew she'd hardly been approachable upon meeting Isabel. Yet if they were to live together she must work to be companionable. She'd spent over two years fending for and keeping to herself so she found the prospect a challenge.

"I'm sorry for your loss."

"Aye." Isabel gave a sad smile. "Ursula grew ill on the journey over. She died not one month after we landed and staked our home. My good husband, rest his soul, died from an attack of the heart whilst he built our cabin." She motioned toward it. "I have lived alone ever since." A sudden fit of coughing overtook her. "Come inside. The wind stirs up the dirt."

Seona followed her into the cabin. The main room held an open hearth, a cupboard, a loom, and one table and three chairs. An alcove with what looked like a plaid, only larger, hung above and shielded the room where Isabel must sleep.

"Leave the door open," she instructed when Seona moved to shut it. "I only close it before I turn in for the night." She coughed again and shook her head in disgust, lightly patting her throat.

Seona watched Isabel take a bottle from the cupboard and measure a small amount in a tin cup. She looked at Seona. "Pine tar and honey. Colin tells me you're a healer. . . ."

Seona remembered seeing the cousins together earlier and felt uneasy to realize she must have been the topic of their conversation.

". . .And you saved Evan's life." Isabel drank the mixture, grimacing at the taste. Clearly the honey did not help sweeten the bitterness.

Seona fidgeted. "I did what anyone would do."

"Nay, not anyone." Isabel looked at her thoughtfully. "You maun show me what you have learned. I, too, have an interest in home remedies."

"I have nothing left." She patted her flat pouch at her side. All of her herbs, tinctures, and tonics were depleted in helping other passengers aboard ship.

"Ah, lass. Plenty of herbs grow in the colony's forest, some like Scotland's I expect."

For the first time, Seona smiled. Isabel seemed a kind soul, tolerant of Seona's ways, even intrigued by them.

She grew eager with the idea of sharing what she knew then sobered. "Is it safe?" She looked out the entry toward the trees beyond Colin's cabin, as if expecting a furry mammal to appear and come charging toward them. "Because of the bears," she all but whispered.

Isabel laughed and picked up a rifle leaning against the wall. "They canna hear you, lass. Have no fear; we'll not go unarmed. Here in the colony, there be less likelihood of running into a dangerous beast than of taking yer chances with a pitiless landlord from our homeland. Though some, myself included, would call them one and the same."

Seona wondered if she spoke lightly to assuage her fears. Otherwise, why take such a weapon if the risk was not great?

"I imagine ye'll want to keep such adventures for later and rest after your journey. Ye may have the cot Ursula used. We can wait another day to inspect the grounds."

The weariness Seona earlier felt had departed upon arriving to the colony and seeing her fear of discovery unfounded. She had no wish to lie down. The desire to replenish her supplies with herbs—and learn the value of new ones—tantalized her hopefulness to begin the search.

Remembering Murdag had entrusted her to issue a different search, for Rory, she carefully phrased her next question.

"The settlers that came before, with you. Where do they abide?"

"Some near, some far. All live within these lands of the

Duke of Argyll, a third cousin of Colin and my husband's. Now that the first shipload of settlers has arrived, men will gather to build the town."

Seona stood immobile with shock. Colin was related to *a duke*—the *owner* of this land?

She had known he was well learned with books, being an agent for the migration. She did not realize his family claimed nobility. He never acted superior or cruel, such as the few men of wealth and title whom she'd had the misfortune to meet. And it was through one such encounter her life had come to danger and she had been forced to flee Scotland.

No! she sternly and silently reprimanded herself. She must desist with this. The days of fear and superstition were another continent behind her and good riddance. She had escaped certain death, had survived storms and starvation. And bears or no bears, like Isabel, she would carve for herself a life in this new land.

Chapter 4

With arms folded across his chest and leaning against the frame, Colin stood just inside his cabin and stared out the open door at the log cabin across the way. A slow and steady rain fell, as it had been falling without end since yesterday, and he felt cooped up like a rooster in a henhouse. Yet no womenfolk shared his abode, though he had begun to hope one lass might consider it in the future. If he could ever work past her frustrating wall of defense to ask her, that is.

Two months had elapsed since they landed on the shores of the Carolinas and Colin knew as much about Seona now as he did then. Which amounted to nothing. He was sure she kept more than one secret hidden, the mystery that composed her mounting daily. What he felt uncertain about was why she still mistrusted him. Had he not proven to her he had her welfare at heart? Had he not protected her from sure imprisonment aboard the *Thistle* and found her sanctuary with Isabel upon their arrival to the colony? At least the two lonely women had formed a kindred bond. He only wished Seona would consider him a friend as well.

"Colin?" Evan's exasperation could be heard from across the room. "I dinnae understand this problem."

Colin unfolded his arms and moved to the table where Evan pored over an open book in front of the hearth. He leaned over the lad and patiently explained the mathematical equation.

"Will we be eating supper at Cousin Isabel's?"

"Not tonight, laddie." He wondered if his brother had heard a word he'd said.

Evan looked displeased with his answer. But he had been coughing lately, almost as bad as Isabel, and Colin didn't want him to get chilled in the rain. He knew he was becoming worse than a mother hen, but the boy's lungs were weakened from all that he'd suffered and he would not lose him as he lost his mother and wee sister. He had not been there to help them; he would not make the same mistake with his brother.

"Seona might wonder where you are."

At his mischievous tone, Colin sharply turned his head toward the lad.

"We've had supper there every Sunday, though I dinnae understand why we canna eat there every even'."

"Aye, Isabel would like having two more mouths to feed."

"She wouldna mind."

"It will not kill you to eat the meat I cook. Or to roast it yourself."

"Cooking is woman's work," the boy grumbled then coughed.

Colin curbed his tongue from a reprimand and pushed

away from the table. Isabel had been feeling poorly and he had no wish to overburden her with caring for them.

"If ye married Seona, neither of us need cook again."

Evan's words shocked Colin a second time. "Whatever put such an idea into your head?"

He chose not to tell the boy he'd been considering the prospect for months.

"Why else do you stare after her? And mumble her name in your sleep?"

Did he?

Flustered, Colin shook his head. "You can no' qualify such a profound statement on the basis of a dream, lad."

"What?"

"Never mind. I'll fetch the bottle of pine tar and honey Isabel left for you. You should take another dose."

Evan scrunched his nose while Colin pretended not to notice.

Seona stared out the open door, catching a glimpse of Colin walking through the main room of his home. She flushed hotly to think he might have seen her staring toward his cabin, but then there was no crime in looking out one's door, was there? And the cabin was always smoky from the turpentine in the lamp oil so the need to take in fresh air was vital.

"Something must be incredibly interesting for ye to stand so long and stare at the everlasting rain," Isabel murmured in amusement from behind as she worked at the loom. "Is it comin' down in colors now? Or flying upward perhaps?"

Seona grinned at her foolish teasing. "Nay. 'Tis the same as always. Silver and falling downward. Though the sky be an interesting shade of brown."

Isabel chuckled as Seona teased her back. In the two months since she arrived, a slow friendship had formed between them. Isabel showed her how to keep house, how to cook, and how to use the loom to weave cloth. She'd also shown her how to tend the few animals and chickens she owned. Seona valued her friendship yet felt thankful that besides the initial question of her former life in Scotland, Isabel had not again crossed that line since the first time Seona told her she did not wish to remember what happened there.

But she did remember. Every day.

And every day she feared discovery, though their cabin stood remote from other settlers' homes yet too close for comfort from the town's emerging settlement. The one person she wished to see still had not made an appearance. She hoped Rory had not left the Carolinas bound for some distant colony and that she would be able to give him Murdag's brooch along with her message.

She fingered the silver medallion where she kept it, in her pouch she often wore slung across her shoulder and hanging at her side. She rarely took it off, hoping she might run into Rory at some point, wanting the brooch with her in case that should happen.

Had matters been different, had Murdag's mother married Seona's father, as he once hoped, instead of his older brother, this might have been her brooch and Murdag her younger sister. Often during the voyage Seona had wondered if she would have been heir to this treasure—given by the queen to one of Murdag's ancestors for an act of bravery—if matters might have been different. The brooch would fetch a handsome price and certainly Seona could have avoided the perilous fate that had been hers to bear after her grandmother had passed on and the townsfolk began to regard her with greater suspicion than before.

Shivering at the memories, she ducked her head and fished the brooch from the mouth of the pouch, looking at the shiny lion's head with topaz jewels for eyes. At times, to her disgust, she thought of keeping the heirloom and selling it, should she again find herself trapped and needing to escape and make a life elsewhere. But she was no true thief. And Murdag was as dear to her as a sister. She would never betray her trust.

With a faint sigh and an even more determined set to her shoulders she slipped the brooch safely back into her pouch and breathed deeply of the moist air.

The climate wasn't as cold as Scotland's chill nor had there been snow yet, only rain. On clearer days, with the ground not so slippery with mud and water, some of the men left the surrounding homesteads to help build public buildings for their colony. Isabel told her that she and the other women had insisted to the men that they wanted a church straightaway, though there was yet no minister. Seona knew from Colin that requests for a Scottish minister had been delivered, but he also told her that another shipload of immigrants wouldn't leave Scotland's shores until the following year, if then.

Seona still had difficulty putting her trust in others, especially in the Almighty. But neither could she forget that she'd been saved from unjust punishment and death, had been protected during the difficult voyage by an important man who could have been to her an enemy but wasn't, at last finding sanctuary in a stranger's home where she'd been sincerely welcomed. And the bears had thus far kept their distance.

Murdag had prayed for her welfare. Colin said he did as well. Even Isabel offered petitions for Seona that she'd overheard. Seona wanted to believe God would protect her always, but she'd spent so long looking after herself, to turn her life over to another was frightening.

Please. . .help me to trust. Show me who I can trust. . .

In silent petition she asked for guidance, hoping her brief prayer was not in vain, and as she watched, Colin's figure again filled the doorway.

He stood there, staring, while she stared back.

A sheet of slow-falling rain fell between them. Neither of them moved. Despite the distance, Seona felt something unseen link them together. She could barely draw breath and had the oddest urge to step out into the rain, to run across the muddy ground and join him. She wondered if he felt the strange connection, too, when he took a step forward onto the covered porch then stopped.

He looked over his shoulder back into his cabin, and she assumed Evan asked him a question. Colin returned his gaze to her for several lingering seconds, as if undecided, then turned and walked back inside. Shaken by the encounter, her heart beating fast, Seona also stepped away from the door.

Chapter 5

At the sudden crack of a twig, Seona turned in surprise to see Colin behind her, where she knelt on the ground at the fringe of the forest. The days of endless rain and light snow had concluded and spring had come. The ground at last dry, she wished to take every opportunity to replenish her stores, not knowing what the weather of this new land would hold next.

Flustered at the sight of him, when she had been thinking about him almost every minute of every day for weeks, she smiled softly and dug in her pouch for the sprigs of leaves she had just plucked from a small tree.

"Sassafras," she explained, having recognized the fragrant scent and texture from her homeland. "To help Evan."

Isabel had recovered from whatever malady once clouded her lungs, but the lad's cough persisted.

A tender expression filled Colin's eyes. "You have a kind heart to think of the boy."

"You've done much to help me. 'Tis the least I can do, though I could never begin to repay you."

"I dinnae want or need your money, Seona. I've told you that before."

"I have none to give." Surprised that he seemed almost upset, she shook her head. "I meant no offense. 'Tis only that I'm grateful and wish you to know it."

He said nothing, and she wondered at his strange behavior. Every Sunday for the past month he'd come with Evan to Isabel's cabin, to share their supper. Of late he seemed quieter, brooding, and often Seona caught him staring at her, an inscrutable look in his eyes.

Awkwardly she rose to her feet. "I apologize if I insulted you." She kept her gaze lowered. "'Twas never my intent." Before she could sweep past, his hand latched on her arm, stopping her. His hold caused no discomfort, but the heat of his grasp warmed her skin through the sleeve and she hitched in a little breath.

"Seona, it is I who should apologize. Please, don't go. I had hoped. . ."

"Yes?"

He smiled softly, dropping his hand from her arm. "I had hoped you might walk with me."

Her heart gave a mad little jump. This was the Colin she had come to know, warm and companionable and arresting. That he could so scramble her senses with one crooked, dimpled smile that spoke of both mischief and innocence—and alter her breath with one engaging look from heavily lashed eyes of the deepest, purest blue—was beyond disquieting.

She gave a nod of assent, not trusting her voice. He

offered his arm to her as if she were a fine lady and he a great lord. He never treated her as anything but special, though she was little more than a serf and his family held a dukedom, however distant in relation to him. Confused by such attention when she'd never known it before meeting him, at the same time touched by his consideration, her heart melted with a tenderness she'd never felt for anyone, and she realized her feelings for Colin had grown deep. Perhaps too deep.

They walked along the fringe of the forest, Colin filling her in on the latest news of the colony. He spent his days away from the cabin, when it didn't rain, and on the days the rains came, he tutored Evan.

Seona grew pensive, a thought budding in her mind. But he had done so much for her, she could not ask it.

"What is it, lass? What is it you wish?"

At his gentle query she looked at him in surprise that he should know her thoughts. "'Tis foolish," she hedged.

"Let me be the judge of that," he persuaded.

"All right. Would ye be willin', that is, perhaps when ye come to the cabin for dinner one night. . ." She took in a breath. "Would ye be willin' to teach *me* to read, too?"

She hoped he didn't think the idea foolhardy for a woman of simple breeding and was rewarded when he stopped walking and turned to her, his smile inviting.

"I think that would be a fine idea."

The warmth in his eyes seemed to trickle into her heart; her skin flushed with the sensation. His eyes grew intent as they looked deeply into hers. A change seemed to alter the air around them. It felt as if a physical force pushed against her chest, making it difficult to breathe.

"Come," he said, his voice quiet as he slipped his fingers around her elbow and resumed their walk. "There is something I wish to share with you before it grows too dark to see."

She looked to the west, noting the sun had dipped lower than she first realized and silently questioned the logic of walking farther from their cabins with night descending upon them. With Colin, however, she felt safe.

He took her through a break in the trees. "I came across the spot last week when hunting for game," he explained, and she gasped when they entered an area of the creek heavily shaded by the boughs of long-leafed pines. A fall of water rushed into a pond from a ledge of rock as tall as she stood. "If you remain very still," he whispered near her ear, standing partly behind her where they were hidden beyond the low-lying branches, "you might see something special."

Holding her breath, as much at the nearness of Colin as by the expectation of what would come, Seona waited. A branch cracked nearby. Alarmed, she took a step backward against him and reached behind to clutch his arm.

"A bear?" she whispered and turned so that she could see into his eyes. Her action brought her closer to him than she realized, his mouth only inches from hers.

"No bear," he whispered. "Only a raccoon. See." His eyes flicked past her a moment then returned to her face. She directed a swift glance to the pond's edge and the small, furry creature. Her heart beat hard and fast, but no longer in fear of a wild beast. She licked her lower lip in uncertainty, her eyes again finding his. The blue in them had darkened, his gaze intent.

"Seona," he whispered, his fingertips lifting to her jaw.

She felt his faint touch like a brand of fire. Her lips parted, her eyes lowering to his mouth. For a breath of time neither of them moved, then slowly he leaned in and brushed his lips over hers. Her eyes falling shut, she clung to his shoulders, certain she might faint. With a little groan, he increased the pressure, drawing her into his arms, and kissed her more deeply. When he pulled away to look into her eyes, both of them were breathing fast.

"I will not apologize," he said, his voice husky. "I have come to care strongly for you, lass. My heart is bound to yours and has been since I first saw you aboard the *Thistle*."

She exulted to hear what must surely be his profession of love, but doubt ate into her conscience. She pulled back and his eyebrows drew together in uncertainty. "Do ye not have the same feelings for me?"

"No—that is, yes. I—I do care, but. . ."

She broke off, loath to explain her fears.

Relief at her admission filled his eyes but he persisted. "What has you so frightened? It is more than bears, I'll warrant." His voice came deep and soft, coaxing her to trust him. "Do I scare you?"

"No." Her response came incredulous and swift.

"Then what does?" He took gentle hold of her upper arms. "What had you stow aboard a ship and flee from Scotland, lass?"

Alarmed that he so aptly targeted her chief concern, she tried to step back but he would not release her.

"Dinnae ask for such confidences, Colin. I canna give them."

"Why can you not?"

She shook her head in frustration. "'Tis not in my nature to trust."

"After all we've been through together, you still believe I would bring you harm?" Hurt disbelief filled his words.

"No. I just—I cannot," she ended helplessly. If she told him the truth, he would despise her, and she could not bear his suspicion or hatred. "Please, Colin. Dinnae ask me again."

Great sadness filled his eyes. "A bond without trust is doomed to fail." Softly he released her. "If ye cannot put your faith in me for a matter of the past, there is no hope for a future together."

Hot tears pricked her eyes at his solemn words. In disbelief she looked away, so he could not see the pain they caused.

Their love was over before it had been given a chance to flourish?

The silence stretched thick and heavy between them.

"It will soon be dark." His words came short and clipped, and she gave a little startled jump to hear him speak so suddenly. "I maun get you back before Isabel worries."

She wanted to apologize for her silence, to plead with him to change his mind, above all, to open her heart to trust him. But she said nothing, nor did he, the entire walk back to the cabin.

Seona set her hands to work, hoping to force her mind to forget.

Isabel came into the cabin just as she set aside a bowl of berries she had picked on her hunt for more herbs. With many of the colony's plants she yet needed to learn their full use, but Isabel was a wise teacher. Some herbs were similar to those in Scotland; others were dangerous or deadly. In the week she first arrived, Isabel just prevented her from touching a plant she spoke of as poison sumac, warning it would severely harm the skin. In Scotland Seona had needed to be aware of other plants, such as the poisonous hemlock, which would kill. Again, she became something of an apprentice, but felt confident that she could continue her calling as a healer.

And some of the settlers had sought her help, through Isabel.

Seona at first had been anxious to accompany her friend to their homes, to aid the sick or wounded who had no knowledge of the remedies that grew in their midst. Sequestered away as she was in the small cabin Colin had arranged for her aboard the *Thistle*, often taking in the sea air when none of the other immigrants were above, she'd never met all the ship's passengers. Colin told her that over three hundred Scotsmen came to this new land. She presumed she had seen or met perhaps fifty on board ship during the two-month voyage, and most had stayed behind in Wilmington when they first landed to await the spring before choosing their land. Now, as the days elapsed and she met some of those colonists, all strangers to her, her fear of discovery once again dissolved.

"Hello, lass," Isabel greeted with a cheery smile, breaking Seona from her reverie. "My, but the place looks well kept! You've been busy." She set down a basket filled with goods.

"Do you think both Colin and Evan will join us tomorrow night?" Seona hoped Isabel couldn't hear the wistfulness in her tone. "I thought I would cook, you've been so busy, and wondered how much food to prepare."

"I canna say. Evan will be here but Colin has been busy of late and absent from the cabin."

Seona knew that but had a strong sense Colin's excuses were only that, his absence deliberate due to his anger with her refusal to speak of her past. It had been over two weeks since their talk in the forest. Would he avoid her forever?

"I visited the trading post today." Isabel began pulling items from her basket. "Three of the men returned from their trading expedition. They stayed the winter with natives. One man seemed very interested to learn that you're here."

Seona's heart ceased to beat. "You told them about me?"

Isabel looked at her in confusion. "Is there a reason you wish to hide?"

Here was an opportunity to confide in her friend, to at last share her great burden. . .

Seona shook her head. "I'm only surprised."

"I spoke because one of the men was injured. His arm was badly cut two days ago, and I told him that you're a healer and he maun come to the cabin to seek your aid. He was surprised to learn of your presence in the colony."

Seona clutched the back of the chair. "Did he give his name?"

"Nay, 'tis sorry I am. We didna talk long."

Seona collected her breath, telling herself she made too much of Isabel's words. Perhaps he was only surprised to hear that a healer lived among them. . .not to hear that the healer's name was Seona, the same who had fled being burned at the stake by an angry and superstitious mob.

Chapter 6

Colin felt as crusty and low as a barnacle on a ship's hull for the manner in which he'd treated Seona.

He should have been more understanding; he knew that whatever curbed her tongue was her greatest distress. Her heart was wounded, enough to flee her homeland for fear of reprisal. At least that's what he gleaned from the little he managed to eke out of her during their voyage.

In truth, he *had* been busy, but his wounded pride had been what prevented him from seeking her out. He'd seen the hesitant, uncertain looks she'd given, when he would return home and catch her gaze as she toiled outside. But he had only nodded briefly and turned away.

Tonight, he would go to her.

Armed with new resolve, he took the path home then stopped in his tracks, shocked when he noticed Seona speak with a stranger in front of her cabin. In the twilight he made out a burly man with a dark beard. Seona put her hand in his and clasped the back of it with her other one. The man looked down. Suddenly he grabbed Seona's waist and twirled her around, both of them laughing, then set her back down on her feet and kissed her cheek with gusto.

Colin felt as if he'd been punched in the stomach. Seona didn't appear one bit upset by the man's familiar advances. Quickly Colin sidestepped, so they wouldn't see him. Seona never told him she had an admirer or beau. But then, Seona rarely told him anything.

Where had she met the man? She seldom left her cabin, and Colin wondered if he was someone from Seona's past. He must be, and she appeared well pleased to see him.

Capping the hot spurt of jealousy proved difficult, and on into the next morning Colin fought resentment as he left his cabin to visit the growing town site. He had taken every opportunity to stay away from Seona these past weeks, visiting others, helping with accounts, even putting his hand to a hammer, though he was no builder just as he was no farmer. He saw no reason to change his habit.

Isabel caught up to him before he made it to the path.

"Colin, where are ye off to in such haste?"

He muttered something noncommittal then remembered his manners and gave her a tight smile. "Hello, Isabel. You look as if you're faring well."

"Not that you'd know it," she said with a scolding lift of her eyebrow. "You've not been to see us of late."

"I've had much to do."

"Mm." Her tone suggested she didn't believe him. "And will ye be joining us for supper tonight?"

"I doubt I'll have the time—"

"You have to eat."

"I might not be back before dark—"

"She asked if you would be there."

"She asked?"

Isabel's eyes twinkled with ill-contained mirth that she had rightly discerned the source of his agitation. "They were the first words out of her mouth when I returned from the trading post yesterday."

He glanced past her, to the cabin she shared with Seona. "Perhaps I might be able to return sooner than planned."

Isabel laughed outright. "You are smitten, cousin!"

His face heated like fire. "No matter. She doesna trust me."

"I say she does."

"She won't speak to me of what ails her. She never has!" He let out the core of his frustration.

"Give her time. She's not the same frightened girl who arrived last year. Aye, she struggles with her troubles, whatever they may be, and it is often I pray for her soul to find peace."

He nodded tensely, having done the same.

"Look to the Lord, Colin. Look to see all that He has done. You survived the crossing over the waters, not once, but three times. I have no need to remind you that not all survived once. Put your faith in the Almighty, as your good mother taught. Even after tragedy befell your family, you struggled and stayed strong. Trust Him to help you through this difficulty as well."

Her gentle words calmed his troubled soul. Patience never had been his fortitude, and he often prayed for more of it. How easy it was to forget past victories in the face of present difficulties.

He smiled at his wise cousin in gratitude. "Evan and I will both be at supper."

Her answering smile was huge. "'Tis pleased I am to hear it."

There was still the matter of the man who had been so familiar with Seona, but Colin had no claim on her life and shouldn't feel as if he did. With Isabel bringing up his tragic family history, perhaps therein laid the answer. If he confided in Seona of his own past misfortunes, she might feel more at ease to be open about hers.

He was acting like a prying fool but couldn't seem to help himself. He wanted to know everything there was to know about her. He only hoped he wouldn't blunder tonight and make matters worse.

Seona's eyes focused on her task of placing venison and beans on plates, but her mind was fixed on the guest sitting behind her at the table. He had agreed to come, and she still could not believe it.

For weeks she had mulled over their last meeting and came to the conclusion he was right. If she couldn't trust the man she loved, then they had no future together. Warm tingles rippled along her skin at attaching such an emotion to Colin, but she couldn't call it by any other name. He had been kind to her and faithful to keep his word aboard ship. In order to survive, she *had* become a stowaway and thief, but, except for their initial altercation, he never treated her as anything less than special. If he could extend such consideration when she wasn't deserving of it, surely he wouldn't be harsh when he learned of the past she had run from, the past of which she *was not* guilty, contrary to the belief of many in her homeland.

Her decision made, she felt as if a burden had been lifted from her soul. But once they ate supper and Isabel excused herself, asking Evan to come with her outdoors to help feed the animals, Seona's stomach again prickled with anxiety. Her pulse raced, her sense of awareness heightened. Colin rose from the table and walked toward the hearth fire, the suddenness of his movement making her jump a little in her chair.

"I noticed you had a visitor last night," he said quietly.

Confused, she looked at his profile. "Yes. A friend from Inverary."

"A friend. Ah. You did seem quite taken with him."

He closed his eyes softly as if trying to seek patience, and she parted her mouth in astonished disbelief when she heard a slight ring of jealousy in his tone. She smiled faintly. At least he still must hold some interest in her.

"His name is Rory Stewart. I had a message to deliver to him from my cousin, Murdag. It was her brooch you saw me with, to seal the message that she would soon join him. He was very happy to learn that with the next ship to come from Scotland he would gain a wife. He simply couldna contain his joy."

At the blithe candor of her words, his shoulders relaxed

and he turned to her, contrition in his eyes. "I thought. . ."

She nodded. "I know."

He exhaled a lengthy breath and shook his head. "It seems I also have much to learn on the issue of trust."

His light retort and faint grin made her heart race, but the crux of his reply left her trembling with the knowledge that the time had come to speak. She wrung her hands nervously in her skirts. Before she could drum up the nerve to say what she must, he pulled a chair before the glowing hearth, then a second one.

"Please, lass. Sit down with me by the fire. I have something I maun share with you."

The solemnity of his tone made her stiffen with a new concern, and curiously she rose from the table and took the chair across from where he sat.

"When I was a lad, my family never wanted for anything," he began, holding his hand with the other, his elbows propped on his lap as he leaned toward her in confidence. By the agitated manner he rubbed his thumb against his palm, Seona could tell this was difficult for him.

"My father was prone to gamble. That one vice became the bane of our existence, especially my dear mother's. She was raised in a genteel society and didna know how to manage with so little. The funds dwindled, you ken. Many were the nights we had no meat on our table. One of my sisters died because Father could not afford a physician's medicine. The day came when he lost everything and we barely had enough to scrape together. Evan was a wee bairn then; he doesna remember and 'tis the sole blessing of our misfortune for which I'm grateful. No lad should have to witness what I did at the age of thirteen—seeing my father's body lying in a snowdrift, the handle of a dagger sticking from his back."

Seona gasped in horror, and Colin's eyes fell shut. "They never found his killer—the brigand stole away. I swore as a boy I would one day find him and seek vengeance. Mother was devastated but maintained enough faith to help me through my struggle. Once I grew into a man, I traveled here with the other founders of our colony, hoping to find a better place for my family. I *did* find it. . ." Colin lifted his eyes to hers, blinking away the tears that glistened there. "But upon my return to Scotland to collect my mother and siblings, I found two graves to greet me. My mother and sister died when a harsh winter hit. Evan is all I have left."

Moisture burned her eyes at the tragedy of Colin's past, her misery twofold.

She ached for his pain, feeling closer to him than before, but dare she tell him her burden now, what with his father's unsolved demise and the hatred Colin bore? Did he still wish to seek vengeance? Would he believe her equally wretched story?

And she, too, had run away.

She wasn't given a chance to decide as Isabel and Evan walked through the doorway.

Colin quickly stood facing the fire, his back to them, and briskly wiped his cheek on his sleeve. Seona wished she could so easily wipe away her past—oh, why couldn't she have met Colin under different circumstances? Before that horrible morn when she, too, had stumbled across the body of her most despised enemy—and had been running ever since.

Chapter 7

To speak of the past helped Colin, more than he first realized. Isabel knew, of course, but Isabel was family and had watched much of his life unfold. Seona had been the first person with whom he had shared the heartache.

In Seona's presence the pain ebbed, and time spent in her company became precious. She was to him the essence of beauty and warmth—her very features depicting the sentiment in the fire of her hair and the glow of her eyes—but she still grew coldly detached when he would probe into her past. Through sheer force of will, he learned not to push, and lately, she had divulged bits and pieces of her history, childhood memories of life with her grandmother. When she spoke of the woman, a faraway glint troubled her eyes, but Colin kept quiet, knowing that to nudge her led to sudden silence.

As the months fell away, one into another, he watched her grow, her fledgling faith watered with the godly wisdom of Isabel and what nuggets he could share from his own hard-learned experiences. Visiting their neighbors to give aid had given her a sweet confidence, and she'd made friends with some of the women. He taught her to read and write and was amazed at how quickly she adapted to the skill. Much more swiftly than Evan, though he didn't tell the lad that, not that it would have mattered or generated envy. The boy regarded Seona as if she hung the moon and scattered the stars. If he were ten years older, Colin had a strong suspicion they would be rivals for her heart.

He chuckled wryly at the thought as he came near where she knelt in the grass among a wild patch of dandelions. She loved the outdoors and often he found her there, once she got over her anxiety that a bear might appear every time she set foot outside her door.

She looked up and smiled. His heart constricted to see her regard him with delight. Soon, he would again speak. She had begun to trust him, giving what she could manage in sharing of her old life, and he had learned to be more patient. Surely, there must be a future for them.

A melancholy look touched her eyes. "'Tis a pity how the wind comes to steal their fragile blooms away." She lifted one stem, almost completely denuded of white froth.

He crouched down in front of her, taking the stem from her hand. "Aye. But 'tis that same wind that carries the blooms of this one flower over the land, to find root in the ground and make more. You could say it sacrifices itself to ensure that others of its kind will be given a chance to grow."

Her expression softened. "I love the way you put things, Colin. You're a wise teacher."

He smiled at that. Isabel would laugh and tell him it was

just a useless weed and his head was full of poetic nonsense. Seona understood him; in many ways they thought alike.

"Will you come to town with me, lass? There's a meeting this afternoon to deal with several issues that have arisen. The women will be there with their husbands and families. Afterward we will sup together."

He was encouraged to see her face light up with the prospect.

"I would like that, Colin."

Her manner was shy as he held out his hand and helped her from the ground. The desire to draw her close and kiss her came strong, but he curbed it and nodded. "I maun go tell Isabel. She will likely wish to take food to share."

"I baked a loaf of bread. I can bring that."

"As long as it's not dark rye with molasses."

At his jest of that long-ago day aboard ship, when he caught her filching the captain's supper, she laughed outright. At the delightful sound Colin couldn't help but draw her hand to his lips and kiss it.

Her eyes widened, the message in them bringing his pulse to a faster beat. He pulled her closer, to give her the kiss for which she silently beseeched him. Evan chose that moment to appear and greeted them with an exuberant shout and a wave. Colin sighed, releasing her hand.

"Until later, sweet lass."

He turned to acknowledge his brother but didn't miss the glow in her eyes at hearing his endearment. And in that moment, he made up his mind.

He would speak what was on his heart this night.

Seona walked beside Colin, with Isabel and Evan trailing behind, to the area that once held little more than a post office at a crossroads. She was amazed at the progress the men had made. Six new buildings stood in the area, as yet with no signs on their fronts, so Seona didn't know what they would be. The sweet aroma of freshly sawed timber from the felled trees came to her in the cool wind, a refreshing smell after the misty rain they received yesterday.

Like the emerging town, Seona had made progress. Slowly, she had reached out to the God Isabel told her about—a good sight different from the fearsome being her grandmother had taught her to fear. Outside, among the plants she enjoyed, she had drawn near to her Creator and in so doing found a measure of peace, a strange but pleasant calmness of spirit she'd never known existed.

Her next step on the road to trust would be to share with Colin and tell him everything.

Every day that passed she felt the desire to do so come more intensely. Colin surely would not react in the negative ways her mind had dredged up months before when faced with the fearful prospect of telling him what he wished to know. He no longer harangued her to get at the truth; instead he held back, though she realized how strongly he desired to persuade her. And it was in his prudence and consideration for her feelings that Seona grew to believe he would never harm or think evil of her.

Tonight she would tell him all he wished to know. For

now, she would enjoy being escorted by what surely must be the most handsome and eligible bachelor in all the Carolinas.

Many settlers had gathered at the town site by the time they arrived. Seona nodded in greeting to several citizens she recognized and had treated. Rory stood between two men and gave her a huge smile and wave. "Hullo, Seona," he called. "Fair weather we be havin'."

"Aye. 'Tis nice to be without so much rain."

"Would you like to go over and speak with him?"

No jealousy rang in Colin's tone and she turned her smile his way. "Later. I wouldna wish to intrude. I should visit with the women." In the small crowd of ladies, she noticed two young lasses she'd never seen before. They looked around the area with interest. One settled her attention on Colin and pulled at the sleeve of the other to say something.

"Did a new shipload arrive?" she said more to herself than to seek an answer.

The second woman looked their way, her eyes filling with suspicion when they lit upon Seona. A strong dread washed through her the moment before the shout came.

"Witch!" a boy's voice cried. "*'Tis the witch!*"

Seona's peaceful world crumbled as she turned slowly to face her accuser and saw the lad who had unexpectedly turned a corner of the stables half a year ago—to find her standing over the landlord's dead son.

Chapter 8

Colin swiftly looked around the area to find whom the boy was yelling about. From that moment, everything happened so swiftly he could hardly follow the events.

"It *is* the witch!" a man cried. "Grab her 'afore she gets away this time!"

Colin watched two strangers run toward and past him. He spun around to see Seona had backed up and now both men held her arms.

She struggled between them. "I'm no witch!"

"You lie, Seona MacKay." The man who had spoken walked toward her. "My son saw you standing over Gregor's body! 'Twas the evil herbs you gave that saw his demise."

"I gave him no herbs. I gave him nothing. I had just arrived—he was lying there, dead, when I came upon him!"

"Again you lie. 'Twas no secret the fool had his eye on you. Many a time you were overheard warning him away. You murdered him with your devil witchcraft to rid you of himself."

A crowd gathered. Colin stood among them and watched the proceedings in a daze of horror, shock muting his tongue.

"How did ye escape the punishment owed you?" the man continued. "Did ye fly across the waters to escape the stake? Is that how ye came t' be in this land?"

"No, please." Tears shone in her eyes. "You dinnae understand. Ye never have—"

"She's a witch like her auld-mither! That woman cast a curse on the village 'afore she died."

"She told MacGrady she had a dream of his dying and a week later he was stone dead!"

"Angus MacGrady was three score and seven. My auld-mither grew senile at the last—half the time she dinna know what she said—"

"'Twas the devil that spoke through her mind!"

"'Twas the sickness. She was ill!"

"She was a healer—could she no' heal herself?"

Seona gave no reply.

"And she passed her evil works to you!" the leader exclaimed.

"Burn her!" someone cried.

"Tie a millstone 'round her neck and throw her in the river to drown!"

The alarming threats broke Colin from the manacles of profound shock that had him bound and he rushed forward. "Let the lass go," he ordered in a voice not to be refused. "Anyone who lays one more hand on her will answer to me."

The two holding her looked uncertainly at their leader. He narrowed his eyes at Colin.

"And who might you be?"

"I'm Colin Campbell. An agent for the migration and one of the founders of this colony."

"Then mayhap ye dinnae know—the wench be evil, a handmaiden of the devil. She maun be destroyed. Only then will the evil be cast from our community."

"This woman is *not evil* and she is certainly *no servant of Satan*." Colin glowered back at the man. "Did anyone see her give the man she was proposed to have killed herbs before his death? *Anyone?*" He looked around her circle of accusers. They looked at one another, uncertain. "I thought not."

"The boy saw her standing over Gregor's body!"

"I told you, I got there only moments before he did."

"Silence, witch!" The man raised his hand to strike, but Colin grabbed his wrist.

"I wouldna try that if I were you." His voice came deadly silent and the man's eyes flinched. He growled, yanking his hand away from Colin's grip but stepped back. "I said unhand her," he directed his order to the other two men.

They looked between themselves then let her go. She rubbed one arm where they had gripped her hard.

"'Tis likely she's cast her spell upon ye that ye canna see truth," the leader said.

Colin forced a calm he didn't feel. He wanted to throttle the man—all of them—for their ignorant superstitions. "'Tis far more likely that you cast grave aspersions on a woman's character without having all the facts."

"Others from the village have heard her chant over the sick!"

"Chant?"

He looked Seona's way. Still she would not look at him, her eyes downcast.

"Explain that, if ye will, witch," the man snarled at her.

"While tending my patients, I pray to the Lord above for their well-being," she said quietly. "I'm no witch."

Colin remembered hearing her do the same for Evan aboard ship. "If that is considered a sin, then ye best throw all of us in the river," he said, his voice deathly still.

"She escaped her punishment in Scotland by flyin' across the waters to this new land!" the boy argued and his father agreed.

"She did *not fly*. She came by way of ship, as all of us did."

"If she was on the ship, how come we never did see her?"

"She spent most of her time helping my brother, who would surely have died without her aid. For that purpose she dinna live or sleep in the hold with the rest of you lot. Nor did she take her meals there. As to why you never crossed paths when spending time on deck, perhaps divine Providence prevented the encounter so you wouldn't toss her in the seawaters before she had a chance to be heard. She said she had no hand in this man Gregor's death and is no witch. I believe her."

He marveled at the ignorance of some men that they could put faith in such implausible tales. He also had grown up hearing superstitions of their land, his daily life infiltrated with them. But once he became a man logic told him what was true and what was false. He prayed a silent prayer for guidance to persuade her accusers to give up their foolish witch hunt. He wished these men and their families had stayed in Wilmington and away from the colony.

He looked at the other settlers he'd come to know these many months, shocked to see doubt etched on some of their faces.

"Surely you dinnae believe the nonsense these men have spoken? Tavish—was it not her skill with herbs that healed the gash in your leg when it grew septic?" The farmer looked somewhat remorseful. "And, Duncan—did her tonic not aid you with the illness you fought a fortnight ago?" At the trapper's grudging nod, Colin turned his attention to all of them. "Have any of you heard her speak one heathen word? Seen her do one evil deed?"

A woman Colin recognized as Maggie, one of the farmer's wives, stepped forward, her child in her arms. Alarm clenched his middle, making it difficult to breathe, as he waited for what she would say.

Shyly she looked at Seona and the newcomers' leader, then swiftly turned her attention to Colin. "When me wee Keitha was badly sick, she gave her plant medicine to heal her and stayed by her bedside for hours. I heard her pray to God to strengthen her and make the fever go away. I dinnae believe anyone who prays t' the good Lord for a stranger's child t' be a witch."

"Pway!" Keitha cried gleefully and gave an endearing little laugh, then bashfully hid her curly head in her mama's shoulder.

A few in the crowd chuckled.

Colin could have kissed the woman for speaking up and

the child for saying just the right word in learning to talk, thus lightening the heaviness in the air. He just held back from embracing them both.

"I think Seona's actions speak for themselves," he said, facing her tormentors again.

"What about Gregor's poisoning?"

"Do you know for certain he was poisoned? Did you consult with the physician who tended the body?"

The two men who'd held Seona captive looked at each other. "No sane man would have lingered for the landlord's arrival tae learn the truth," one admitted. "They were tyrants, the father and the son. 'Twas the landlord's order the woman be caught and burned for witchcraft, but we dinna stay to see it carried through. We were preparing to leave for the ship the day his son died."

Cold fear gnawed through Colin's gut at just hearing the words. The last woman he'd heard of who was proclaimed a witch—for giving birth to a child with deformed hands and feet—had been burned alive a little over a decade ago in Dornoch. A powerful landlord who wanted to make anyone suffer in his desire to strike out in revenge for the death of his son could easily find a way to mete out such injustice on Seona, with those in power supporting him and with the theoretical proof men such as these had gathered against her.

He maintained his calm though he wanted to grab Seona and run deep into the forest where no man could find them. "Unless and until you can bring proof that she murdered this Gregor, the matter should be closed. The woman you describe doesn't resemble a citizen of this colony. Nor do I agree with you that she's a witch based on the ambiguous grounds you've given. I say Seona MacKay is no witch. Others here who've come to know her and been helped by her generosity agree with me."

The men looked undecided. The leader appeared sullen.

Colin turned to include everyone. "We came to this colony to find a better way, a new start—freed from all oppression. Let us not begin this new life by making the same mistakes of those landlords whom we left, and oppressing one of our own."

Several men in the crowd nodded in agreement.

Rory stepped forward. "Colin speaks wisely. I have known Seona for years. She is none of the things these men say."

"I agree. Colin is a man I would put my trust in," a farmer he recognized as Finley MacBride said. "Even my life. He's proven his intelligence and always has been one to lend a hand where needed. If he says we should drop the matter, I'll have no more of it."

A general murmur of approval went up and the leader looked at Colin.

"You're making a mistake you may come to regret."

"I'll take that risk." He barely prevented himself from lashing out with words, managing to keep his tone quiet. He took Seona by the elbow. "Come," he said quietly.

Moving past the men who stepped away from him on both sides, as if he were Moses parting the Red Sea and escaping the Egyptians, Colin walked with Seona toward the stillness of the forest.

Seona's mind still in a whirl—one moment sure she would be tossed in the river as fodder for the many-toothed creatures there, the next walking with Colin and away from her would-be executioners—she struggled with what to say.

"I wanted to tell you. I planned to tell you tonight." She shook her head. "MacBride spoke well—you're a man to be trusted—I've learned that."

Colin said nothing. Her sidelong glance showed the tension pulling his jaw tight.

He was angry with her.

He had every right to be.

She had been too late to speak but at least could try and remedy the matter with what none of those men had known. "There is more I maun tell you. Gregor did more than make his interest known—he tried to have his way with me, but I fought him off. Two days later I found him dead. Both times, someone came unexpected. The first time was a blessing. The last time became my curse. . ."

They walked through the fringe of trees, blocked from view of the others.

"And my auld-mither went senile two years past," she went on, nervous when he did not respond. "She spoke to flowers and trees as if they were mortal and said the oddest things that made no sense. As if she was no part of this world. They might have burned her, had she not died. But she was no witch either—oh!"

She exhaled a surprised breath as Colin stopped walking

and brought her swiftly around, pulling her into his embrace. "Dear God. . ." he whispered in what sounded like a quiet benediction of humble gratitude. Immediately he pushed her away, holding tightly to her shoulders, his expression both stern and frantic. "I almost lost you. If public opinion had not gone in my favor. . . Seona, I canna bear the thought of living life without you!"

"You spoke up for me," she whispered, her heart beating fast at his emphatic response.

"Of course." He looked confused. "I couldna let those men harm you! I would move heaven and earth to ensure your safety."

"Then you believe me innocent? Of all they accused me?"

His eyes grew gentle. "You are no more a witch than I am a sorcerer. Anyone who takes the time to know you knows that."

"And Gregor?" she asked quietly, remembering his feelings toward his father's escaped murderer. "He was a beast, but I would never kill a man."

"I believe you. I think no ill of you. I could never. . ." He shook his head and brushed away the tresses that clung to her damp face. "In these months we've come to know one another, you've become the healer of my heart. I believe God sent you to fill an empty place I thought no one could. Seona, I *love* you."

Her heart flooded with joy at hearing the cherished words—and at his warm, tender kiss that followed his whispered but fervent proclamation. She melted against him, at last beginning to feel whole again. Just as she had helped to heal the void in his life, he had done the same for her.

He softly broke their kiss to look into her eyes. "My sweet lass, I was wrong to expect so much from you so soon. I fear I scared you away those first months. Though had I been prepared I might have been able to prevent what just happened," he added wryly, and she lowered her eyes in remorse. With his fingertips against her cheek, he brushed his thumb along her chin. "After this, after what could have happened, I find I can wait no longer. And now I must ask for even more from you. . . ."

She looked at him, bemused, and he smiled.

"Will you become my wife, dearest Seona?"

She gave a laughing sob and could only nod as she slipped her arms around his shoulders. Colin responded with a heartier kiss that warmed her all over. He embraced her fully, picking her up where she stood and holding her against his strength.

"I love you, Colin Campbell," she whispered once he set her down and she again had the breath to speak. "I would be proud to call you Husband."

"Seona MacKay. . ." He smiled. "At last I know the surname of the woman who captured my heart, though I pray she will relinquish the name soon." His eyes glowed with his excitement. "I dinnae wish to wait for a minister to come with the next ship. Let us go to Wilmington and find a man of the cloth to marry us there."

His words sounded like manna to one who'd been starving; she had wished for his love for so long she could not recall the day she first realized it. "Aye, Colin. I want that, too."

She had escaped Scotland without a hope and a prayer, and in her new home had found acceptance and faith. . .and, along the journey, the incredible man who had taught her the meaning of both.

Epilogue

One year later

Seona could barely contain her enthusiasm as she swaddled her daughter, Finella, in a soft woolen that Isabel had made for the child. Her husband stood at the door, patiently waiting, his bright eyes alight with his smile. As she neared he bent to place a kiss on his daughter's forehead, then leaned down further to brush his lips with Seona's.

"If I could bottle the joy on your face, I would make a fortune."

She laughed. "How can I be anything but joyful? I have you for a husband, our wee Finella, and today my happiness is made complete."

He smiled and rested his hand at the small of her back. "Are you ready then?"

She nodded.

"Evan?" Colin called to his brother. "Are you coming with us?"

Evan had been the one to bring the news, and he could barely stand still for his excitement. A wide smile splitting his face, he ran to the path.

"I take that as a yes," Colin murmured in amusement.

Isabel poked her head from her cabin. "You two go ahead," she called out to Colin. "The meal will be waitin' for all of you on your return."

"I was beginning to think I'd never see this day," Seona admitted as she walked beside Colin along the sun-filled path leading to town.

"Where is your faith, woman?" he teased, and she grinned.

"It's been a learning experience, but I'm finding my way."

"We all suffer through the steps, my love. 'Tis like a voyage. Leaving all that one knows behind, in uncertainty and hope, sailing across dangerous waters, at last arriving to the promised destination. But the voyage of faith is everlasting, to be taken again and again as long as we live on this earth." He gave a gentle rub to her back, where his hand rested. "And you have come through many of them unscathed."

She regarded him in wonderment. "Perhaps you should have sought to be a minister instead of an attorney, though the people are blessed to have you and know it."

Ever since he stood up for Seona against her accusers, other settlers had sought Colin's aid in their injustices, and the step to representing them came natural. It was what he felt he'd been called to do.

"I never thought I would see the day when I looked forward to a minister coming here." She looked at him suddenly. "You do think they sent one?"

"If not, they will send someone to officiate soon; we've sent enough correspondence asking for it."

"I hope Murdag received mine." Once she learned how to form letters to flow and link together to look legible, she had written her dear cousin often. At the end of every letter, she bade Murdag to join them soon, telling her about the colony and what she could expect when she arrived. Since Rory had no ability to write, Seona often added little tidbits from him that he would relate to her and she would pen at the bottom.

She knew Rory must be excited. He had gone to Wilmington days ago to trade his pelts and surely must have been there for the event.

At last they arrived to their destination beside the river.

"There's Tomas!" Evan ran ahead, catching sight of someone he knew. People milled about, in clusters, disembarking from longboats—a few she recognized from the colony, others were strangers and looked bone weary. She remembered her own arrival and the exhaustion from traveling. At last she spotted Rory's husky build and there, standing next to him, the owner of a sweet face that hadn't changed and she thought never to see again. Tears clouded her eyes the moment Murdag looked her way.

"Cousin!"

The two women rushed toward one another. Awkwardly and eagerly they embraced, Seona holding her baby, Murdag carrying a cloth bundle held to her chest with one arm. Finella gave a sound of protest at being muffled between them.

Drawing away, they laughed at their situation. Murdag set down her bag and put a gentle hand to the babe's thick russet ringlets. "Hello, Finella, I'm your cousin," she cooed. "She's as bonny as you said in your letters."

Finella smiled bashfully, lowering bright blue eyes, and Seona felt thankful that the fussiness of last week had ended; the cutting of her tooth must at last be complete.

"This is my husband, Colin." Seona motioned to him as he walked up with Rory.

"Colin, 'tis a pleasure to meet you at last," Murdag said, taking his hand in both of hers. "Seona wrote of all ye did for her aboard the *Thistle* and afterward, and Alec told me also, on his last visit home. I'm pleased to make the acquaintance of such a fine man."

"Anything I did, Seona gave me far more in return. If not for her, my brother might not be alive today."

"Aye, the good Lord has given our Seona a powerful gift, t' help and heal others."

Embarrassed, Seona turned the subject from her. "How is Alec?" Since Colin had become her husband, she had confessed her cousin's hand in her escape. To her surprise, Colin wasn't upset but had responded with amused relief—thinking "the gangly redhead" had been her ardent admirer, admitting on a few occasions he had seen them speaking together from afar and had come close to throwing him overboard due to his "interest" in Seona.

And she had thought they'd been so sly to evade his knowledge!

"He's still very much the seafarer, though he said when he's ready to grow roots in the soil he'll join us here." Murdag's face grew brighter. "But I have news I've not shared." She looked at Rory, slipping her hand through his arm. "I also have a husband."

Seona's eyes widened in shock. "Murdag! You two were wed?"

"Aye, once her ship docked I wouldna wait another hour," Rory chuckled. "Of course, when I told Murdag there be no minister in our colony yet, it did help to aid her decision."

"Och," she grinned. "Foolish man. Why else do you think I crossed an ocean if not to marry you?"

Overjoyed for her cousin, Seona hugged them both and Colin offered his hearty congratulations, having learned of their story through both Seona and Rory.

She felt grateful that Murdag at last realized her dream of wedlock to her childhood playmate and sweetheart. Their love had withstood much, proving faithful over the years, each of them committed only to the other despite problems within their families that prevented the union. Colin and she had not had as lengthy a relationship or endured anywhere near as much strife, but through the past year of marriage their bond of love had grown stronger with each day and Seona was certain it could only improve.

As the four walked along the bank, the two women between their men with Finella resting her head on Seona's shoulder, Murdag slipped her hand into Seona's free one. "I knew in my heart when I sent you off that night that God would be faithful to protect you. And He has. He brought about good from the troubles and gave you a new life. Just look at all He has done!"

Seona smiled secretly. "More than ye know." Or Colin did, for that matter. She had not yet told her sweet husband, she would share alone with him tonight, but she strongly suspected that she was again with child. She squeezed Murdag's hand as they moved toward the growing settlement, blissfully content to have her loved ones all around her.

"Once we bade one another a tearful farewell, but that unhappy time has long passed. Now I bid you joyful welcome, dear cousin, to our Argyll Colony."

Pamela Griffin lives in Texas with her family and fully gave her life to Christ in 1988, after a rebellious young adulthood, and owes the fact that she's still alive today to an all-loving and forgiving God and to a mother who steadfastly prayed and had faith that God could bring her wayward daughter "home. Pamela's main goal in writing Christian romance is to help and encourage those who do know the Lord and to plant a seed of hope in those who don't.

PRINTED ON MY HEART

by Laurie Alice Eakes

Dedication

To Gina, Jennifer, and Pamela, for being
such a supportive and talented team to work with.

And it shall come to pass, after that I have plucked them out I will return, and have compassion on them, and will bring them again, every man to his heritage, and every man to his land. And it shall come to pass, if they will diligently learn the ways of my people, to swear by my name, The LORD *liveth; as they taught my people to swear by Baal; then shall they be built in the midst of my people.*

JEREMIAH 12:15–16

Chapter 1

Cross Creek, North Carolina
October 1758

The ropes burned Fiona MacGill's wrists like rings of fire, and she stiffened her shoulders, bracing for the whip to blaze across her back. Two days in Cross Creek of the North Carolina colony, and already she was a criminal, a felon, sentenced to a whipping for showing no signs of employment.

"As though I haven't done the looking, Lord."

As though the Lord were listening to her. If He were, she wouldn't be bound by the wrists to a post with a jeering throng of what sounded like schoolboys behind her, and a man with a Scots accent as thick as her own reading out some proclamation as to what gave these people the right to treat her worse than a stubborn plow mule. Some new law in the colony came from the reading man. *Lazy* emerged as the nicest word from the crowd. She'd never even heard some of the language from the Scots-hating *Sassenach* in Glasgow. Her ears burned. She bowed her head, but not to pray. Praying was for people like her long-lost sister Murdag, who had started all the badness in their lives.

"When your punishment is done," pronounced her fellow, but heartless, Scotsman, "you will leave this town at once, you ken?"

Fiona nodded. She wouldn't want to stay. Surely in this vast new land someone somewhere would want a hardworking woman of four and twenty. She could cook simple fare. She could sew a good, if not fine, seam. She could read. *Faither* hadn't often been able to put food on the table after the uprising against the Sassenach twelve years ago, but he could put learning in their heads. If they'd have devoured *parritch* like they'd devoured the written word, they'd have grown as sleek and fat as the cat belonging to the woman Fiona worked for in the city. That cat could have withstood a whipping without feeling a thing it carried so much blubber on its bones.

Unlike Fiona, who wondered how she would leave town without her back, which bore no spare flesh, and probably her shift and bodice, too, cut to ribbons by the leather lash she now heard whistling through the air. Whistling like wind around the corner of the croft on a cold winter night, loud in the suddenly quiet throng. Fiona's stomach knotted. She'd be sick if she'd eaten recently. Her head spun. Black spots danced before her eyes. Any moment pain like she'd never known would cut her in two—or feel like—

"What do you think ye're doing?" The man's voice sounded like music with its gentle lilt. Not a Scots voice. Not English. Something rich and poetical and, at that moment, angelic. "You are all fools and no better than animals for thinking to whip a *merch* like she's a criminal."

"But she is a criminal." A chorus rose from the onlookers, explanations drowning out one another.

"Vagrant."

"No work."

"The law."

"Not need her kind."

The newcomer's voice vanished in the hubbub. Fiona didn't care. Her wrists still burned. She didn't care. The lash hadn't fallen. Someone people knew, seemed to perhaps respect, had intervened somehow. Possibly, the lash wouldn't rip up her back after all.

"Lord, are the old ones right? Will it be well because I'm on the same side of the water as the brooch?"

The old ones, the wise women from the village, weren't there to respond, but Fiona heard their voices, their sibilant Gaelic sliding through her mind. *"You find that brooch and make things right with the land before the bairns all starve."*

If she was saved from the lash. . .

She was saved from the lash. Muttering their disappointment, the horde of schoolboys and townspeople, who appeared not to have work themselves, shuffled away. She didn't look, but felt their absence behind her, cold air where the heat of contempt had seared her spine. Even MacFarlane, Jordy MacFarlane, left, though his, "I will be back in a wee bit," came through loud and clear.

So perhaps she wasn't saved after all. Perhaps this newcomer had simply dispersed the crowd to give her a measure of dignity in her punishment.

Yet light flashed, silvery-gray in the cloudy afternoon,

and the blade of a knife slid between her wrists and the rope. The rough hemp parted. Fiona crumpled to a heap on the dusty track these colonists called a street. From the corners of her eyes, she caught a glimpse of feet in fine leather boots draw near. She curled up into a ball and covered her head with her arms, preparing for a kick. *Just not too hard, please.* Just enough to encourage her to rise and get out of Cross Creek. She'd do so gladly.

No kick struck. The crowd noise dwindled further. More footfalls pattered away. The town seemed to grow eerily silent after the jeers and sneers and just plain meanness.

"Can you rise on your own?" The lilting, angelic voice spoke directly over her arm-protected head. "I'm that sure I'll have no trouble in carrying you, but 'twill look better if you can walk."

Slowly, aching in every limb and as weak as an unweaned kitten, she lowered her arms to the ground and raised her head to look straight into the darkest, clearest eyes she'd ever seen. She drew back, scuttled away a few inches like a crippled crab. Angels should have blue eyes. Faither had said she possessed eyes as blue as an angel's.

"I will not hurt you." He spoke in that sweet, musical voice, and she didn't care if his eyes glowed like midnight at a new moon. "But you have to come with me. 'Tis the law."

The law! she wanted to shout at him. *I'm sick to my soul of your colonial laws!*

She kept her mouth shut.

He drew his brows—nearly black like his eyes and hair—together. "Do you understand English? If not, we have a bit of a problem, as I know little of the Gaelic."

"I ken the English." Her voice emerged as a croaking frog's must if he were out of water too long.

Asking for a drink of water had gotten her strung up awaiting a beating.

"I took the Sassenach sil'er for a year to get myself over here, and this is what I have to show for coming to this great new land." Her tone rose with every phrase. So did she, shakily, slowly, but stand she did, all of her full height—several inches below his shoulder. She tilted her head back, and her hair fell around her like the cloak someone had stolen even before MacFarlane had the ropes knotted around her wrists. "I heard this is a land of plenty and I'm thinking they're right—plenty of meanness and thieving and treating the unfortunate like a mad cur. Now if you'll be excusing me, I will be on my way like the good constable said I must."

"That has all changed, Miss—?" He arched those enviably curved eyebrows in a question.

"I cannot see where that is any of your concern." She took another step backward.

She could never outrun him. Before she reached the next cross street, she'd be flat on her face, fainting from weakness and hunger. But if she could outwit him, perhaps she could get away from this horrible place. She could climb as well as any of the sailors on the brig that brought her across the Atlantic. She'd learned when climbing trees to hunt birds' eggs so she could serve Faither something for dinner. If it wasn't wrong to do so, she'd bet her shift she could outclimb this handsome man who sounded like he should be singing in the kirk in Glasgow, instead of standing with her in a dusty and mostly deserted street in a colonial village.

"I will explain all to you, miss, but I need to give your name to MacFarlane within the hour to keep you from that beating." He took a step closer to her, more a half step, not close enough to touch her, not close enough to grab her. "He's getting the papers now."

"Papers?" Fiona flattened her hands across her middle and looked down. Against her drab brown bodice, her fingers, grubby as they were, shone as white as bleached bone. Inside, her stomach felt like it rubbed against her bones. Nausea rose. She swallowed. "What papers?"

"Your indenture. Now then, be a good merch and tell me your name."

He spoke as though she were ten and four, not twenty and four, and looked not much older than she. He spoke to her as though she were a mere child, chattel.

Chattel. Indenture.

The old ones were wrong. Being on the same side of the water as the brooch did not bring back the good fortune if her understanding of what he was saying proved true and starvation wasn't making her crazed.

She licked her cracked lips. "What is a *merch*?"

"A girl." He smiled.

She wished he hadn't done that. It brought starlight into his dark eyes and a softness to the chiseled lines of his face. It touched something deep inside her she thought long dead. "But now that I am looking at you, I think maybe you are a *gwraig* instead."

Sweet-voiced or not, his words sounded barbaric.

"Woman," he added. "Are you over one and twenty?"

She glared at him.

"Miss, I am trying to save your back." For the first time, he sounded impatient, though he kept that annoyingly beautiful smile in place. "If I do not have the information to give MacFarlane, he will be more than happy to carry out the law and beat you."

Fiona gulped and glanced around for the nearest and easiest building, tree, or wall to climb. "How can you stop him if you simply ken my name and age?"

"You were going to be whipped for not having work, aye?"

She inclined her head in acknowledgment, choked by the memory of the pronouncement in the street. Then she raised her head and looked into his eyes. "I have sought the work for two days. None would have me, as I have no family and no references. So I was to be punished. I still do not have the work, so how can you change this law? Are you so important?"

An odd look crossed his face, a dancing to his eyes as though he suppressed mirth, but he sobered before shaking his head, sending his heavy queue flipping over one shoulder. "I am a mere printer, miss, but work I do have for you."

"Oh, nay, you do not." Fiona slid sideways, laid her hand on the post to which she'd been hitched like a horse. If she could use it to get to the roof of the nearest building, a tannery from the smell of it, she could escape. . . "I asked at the print shop. I was told they are not hiring anyone."

"Nay, we are not. Our family can do the work ourselves."

He stepped between her and the post as though he understood her intentions. "But I have purchased your service for a year to keep you from the beating."

"Are you saying—" Fiona's throat burned with bile. "I am your slave?"

"'Tis an indenture. 'Tis another option the law offers for vagrants. You will be free twelve months from this date." He moved close enough to take her hands in his then, strong, uncalloused hands with ink-stained fingers. Gentle hands warm in the autumn chill. "But no papers have been signed as yet. The choice is still yours. You can be my bond servant for a year, or you can let MacFarlane give you the whipping and then put you into servitude wherever MacFarlane pleases to pay your fine, as the law requires."

Chapter 2

Filthy, a bit odorous, and fragile enough to look like that whip of MacFarlane's would have cut her in half with a single blow though she might be, the glow in her blue eyes heated Owain like a Carolina summer sun. Burned him more likely. And it wasn't a good feeling.

He set his mouth and resisted the urge to look away from her glare, to step away and let her attempt to escape. He'd caught her glancing at the post then the tannery roof. He wasn't about to make a fool of himself chasing her over the rooftops and trees of Cross Creek in broad daylight. He was already making enough of a spectacle with the few occupants of the town who hadn't found business to do once MacFarlane had postponed the whipping, the entertainment. One of those lads or ladies was bound to be talking to his parents at that very moment. Either one of them, even his sister, appearing on the scene would humiliate him enough he'd want to escape Cross Creek himself for someplace like that great river he'd heard about in the west.

But since he'd already made a fool of himself, he might

as well continue the action and persuade her to take his offer over the whipping. Only one had set his hackles rising, and that had been on a full-grown man who'd stolen a whole chicken from the bake shop.

Yes, he would do what the situation called for, even dash across the rooftops like daytime thieves, to keep her from that kind of pain, humiliation, even death.

He took a deep breath. "So what will it be?"

"I will be taking the whipping rather than dishonor myself with you." She spoke with such dignity, despite her rags and filth and nothing to show for herself, Owain's heart twisted in his chest like a fire spill.

Then her words sank in and he jerked back as though she'd smacked his face. "Dishonor yourself? What are you saying, miss? I would never dishonor a lady."

"But I am so obviously not a lady." One of her feet, shod in rough wood and leather brogans, slid back half a step.

Owain remained motionless. "You misunderstand me, miss—will you at least give me your name?"

"Nay, you will not be needing it." And she spun on those clumsy shoes and fled.

"Catch her," shouted the bystanders, who'd watched the proceedings like a play.

"The vagrant is getting away."

"We'll miss all the fun of it."

Sickened by the cries and the men giving chase, acting like vagrants themselves, Owain sprinted past them and caught hold of Fiona's sleeve. The threadbare cloth tore away in his hand. He held naught but a dirty rag. One arm bare, pale as magnolia blossoms, as thin as broom straw, the girl slipped between two buildings.

"She'll get free thatta way," someone protested.

No, she would not. Owain knew Cross Creek in the dark. Even in the gloom of the autumn day, he knew every narrow alleyway, every tight passage, each shortcut.

He knew how to run and hide in plain sight.

He didn't crowd into the gap between the buildings. He let the others bottle up the opening, darted around the side, and climbed a low fence. Chickens squawked and gabbled at his intrusion. He leaped over them, then the low wall keeping them in the yard on the other side. The owner's shouts rang behind him, cackling much like the fowl.

"You'd better not stop them from layin' tonight, Owain Cardew, or your faither—"

His *tad* would know every detail of this day in five minutes if he didn't already. Mrs. MacLaughlin and her hens didn't frighten Owain. Neither did his tad—much.

Losing the girl—the young woman—to the crowd or worse, MacFarlane's lash, did concern him. He paused, glanced up the street, and saw her stumbling toward him. Her footfalls slapped down at an uneven gait. She'd lost a shoe. She was losing energy. If she'd eaten in the past two days he'd be surprised.

He caught her as she tripped over a rut in the road and swayed forward.

"Now look what you have done. I will have to carry you home to Mam, and the explanations she will be demanding. . ."

The girl made no response. She didn't move in his arms. She had fainted.

He should set her down, lower her head, let her regain consciousness. With townsfolk striding toward him, he turned on his heel and headed for home with the young woman cradled in his arms. He took every back way he knew, which was most of the way. Most people stopped following after the first block. Everyone stopped after the second. They and MacFarlane knew where to find him. The Cardews, besides being nearly the only Welsh family amidst the scores of Scots who'd settled North Carolina in the past twenty years, were the only printers.

Though the female weighed nothing to a man used to lugging a hundred-weight of paper from storage to shop, Owain's heart pounded like a running man's by the time he reached the kitchen door. It stood open to the alleyway, smoke billowing forth and reeking of burned bread. Bronwen, his sister, had been baking again, which meant Mam wasn't feeling well.

Perhaps this girl was safer with MacFarlane.

Owain pictured the lash and shook his head. His queue flipped against her cheek, and she opened her eyes. "You, you—" She muttered something in Gaelic he was glad he didn't understand and set her on her feet before she struggled. He didn't need Bronwen emerging from the house to see him fighting to hold on to the slip of a girl.

Bronwen emerged from the smoking kitchen in time to see that girl slap Owain across the face. As far as blows went, she was a kitten smacking a lion. He barely felt it. But the look in his sister's dark eyes, as dark as his and sparkling with laughter, encouraged him to leave the women to their own devices and retreat to the print shop. He knew what he was doing in there. At least he knew more than he knew about what he was doing with females.

"Did you have to go abduct yourself a bride, Owain?" Bronwen asked through her snorts of mirth. "She's a poor enough specimen if I ever saw one, will blow away faster than one of your pamph—"

"Hush then." He barked out the words.

Bronwen slapped her hand across her lips and the laughter died from her face, for coming toward them, town elders and half a dozen men from what the Scots called their kirk, though it boasted no regular parson, had just rounded the corner. They removed their bonnets at sight of Bronwen, who dropped a curtsy, all grace and poise despite a flour-smudged apron and, yes, nose. "To what do we owe this honor, sirs?" she asked in English better than that of any of the men, having been born in the colony nineteen years earlier and educated by their English mam.

"He has absconded with property of the government." MacFarlane pointed at Owain. "If he does not sign these indenture papers and pay in full, he will be lashed along with this female."

"I have not absconded with—"

"I am not the property of anyone—"

Owain and the girl spoke together.

"She's with you here, is she not?" MacFarlane interrupted them both. "Not where I told ye to stay."

"She—" Owain stopped himself. If he admitted that she'd run off, the townsmen might refuse to let him take over her fine and indenture for vagrancy.

"I believe," Bronwen said in her calm, clear voice, "the female, who smells worse than my poor bread, needed help. She looked to be fainting when he arrived."

"Is that so then?" MacFarlane asked.

"Aye, sir." Owain bowed his head. "I believe she is hungry."

"Not hungry enough to eat Bronwen's cooking," someone said in the crowd, raising a chorus of snickers.

"Did you faint, lass?" MacFarlane's voice seemed to have softened a fraction.

She, too, bowed her head, hiding her face behind her tangled hair. "And I came to myself in the smoke and found I had been carried off against my will."

"So ye'd rather have the lash and serving the town of Cross Creek than this Welshman, who cannot have the money to pay yer fine, you ken?" MacFarlane's green eyes began to glow.

Owain clenched his fists.

"I would rather keep my honor." The young woman spoke with quiet dignity that wrenched a little more at Owain's heart.

"Owain, do you care to tell me to what this merch is referring?" Bronwen demanded.

"I'd like to have the opportunity to be telling the lady herself." Owain reached for the girl's hands, changed his mind, and compromised by stepping between her and MacFarlane. "I am trying to save your honor, miss. That lady beside me is my sister, Bronwen Cardew. I am Owain Cardew. My mam and tad will be along at any moment, I have no doubt, and you will see that we are a respectable family with money enough for our needs."

"'Tis debatable that," someone shouted. "Printing anything people pay you—"

"You would have to serve anyone Cross Creek chooses after your whipping," Owain continued.

"Nay, you lie." The girl looked past him to MacFarlane. "You said I had to leave the town."

"Aye, so I did." He grinned. "Mine is the first farm along the way. I figured you could serve out your fine there if you made it that far and keep you from anyone—"

"Do not, *brawd*." Bronwen grasped Owain's arm.

He hadn't realized he was about to strike MacFarlane. Violence would serve no purpose, not to mention how strongly the Lord would disapprove. For a man perhaps not being as upright as he should be in the town, he didn't need to draw that sort of attention to the Cardew family. He had already drawn far too much with this day's work.

"But there is no work here." The girl's lower lip quivered, making her appear more child than woman at that moment. "I've asked and asked and. . ." She pressed one hand to her brow and swayed.

Bronwen slipped an arm around the young female's shoulders. "Here comes our tad. He'll make all right and clear."

And, bless him, there was Tad, Owain Cardew the Elder, master printer from Cardigan, Wales—an older, grayer, and slightly paunchier version of his son.

But no less vigorous for all his forty-plus years. His long stride swept him toward the crowd, primarily his two children flanking the stranger, his boot heels digging deep furrows in the dirt of the lane. He skirted his offspring, for which Owain gave a sigh of relief, and looked MacFarlane in the eye. "I cannot get you removed from yer post, Jordy MacFarlane, as I have too many of your clansmen to oppose me, but you cannot stop me from reminding the town that ye were willing to flog a female who was only asking around for work and not of any indecent kind."

"It's the law." MacFarlane seemed to shrink in size, though he was half a head taller than Owain Cardew the Elder. "Passed last year. We are to whip all vagrants and make them work off their fine for a year."

"Unless she's indentured to someone else, aye?" Tad's accent thickened, deliberately, Owain suspected. His tad emphasized his Welsh origins when he thought it convenient. "And my son said he'd buy the indenture, is that not so?"

"Aye, but—"

"Then where are the papers and why are all these people here?"

A dozen people spoke up at once. In the hubbub, Bronwen and Owain turned the newcomer, the female causing so much trouble, into the smoky kitchen, and led her through to the print shop. It smelled of ink and paper and the lead letters, but that was an improvement over burned bread.

"Tad will make it all right if you will cooperate, miss," Owain said, gently nudging her onto a chair. "Now then, do tell me what your name is."

"Fiona." Her voice emerged in a mere whisper. "Fiona MacGill. I never intended. . . I never thought. . ." She stiffened her narrow shoulders and raised her chin. "I arrived at Cape Fear a week ago, and aptly named it is. Since then, I have had someone pretend she could give me work only to lure me to where she could steal my money, people accuse me of vagrancy when all I wanted was work, and a strange man says he has bought my papers. How are you expecting me to feel about you all? Grateful?"

"Yes, that you could," Bronwen began. "Without my brother's intervention—"

"Stubble it, Bron." Owain crouched so he was closer to eye-to-eye with Fiona MacGill. "We do not blame you. We have all made amok of this, but you are safe now. We are printers and of the highest respectability."

Bronwen snorted, quite unlike the lady she was supposed to be.

"Our mam—our mother—is upstairs. She is unwell at times, and Bronwen can use help with the cooking. Can you cook?"

"Plain fare only."

"Any fare will do for us after eating what Bronwen produces." Owain smiled.

Bronwen glared at him, but her eyes danced. "You'll catch yourself a fine wife with your cooking, brawd."

"Now then," Owain continued, hearing the crowd diminishing outside and suspecting what was about to happen next, "Bronwen will take you upstairs to her chamber and find you some clothes and the like. Do you have any possessions to retrieve?"

Fiona shook her head. "Stolen."

Bronwen growled low in her throat.

Mentally, Owain started composing a pamphlet for distribution regarding the mistreatment of newcomers to the colony. But maybe down in Wilmington, not there in Cross Creek.

The back door slammed, sending remnants of smoke puffing into the print shop.

"Go," Owain commanded Bronwen and Fiona. Then he rose to face his tad.

Chapter 3

As she enjoyed the luxury of a bath beside a brick wall that must house the chimney for the kitchen fire, as it radiated warmth, Fiona heard every word of the conversation below stairs. She heard especially since Bronwen held the door open just enough for the voices rising up the stairs to filter into the bedchamber. The accents were odd, but the English clear enough.

"What were you thinking, Owain Cardew?" The father's throaty accent made him sound like he growled. "You will bring ruin upon us, and your mam is not well enough for us to be moving. You should have left well enough alone."

"And see that constable cut her in half with his whip?" Owain sounded just as furious, but added a grudging, "sir."

"You know naught about her. She could be a thieving vagrant."

"I am not." Fiona started to leap from the water, already cooling anyway and gray with her dirt.

"Hush now." Bronwen waved Fiona back. "Owain has the best judgment of character of any man I know, for all he has but four and twenty years."

"My age," Fiona muttered.

Bronwen stared at her. "You're that old and unwed? Or are you a widow?"

"There are few enough young men left in the Highlands, Miss Cardew. Fewer for those of us without a dowry."

Thanks to her half-sister, Murdag, who had taken the brooch, who had left for America, leaving behind her little sister in the hands of a stepmother who hadn't proved as trustworthy as she'd seemed at the time.

"Most of the men fled after the 'Forty-Five,' " Fiona added, recalling the Jacobite Rebellion of 1745.

Like her brothers. Like her faither should have.

Everything had been well in the village until Murdag took the brooch, the gift from Queen Mary Stuart herself for the ancestress who tried to help the beleaguered monarch retake her rightful place on the Scottish throne nearly two hundred years earlier.

"'Tis when the Scots rebelled against the Sassenach, the English, to put a Stuart back on the throne," Fiona explained.

"Yes, I know." Bronwen made a hushing gesture.

"We will not have the money to take your mam to a physician in the city if you keep wasting it on things we cannot afford to buy."

"Aye, sir, but—"

"Do not argue with me. You may be four and twenty, but I can still thrash you for disobedience and disrespect."

Owain's return sigh sounded like someone had used bellows to build up the fire in the kitchen. "Aye, sir, though she says she can cook. I will work twice as hard to make up for it, as I think Mam will get well faster and perhaps not need a physician if she is fed better."

Mr. Cardew emitted a grudging chuckle.

Bronwen blew out a breath through her lips as though she'd been holding it overly long, and closed the door. "Everything will be all right now. Tad will pay your fine and you will work for us for a year to pay us back. We really could use the help, but they want another printing press in the shop so badly, they've been trying to make do with me, and I just *am* such a poor cook. And Mam is unwell and Owain is forever. . ." She clamped her lips shut and moved to where a bucket of water stood. "If you're not too shy about it, I'll pour this water over you so you can wash your hair. I'm afraid you're going to be terribly pretty when you're clean and fed, aren't you?"

"I do not ken if I am or no." Fiona rose with her back to Bronwen, but felt hot all over and noticed even her arms had flushed with her embarrassment. "Only one man ever courted me, and he a widower with six children needing a *mither*."

"Six of my own would be fine." Bronwen sounded a bit wistful. "But not someone else's. Ready to finish up?"

Fiona was ready. The water hadn't cooled too badly. Still, gooseflesh broke out on her arms and legs. Yet the idea of having her hair clean again, to smell sweet from the drops of some fragrant oil Bronwen had sprinkled into the water, an unfamiliar flower aroma to Fiona, pleased her. She hadn't enjoyed a full bath since leaving Mrs. Grant's employment and boarded the ship bound for America. Before all her savings had been stolen, she had at least been able to wash with a cloth and basin and sliver of precious soap, but nothing this nice, and not her hair.

"But I have naught to wear," Fiona thought aloud with a cry of horror. "Those other clothes are ruined."

"I noticed you were missing a sleeve."

"Your brother pulled it off."

Bronwen laughed. "Trying to catch you? He cannot bear to see anyone suffer, which is why he works so hard to save money for a proper physician for Mam."

So he rescued others and she was nothing special to Owain Cardew. Not that she cared. She was a servant for a year, then they would send her on her way, perhaps with a reference this time and clothes that looked respectable so people wouldn't slam their doors in her face when she asked for work.

If she hadn't found Murdag by then. Or the brooch. She must find the brooch and then the means by which to return it to Scotland. The brooch belonged in Scotland, not this barbaric new land. The Old Ones in the village said all would be well again once the brooch returned. All had been well before Murdag sent it away with their cousin Seona, then followed to marry her fiancé, Rory.

"I don't need a knight." Fiona shivered. "I need clean clothes. I'm sorry. Even my cloak was stolen."

"Mam's clothes should fit. A little large, but you'll grow, I expect, once someone starts to feed you." Bronwen glanced toward the door through which footfalls on wooden stair treads reverberated. "I expect that'll be you doing the feeding."

"But will your mither care? I mean, have you asked her then?" Fiona wrapped her arms around herself.

Bronwen enfolded Fiona in a wide sheet of flannel. "This will keep you warm until I fetch some clothes for you. Just sit here by the chimney and brush your hair."

Before Fiona could ask another question or make a protest, Bronwen flitted out the door. Fiona stepped from the tub of now chilly water and did as Bronwen suggested. She settled on a narrow wooden bench against the chimney and wrapped the flannel around her. Heat radiated from the chimney bricks again. Apparently someone had stoked the fire in the kitchen below. The warmth spread through the cloth and into Fiona's skin. Lovely, blessed heat. Voices, no louder than murmurs through the thick wooden panels, drifted to Fiona. So did the aromas of wood smoke and—rabbit stew? If someone in the household could make a dish with such a savory aroma, they didn't need Fiona MacGill's simple abilities in the kitchen. Her talents ran to bannocks and *brideys*. Her brideys were the best in the village, if the ingredients happened to be available, which they had been so rarely in the past dozen years.

Her stomach growled. Her head went light as it had when she'd been running. Goodness, she didn't even have two shoes anymore.

"Just more proof You do not care for me, God. I could have gotten a few pence for the shoes in a pair."

Murdag would never agree with her. If the six-year-old Fiona had said something like that to her much older sister, Murdag would have scolded her, calling it blasphemy against the Bible that promised God would care for all His children, of whom she was one. *"Put your faith in Him, child, not the brooch I sent away with Seona."*

But Murdag had gone, too, and nothing good had happened since, no matter how many hours Fiona spent on her knees. Yet she smelled rabbit stew, was warm for the first time in weeks, and safe perhaps for the first time since Murdag said good-bye.

Instead of brushing out her hair, she leaned her head back against the warmth and closed her eyes. Oh, how her head ached. How her body ached. She simply wished to curl up on the floor and sleep. . .

The door flew open. Fiona jumped and hit her head on the chimney.

"I am so sorry." Bronwen closed the door with a bang.

Fiona stiffened in her cocoon of flannel. "Is—is your mither overset with me being here then?"

"Upset with you being here? Why ever should she be upset with you?" Bronwen dropped a bundle onto the bed that took up most of the room's floor space. "She said it's past time Tad and Owain hired someone to help me until she's well." She frowned. "Which is taking far too long."

"'Tis sorry to hear that I am." Fiona wrapped the flannel more tightly around her. "Is it. . . ? Is she. . . ?"

No, she couldn't ask such a thing of this friendly, kindly woman, yet still a stranger to her.

Bronwen sighed and began to unwrap the bundle. "We don't know if she's dying or not. She caught a chill in a rainstorm last summer and just isn't getting better as quickly as we'd like. None of the healers here know what to do."

"I had—have a cousin who is a healer." Tears filled Fiona's eyes. "Seona. She came here to North Carolina eighteen years ago, but I ken not where she has gone now."

Bronwen swung around and stared at Fiona. "You haven't heard from your family in nearly twenty years? We get letters from Wales on nearly every ship."

"'Tis different in the Highlands, you ken. 'Tis nigh a wasteland since the rebellion and little news gets through."

But if she could find Seona, perhaps she could heal Mrs. Cardew and pay back the family for the kindness they had shown Fiona thus far. Seona's skill had been uncommonly fine even when she was young. Now she must be even better, more knowledgeable. If she still lived.

A chill ran up Fiona's spine despite the warmth of the brick and heated flannel wrap. If Murdag and Seona were dead, Fiona would never find the brooch for the family. What was left of the family.

Oh, but telling Murdag about Faither and the boys would be painful.

Fiona wiped her eyes on the corner of the thick sheet. She must not weep in front of this woman, this stranger. They would think her weak. Of course, she'd already fainted. Still, she practiced a smile.

Bronwen turned in time to see it and smiled back. "Here are a few things Mam said you may have. I'll leave you alone to get dressed. Everything laces in the front, but call if you need any assistance." She whisked out of the room.

Slowly, reluctant to leave the comforting warmth of

the bricks, Fiona rose and approached the bed. The sight of stockings, shift, two petticoats, a bodice, and a skirt, the latter in a pretty deep gray-blue, all spotlessly clean, drew her. Yet she felt a bit like a moth to the flame. Everything the Cardew family did for her, each bit of material goods they gave her, indebted her to them further. She had never been indebted to anyone in her life.

Nor had she been without so much as a shift to her name before in her life, and she couldn't go around wrapped in a towel the size of a tablecloth. So she began to dress, drawing on lisle stockings as though they were woven of the finest silk, blessing Bronwen or her mother for wearing the more comfortable jumps to a corset. Fiona didn't need to lace tightly to flatten her silhouette. She'd eaten so little since leaving Glasgow her ribs stuck out like the strakes on an unfinished boat.

Beyond the thick door, footfalls sounded, the heavy tread of men's boots. Voices murmured too low for her to catch the words. She hastened into her clothes, drawing the tapes of the petticoats tightly, though the waistband bunched beneath the bodice. No matter. She wasn't there to attract attention to any good looks she might possess any longer—which she knew must be not at all, despite the leer MacFarlane had given her.

She shuddered at the memory of him telling her he hoped she'd reach his farm first. She'd eat in the pigsty like the prodigal son before she would work for him.

"Thanks to you Cardews, I need not."

If they were trustworthy. Her experience aboard ship had

taught her that people could seem friendly and then rob one in a trice.

Warm in the layers of linen and woolen clothing, Fiona glanced about for something to wear on her feet so as not to ruin the fine stockings. Lying upside down atop a folded paisley shawl rested a pair of leather slippers with cork heels and ribbons to tie them on, impractical gear for outdoors wear, but comfortable within the house.

She'd owned a pair once, too. They were quiet on wood, marble, and floors with rugs and hadn't disturbed her mistress as Fiona went about her duties. With the ribbons tied around her ankles, the shoes fit well enough, and she was just wrapping the shawl around her shoulders when Bronwen snapped open the door again.

"Do you never knock, *chwaer*?" Owain's voice sounded close.

And a little tingle, like warmth after being cold, ran through Fiona at the sound. She wondered if he sang. He talked like he was about to burst into song, so rich and melodious a voice did he have. What did it matter if she didn't know what some of the odd words he used meant?

"Mam is ready to see you," Bronwen announced to Fiona, completely ignoring her brother's question. "In truth, we're all going to talk to you."

Chapter 4

Fiona sat at the kitchen table with the entire family, as though she were one of them, not their servant. Yet their servant she was. Papers had been signed by everyone—town leaders for accepting the Cardews' money to pay her vagrancy crime, the Cardews for taking her on as a responsibility, and her for pledging that she would work for these people for a year to pay them back for their money spent on her behalf.

Money they wanted to use to get their mither well.

Printers in a small town like Cross Creek must not make much money, though they did have a shop with many goods. A press resided in the front room of the house, which was the shop full of books and news sheets, invitations to parties, and words to songs. The ground floor consisted of two other rooms, also. One seemed to contain nothing but supplies for the print shop—paper, ink, the pads with which they inked the press, and extra letters. Food stuffs stood in one corner like humble refugees with nowhere else to go just like her. The fourth room was a parlor, spotlessly clean, but so cold and dark from drawn draperies across the window it appeared barely used.

The heart of the house lay in the kitchen, warm, fragrant now that the rabbit stew had overpowered burned bread, and filled with Cardews. The men weren't as large as the Highlander males with which Fiona had grown up, not as tall and broad. Neither were they small, as she always thought Welshmen would be, stuffed underground in coal mines so much. Bronwen was tall for a female, dark like her brother and faither, not small and fair like her mither.

Mrs. Cardew resided at the foot of the scrubbed pine table, as fragile as the best china Fiona used to serve her mistress's tea in Glasgow, all ivory and gold except for her blue eyes. Despite her obvious illness, she was still a lovely woman, and her smile, a full curve of her lips, twisted Fiona's heart, reminding her of how once upon a time she had a mother who smiled at her. Fiona wanted to do anything the woman asked if it would make her smile with that loving warmth so long missing from her life. The first request had been for Fiona to consider herself welcome.

"My son did the right thing in saving you." Mrs. Cardew squeezed her husband's hand as she spoke in her breathy, clear English voice. "Owain is truly his father's son."

"But the physician." Owain stared at the toes of his boots. "I am that sorry I did not think about money for your physician."

"The Lord will take care of us, my son," Mrs. Cardew said. "Now it's settled. Let's get those papers in order to satisfy Constable MacFarlane and the townsmen. Miss MacGill, you will join us."

It wasn't a question; it was an order.

So Fiona had joined them, but insisted she finished making the meal. Owain didn't argue with her. Nor did Bronwen. They escaped into the print shop as though they couldn't wait to be away from her, and Fiona set about seasoning the stew a little more, then mixing up the only bread she could in a short time—oatcakes. If they hated her bannocks. . . But there was nothing they could do now. The papers were signed, and she crept about on her cork-soled shoes, trying to disturb the family as little as possible, and listening. She listened to the light click of type going into the galleys. She listened to the rumbling swish of the ink pad sliding across the paper to ink the page with words. She listened to a bell ring over the shop door, as customers came and went.

She listened for the voice of the younger Owain Cardew.

She didn't hear it until they gathered around the table for the meal. Mr. Cardew carried his wife downstairs and set her on her chair with loving tenderness that set an ache sliding up inside Fiona's heart. As a child, she'd dreamed of a man treating her like that. Then the rebellion came and the young men went. Her brothers died or fled to America never to be heard again, and Faither faded slowly away along with any hope of marriage for Fiona.

Head turned away from the family, Fiona set the dishes of stew and plates of oatcakes and jar of honey on the table, then crouched beside the hearth to partake of her own meal.

"Eat slowly," she mouthed to herself. "Do not make

yourself ill with the gobbling."

Her stomach growled.

So, it seemed, did Owain Cardew. "You're not the family dog, Miss MacGill. Get yourself up to the table to eat."

Fiona caught a gaze flash between his parents. They smiled and nodded. Bronwen rolled her eyes, as though Fiona were a simpleton to think anything else.

"But I am a gilly—a servant—no?" she murmured.

"We are all servants of the Lord and equal in His eyes," Mrs. Cardew replied. "You will eat with us and share Bronwen's room."

"But—"

"Where else did you plan to go?" Bronwen asked. "We haven't another chamber."

"The kitchen here." Fiona glanced at the hearth. "I had a blanket before the hearth when I served in the home of an English officer in Glasgow."

"And they think themselves civilized." Owain muttered the words, but didn't look at her.

In truth, throughout the prayer before the meal, throughout the dinner, he avoided so much as glancing her way, though he sat across from her and beside his sister. He spoke to his family. He pronounced the food tolerable, as did everyone, but he said nothing to her either.

Mrs. Cardew asked Fiona questions like, "Why did you come to North Carolina?"

"To find my sister, Murdag Stewart."

Surely people who printed news sheets and dealt in printed matter would have heard of many people.

They shook their heads. "We know many Stewarts, but none named Murdag," Mr. Cardew said. "But her name isn't the same as yours."

"She married a Stewart. Rory," Fiona explained.

She took a bite of stew, but tasted nothing.

"Murdag MacGill perhaps?" Bronwen asked.

"She was my half-sister, a Mac Kay. Or Seona Campbell," Fiona offered, "my cousin."

Nothing.

"Perhaps you have not been here long enough?" It was, perhaps, a rude remark, but she was stranded in Cross Creek now and couldn't go looking for Murdag, for the brooch.

"We have been here in Cross Creek five years," Mr. Cardew said. "Twenty years in the North Carolina colony."

Bronwen made a face. "We've moved twice since I was born."

"I am thinking we will be here awhile," Mr. Cardew said.

"So this one can find a husband." Owain tugged a loose strand of Bronwen's hair.

Such affection, such love in this family. It glowed from all of them as they addressed one another, even when Mr. Cardew spoke sternly to his son about work being late, about too much ink on the press, about not knowing his Bible verses for the day.

Fiona hastened to gather up dishes and begin to boil water for the washing up. She didn't want them to quiz her on what she knew of the Bible. She quit reading hers at the age of twelve when she learned her eldest brother had died on the field at Culloden. She'd doubted God's caring for her before that day. She knew it then.

"Come sit down again, Miss MacGill." Mrs. Cardew spoke from the foot of the table, the place closest to the fire. "We share our favorite passage from the Bible reading before we clean the supper dishes."

Fiona froze in the act of tipping a bucket of water into the kettle hanging over the fire. If she admitted the truth, they might sell her back to the lecherous constable. If she lied. . .

No, she couldn't lie to these good people.

She stared at the red and gold flames, wishing she could conjure verses from the dancing light. "I do not read my Bible."

"If you can't read, we'd be happy—"

Fiona swung around, splashing cold water across the front of her gown, and glared at Owain. "I may come from a poor village in the highlands of Scotland, not that there is naught else there now, but it does not mean I cannot read. My faither taught me weel to ken my letters and many books and—and. . ." She trailed off, her face flaming. She dropped her gaze to the now wet floorboards. "'Tis sorry I am for speaking so."

"No need to apologize, child." Mrs. Cardew grasped the edge of the table and rose. "My son should apologize for being so thoughtless."

"My brawd is a clod," Bronwen muttered.

"That I am." From the corner of her eye, Fiona saw Owain blushing. "So few of the Highlanders here can read. . ." He mumbled something in Welsh.

"Was your Bible stolen with all your other things?" Mr. Cardew asked. "We sell them in the print shop."

"No, no, they are too dear for that." Fiona shuddered at the thought of such an expensive gift. Six pounds or so, more money than she had seen in her lifetime. "I—I have not had a Bible since we sold it to an English soldier in exchange for food twelve years ago." She blurted out the words. Then, because they were all gazing at her with such sympathy, she lifted her chin and added, "But I do not care. God had already left me."

She expected them to gasp, to look horrified, to throw her out as God had done. But all of them gazed right at her, even Owain for the first time since she had gone upstairs to bathe, and compassion filled their eyes.

"God has not left you, my dear." Mrs. Cardew, wavering in her weakness, closed the distance between herself and Fiona and slipped an arm around her shoulders. "Nothing can separate us from the love of God. He has a purpose in all His actions. We have seen His hand in our lives again and again. But you are weary. Bronwen, take her to your room so she may sleep."

Bronwen did so. Though the autumn darkness was just slipping over the sky, she tucked Fiona up in her own bed and then sat on the bench by the chimney, reading her Bible by the light of a tallow candle. Bronwen said nothing condemnatory or disdainful.

None of the Cardews did, as Fiona learned her way around the household, found everything that needed to be done, and then took over more during the next few weeks. She worked so hard cooking, cleaning, and trying to remember what herbs would best return strength to Mrs. Cardew, she gave none of the family time to talk to her. Not that they enjoyed much time to do so. Mrs. Cardew sewed and slept most of the time, and the others worked in the print shop, except when carrying parcels to customers, buying supplies from factors, or taking their meals. They worked from dawn to dusk and then, as she drifted off to sleep, Fiona heard the press sliding across the paper with its gentle *thump, thump, thump*.

And all the while, they found time to read their Bibles, pray together, and talk about special verses to them that day. Mr. Cardew seemed to expect his two children, grown as they were, to memorize verses, too, and recite them like schoolchildren. Bronwen was better at it, but Owain's recitations, though flawed in perfection of the wording, sent a tingle of pleasure through Fiona, his voice like he was singing the words. Only on Sunday, when they gathered with others for worship, despite the fact that a minister only arrived in town occasionally, did Fiona hear Owain sing. Deep and rich, his voice sang words of praise to God in a way that nearly made Fiona believe she was wrong in thinking the deity no longer cared about humans.

Owain didn't speak to her a great deal, not more than necessary. He didn't talk to his family much either, other than teasing his sister about her beau or discussing business with his faither. He talked a great deal to customers. She heard him in the shop, as she worked in the kitchen. Young women slipped in to peruse the same stock of books and sheets of music, asking him questions. Fiona figured it was simply to hear him talk. She wanted him to talk to her, tell her about himself, his family, anything. She wanted to hear him sing more than the kirk music.

Then one morning, determined to make real bread instead of bannocks, she slipped from bed without disturbing Bronwen and descended to the kitchen. She needed flour, but the supply in the kitchen ran low. Having seen some in the storage room, she pushed open the door between it and the kitchen and heard Owain singing a melody of love and loss, a ballad of the heart. As soft and low as a lullaby, the song hadn't penetrated the timber walls of the house. But they penetrated the pain of loss around Fiona's heart, and tears stung her eyes. Hoping she wouldn't weep, she stood in the doorway swallowing for several seconds before she realized what Owain was doing as he sang to himself.

He had uncovered a second printing press and was turning out some sort of news sheet with the rapidity of a master printer of great experience. But the printing press lay in the shop. So why would they keep a second one hidden in the storage room?

Chapter 5

Owain's hand slid off the arm of the secret press, ruining the sheet on the bed before him. His song choked in his throat, and he spun to face the doorway, to face Fiona. "Miss MacGill, you are awake so early."

"I was wanting the real bread." She glanced toward the barrels of food stuffs in the far corner as though not noticing the press. "I was not spying, truly."

She didn't need to be spying to have seen far too much. He should have been paying attention to the noises around him, but he was so tired from being awake all night to get out the new pamphlets, he'd sung to keep his concentration. Now all he could do was brazen this out. "Do not say anything, please." He smiled at her. "Fiona."

"Do not try any of those pretty words with me, Mr. Owain Cardew. I may be naught but a gilly, but I am Miss MacGill to you. At least I think 'tis best that way." She ducked her head, and feathery strands of her pale gold hair caressed her cheeks like delicate fingers.

His own fingers, ink stained now, twitched. He wanted to brush that fair skin as he'd wanted to since seeing her walk into Mam's room all clean and smelling of summer flowers, her hair like something out of a tale of knights and ladies, her stance both shy and proud. He'd dared not look at her since for the wishing she weren't his family's bondswoman and worse, he soon learned—an unbeliever. Now she knew he owned a second press he kept hidden away, and that could spell ruin for them all, force them to move when Mam was not well.

He took a step toward Fiona. "Please, Miss MacGill, I will call you whatever you like, just say nothing of this press or finding me here."

"Are you breaking the king's laws then?" Her gaze darted toward the stack of pamphlets he'd taken from the drying lines. "Is there not a war on or something?"

"Aye, another war with France up north and west of here. But these pamphlets are not sedition. They are—" Footfalls sounded on the steps, heavy ones. Tad's. "Please go. I will tell you all later."

Without a word, she spun on her heel and slipped from the storage room and into the kitchen. A moment later, Tad greeted her and offered to fill the wood box. She asked his permission to fetch flour from the storage room. By the time she returned, Owain had the press covered, the pamphlets tucked away until nightfall. She said nothing to him, nor he to her. But he would. He must. Somehow he needed to find a way to talk to her alone, ensure her loyalty to them in her silence if nothing more, a difficult task in the house.

At each meal that day, the only times he saw her once the shop opened for business, Owain wondered why he worried about Fiona saying anything. She scarcely spoke. But she listened. Her gaze switched from Tad, to Mam, to Bronwen, and almost to him when each of them spoke. She said little unless asked direct questions. Gradually, though, they learned of how hard her life had been in Scotland, her mother dying, then her stepmother leaving when times got difficult. Her brothers vanished during the Scottish rebellion against England, leaving her alone with their father and little to support them.

Owain knew how his own family had struggled over the years. He worked late into the nights on his secret press to keep from being as poor as they had been when he was a child. But he hadn't turned his back on the Lord as much as she had. He worshiped with others when they had no minister in town and believed that, surely, God would make things better. Perhaps she would prefer her own Scots worship. A few weeks after her arrival, a minister did plan to preach at the kirk.

"We like to go there when they have a minister present," Owain said. "Bronwen will come with us, too."

"Especially if Jamie MacLaughlin is there." Tad winked at Bronwen.

"Him." Bronwen tossed her head. "He thinks he'll get rich selling eggs, but he really wishes for a bride with a dowry, which I don't have."

She would if Owain hadn't bought Fiona's indenture.

"He's doing well enough with his mam," Tad pointed out.

"We will go to services," Owain blurted out. "I will ask Jamie to join us."

Bronwen blushed. She liked the young man, who had moved to Cross Creek with his widowed mother a year before the Cardews arrived. Like Owain, he wanted to see things in the colonies change, wanted more than those with royal land grants to have the opportunity to prosper.

During the walk to church or after, if the weather proved fine, Owain could talk to Fiona, ensure her silence—he hoped.

If he could find the words to speak to her. When she descended to prepare breakfast Sunday morning, she wore a different gown, another one belonging to his mother, but better fitting, a rich brown that brought out the gold in her hair. And someone, Bronwen no doubt, had tied a ribbon around Fiona's braids. All Owain could think was to tell her how pretty she looked. He knew that was wrong. She was their bondswoman after all, if nothing else were amiss with thinking those things of her, so he said nothing.

Yet when Jamie arrived to collect Bronwen, all talkative and vibrant and large enough to make the kitchen appear little more than a closet, Owain could do nothing but offer Fiona his arm for the walk to the church.

The day shone fine and bright with a promise of warmth in the air. Perhaps they could take a stroll after the service. Talking beforehand proved impossible. The streets crowded with other churchgoers. Most of them stared at Fiona as though she were some odd specimen of beast from the forested mountains. Everyone would now know of her near whipping for vagrancy. With each glance, she tightened her hold on Owain's arm until he feared he would lose all feeling in his fingers. So much strength in such a little thing. So much strength of spirit to keep her head up and looking right back at everyone just as he did, glaring down a few of the men who leered and sneered, especially MacFarlane.

"The next one will be to get rid of you," Owain muttered under his breath.

Fiona glanced up at him. "I beg your pardon?"

"Never you mind that. Would you be liking a walk in the sunshine after the service? I'm thinking Bronwen and Jamie would not mind the time to talk."

Indeed, the two appeared so absorbed in one another they were about to pass the door of the church.

"I would not mind the walk, nay." Fiona smiled.

A shiver ran through Owain. He looked away from her, concentrated on fixing his thoughts on God, not matters of the world like pretty serving maids. He needed to pray for her soul. For her belief that God did care about her. Yet she had not been treated well in the colonies thus far. MacFarlane sat in the front, smug and prosperous and righteous-looking, while he had treated Fiona like a farm animal or worse. Men like him needed to be stopped.

Despite the sermon on having a right heart with the Lord, Owain felt anger rising up inside him. Perhaps he was not the man to speak to Fiona about the love and constancy of God.

Yet the warmth of the air with just a hint of coolness in the light breeze, drew them to walk out of the town and toward the farms and forests, the former fragrant with the fresh-cut stalks of harvest, the latter of pine and drying leaves. Jamie and Bronwen strode far ahead, in sight, but out of earshot, a fine young couple with money—or the lack of it—a barricade between them.

While Bronwen's and Jamie's voices drifted back, silence grew uncomfortable between Fiona and Owain. He felt her discomfort in the tension of her hand on his arm. She even tried to draw away once with muttering something about getting home to cook.

"But you made those brideys yesterday. They will do us fine today so no one has to work." Owain resisted the urge to cover her hand with his free one and blurted out, "I need to talk to you about the press you found."

"Nay, you need not."

"I'm thinking it appears as though I lied to you about what I'm doing."

"You have your reasons."

"Which is not godly of me."

"I do not care. I read things in Glasgow about how God exists but is not interested in us as individuals as the man preaching this morning said. I believe this is true."

"That's called deism and is wrong. God cares about every detail of our lives." Owain allowed himself to touch her fingers for a heartbeat, enough to make his beat faster. "My family left Wales because the mines weren't doing well, so people were not buying books or news sheets. We had little more than our press when we came, and now we have a house and enough to eat, clothes and"—he smiled down at her—"even a young lady to cook. Is that not God taking care of us?"

"Your mither is ill."

"One brother back, Mam spends her days praying for her family in England and Tad's family in Wales, for neighbors and for mates for her. . .children. . ." He stumbled over the last, but it had come out anyway, so he hastened to add, "So look how well Bronwen is doing. Jamie is one of the finest men in Cross Creek."

"And she has no dowry to get him to wed her."

"It is the reason for the extra press." Owain waited a moment, as their footfalls crunched on the rutted track. "I print up pamphlets for people in other communities in the colonies. Nothing against the government, I do promise you, but things others do not wish traced back to them. It is not just to persuade Mam to go to a physician. It is for a dowry for Bronwen."

She remained silent for several moments then burst out, "He never provided for me, not a dowry, a sweetheart, or even a brother to help. I prayed and prayed for God to bring relief to my faither and me, to bring at least that, but He didn't and I scrubbed floors and chamber pots for an English officer's wife so I could come here and find the brooch—I mean, find my sister and make all right again."

Owain stopped and gazed down at her, not caring that Jamie and Bronwen were out of sight over a hill. He trusted them to behave themselves. "Will you tell me what this is all about, Fiona MacGill? How can finding your sister make all right again? That is, I can understand wanting to find her, but I cannot understand what you are saying about a brooch."

"'Tis naught you would ken."

"No, I cannot know if you do not tell me, and I will stand in the middle of this road until you do, even if nightfall comes."

For several minutes, he thought she would let him do just that. She glanced around her at the trees, the pale blue sky, everything but him. She removed her hand from his arm and crossed her arms over her middle. Then she sighed. "Perhaps you can help me if I am telling you."

"Perhaps I can." He met and held her gaze for a full minute. Along the road, Bronwen's and Jamie's laughter drifted on the breeze, and what was left of the leaves rustled like sheets of paper or pamphlets. Wood smoke scented the air, sharp and fragrant, blending with Fiona's sweet fragrance, familiar and comforting aromas from home, yet this woman was such a stranger no matter how attractive he found her.

"We had a brooch in the family for nigh on two hundred years," she began.

She told a tale of an ancient brooch that sailed to America with her cousin as a promise to her sister's fiancé. She talked about how nothing good had happened in the family since the brooch left the village, culminating in the destruction of the Highlands after the rebellion twelve years earlier. She told a tale of trusting in what the old women of the village claimed—that the loss of the brooch had brought bad fortune upon them, not the misbehavior of mankind.

"So I must find my sister and the brooch and take it back," she concluded.

"No, Fiona MacGill, only God can heal people's hearts and lands, not a trinket," Owain said. "But I will help you find your sister as best I can just the same. But I would rather you found the Lord instead."

"You wish me to find the Lord, with your sedition and—"

He touched a fingertip to her lips. "No sedition. You can read the pamphlets. They go back to Wilmington and down to Charleston and up to Williamsburg. I am paid to make them far from their sources to protect those who want them distributed. Mostly they are tales of dishonest merchants, warning people. Sometimes they are warnings of certain military officers for the people to be wary of. Or governors. That is dangerous, I know, and I am placing much trust in you to say nothing."

"Then why do you risk it for the money if God will take care of your needs?" Fiona glanced up the road, to where Bronwen and Jamie, their faces glowing in the afternoon sunlight, returned toward town. "'Tis risky for your family."

"I am careful. I only—" He stopped. She knew more than enough. "I will make up pamphlets to send about describing your sister. Can you give me a good description?"

"Aye, I can draw one."

Indeed she could. Owain took one look at the likeness Fiona penned, and decided to talk to Tad about adding woodcuts to their printing. How accurate the likeness, coming from a child's memory, he didn't know, but the details astounded him. If they could add pictures to their pamphlets and news sheets, even sell the pictures themselves, they could increase their legitimate business profits. Until they could set up the wood cutting from Fiona's drawings, he wondered if someone with fingers as nimble as hers could learn to set type. It might save him from so many late nights.

She proved a natural student at slipping the tiny lead letters into their slots, backward so they came out right once the page had been inked. Whoever had taught her had done well. Fiona proved quick and intelligent and excellent company. She talked of her home, the beauty and the devastation, the loss of one family member after another. She had read many books, and they spoke of those. After two weeks of working with him and Tad, she even began to argue with her head ducked and her voice low, but disagree nonetheless. It made Owain smile at her attempt to show humility and strength of will and character at the same time.

If only she trusted in the Lord instead of trusting in the power of some ancient piece of jewelry for a reversal of her lot in life, he could find her a woman worth courting. Perhaps if he found her sister. . .

He sent out pamphlets with a description of Murdag MacGill or Stewart. He worked on setting up their printer to manage woodcuts and began to teach Fiona how to create the blocks of wood on which she could transfer drawings so they could become pictures in ink on paper. He spent more and more time with her, and not one member of his family said a word for or against it. Yet he caught a smile here and there from Mam, a wink from Bronwen, and a frown from his father.

That frown compelled him to speak to his father as they collected a load of paper from the riverboat. "You know I could lose my heart to a merch like Fiona."

"Aye, that I know. She is a fine girl, pretty and quick and so much talent." Tad began to stack the reams of paper onto the wagon they borrowed for such trips, his dark brows knit together. "And I know you've been praying for a lady to love as a wife. But her heart is not right with the Lord and neither is yours."

"Mine is not? Tad, how can you say so?" Even as the words left his mouth, Owain knew Tad was right.

"You have too much anger in your soul, my son." Tad spoke Owain's thoughts aloud. "You are angry about your mam's illness and angry about our lack of money, though we work so hard. Do good with the printings, aye, but do not let all you read fester. And the Lord will heal your mam when He wills."

"Just as He's sent me the sort of merch I could love and has her an unbeliever." Owain clamped his teeth together so hard they hurt, and he knew Tad was right—too much anger in his heart against the Lord's will not being his own, so much like Fiona's.

In silence, he and Tad returned the paper to the shop and found Fiona engaged in selling two expensive books to a young male customer. Her beauty glowed from her, and the young man postured and preened and asked her if she would go walking with him after church on Sunday.

"I cannot." Fiona blushed, making her even prettier. "I'm a bondswoman."

"Well, at least you'll be here in the shop more." The stranger spoke like an English aristocrat.

Owain stood in the shop doorway until the gentleman departed, books under one arm, carriage of head and shoulders arrogant, as though he owned Fiona.

Owain winced at that. Yes, his family owned Fiona, but she was becoming a part of their family in most ways. No English stranger had a right to try to court her. He must speak to her, or perhaps Tad should.

Then she turned to him and held out a slip of paper. "He left this behind in one of the books he looked at but didn't buy." Fear clouded her eyes.

His gut tight, Owain took the paper and read the brief and badly printed words: *Your constable knows what you are doing and therefore so will others.*

The next day, a pamphlet began to circulate around town that the Cardews had not printed. The ink was smudged as though the letters on the press were worn or the papers had been stacked before the ink dried. The wording talked about the dishonest constable, as well as two cheating storekeepers.

And that night, someone threw a rock through the window of the print shop.

Chapter 6

"This isn't our work." Owain's face glowed as pale as moonlight beneath the lanterns his faither had lit to show the damage. "We would never do anything so slapdash."

Fiona wished to go to him, touch his arm, smooth the wrinkle from between his brows. His hair hung loose about his shoulders, and she wished to brush it out and twist it back into its usually neat queue to see if it were as soft as it looked.

Ah, but she wished to touch him too much these past weeks, too often caught herself remembering his queue brushing her cheek, his arm beneath her hand. Once she found herself looking at his mouth as he talked and taking in not a word he said. She'd liked him from the minute he saved her from the whipping, but now, in proximity to him daily, she feared she loved him.

Yet he scarcely paid attention to her outside of her work cooking, cleaning, and concentrating on the woodcuts for the shop. The only personal words they exchanged, if one did not count discussions of poems and books, pertained to no news coming forth about her sister or her cousin.

Now he studied the pamphlet that had been wrapped around the rock tossed through the window. His faither stood behind him, doing the same. Neither so much as glanced Fiona's way. She should have remained upstairs safe and warm in her room as had Bronwen and Mrs. Cardew.

Or she could make herself useful.

As quietly as possible, she began to clean up the broken glass. Chilly air, damp from an earlier rainstorm, seeped through the square. Perhaps a heavy piece of pasteboard would stop that until they could find more glass. Perhaps send as far away as Wilmington. And the cost!

Shivering inside her skirt and bodice hastily donned over her night rail, Fiona fitted a piece of stiff paper into the opening then returned to sweeping up the glass. Across the room, the men talked in hushed tones. Owain's face was pale, his father's mouth set in a thin line. When they vanished into the storage room, she understood—Owain had confessed his secret work and Mr. Cardew was more than unhappy about it.

"Prove it was not one of us." Mr. Cardew grumbled his words, as the two men returned to the shop.

Owain emitted a sound like a growl. "Aye, and prove it was not MacFarlane himself who did this."

"But we are the only press in town."

"And anyone can send from another place as—as others have been doing with me."

"Risking this sort of thing to happen to us, or worse."

"I have earned a good bit of specie for us, something

we have never had."

Hurt crossed Mr. Cardew's face, and Owain reached out a hand. "I apologize, sir. You are the finest printer in the colonies and have taught me a great deal."

"Not enough like about being honest with your parents. Or honoring them."

Fiona crouched on the floor, not wanting to hear anything so personal. But the message was clear—Owain didn't trust God any more than she did. The revelation saddened her. She didn't know why. She wanted him to have that inner calm, the peace that all would be well some way because of a belief that God was in control, that she saw in the rest of the Cardews.

Fiona bowed her head, burdened in her heart. She felt responsible. He'd spent precious money saving her, had deceived his family, and now more trouble had come to them possibly through her if this pamphlet pertained to the constable who had wanted her to work for him. She must say something, point that out.

She started to rise.

"Fiona, I am forgetting you were there." Mr. Cardew gave her his gentle smile. "Go throw away that glass then get to your bed."

"Aye, sir." Fiona obeyed the first part but remained in the kitchen beside the hearth. Embers still burned, and she found some warmth there. She heard nothing of what the men said but knelt and stoked the sparks into flames and began to boil water. They would be wanting tea if they intended to remain awake. She wanted tea, a luxury in the Highlands, but something she had been given in Glasgow as her due for good service. The Cardews were generous, too, though it must be costly in the colonies.

"God, why do You hurt these good people so?" she murmured as she worked. "If You loved them, You would take care of them."

"God is not harming us." Owain spoke from the kitchen doorway. "'Tis other people. We take a risk with our pamphlet printing and now someone is using it to harm us in return."

"But you would have enough money to take Mrs. Cardew to a doctor if God really cared."

"Aye, I struggle with that, I confess." He drew near to her and touched one of her braids hanging loosely on her shoulder. "But do you think your own tad, your earthly father, loved you though he could not provide enough for you to eat?"

"He would have given me his portion if I asked. What did God do for me?"

"What did you ask Him to do for you?"

Fiona glanced down. "The old women said to ask for the brooch to be returned."

"Superstitious nonsense, nothing in the Bible."

"We are superstitious in the Highlands, you ken."

"And I am a fraud, you see." He glanced at the kettle on the hearth, the mantel, the brick of the chimney to one side of her. "I talk of trusting God to you and do not do so myself." He strode to the door. "I am going out. The rain left mud and footprints for me to follow, so I will be cold when I return."

So would she, for Fiona intended to follow him. He could claim all he liked that God was taking care of his family, but Mrs. Cardew still looked wan, Jamie MacLaughlin wasn't coming up to scratch in proposing to Bronwen and. . . Well, Fiona couldn't be sad that God had provided Owain with a wife or even a young maid in whom he was interested. His life centered around his work in the print shop and the extra work at night. Fiona would not trust God to take care of him when she could carry one of the kitchen knives and follow, ensure his safety or run for help if something bad happened to him.

Moonlight brightened the once cloudy night sky. Along with the stars, clear there in the fresh air with its sweetness of wood smoke rather than the sourness of coal. Silent on her cork-soled shoes, knowing she was likely ruining them, hoping the soughing of the wind would mask the rustle of her skirt, Fiona slipped behind Owain.

He walked bent over. Occasionally, he stooped to examine the lane then would head off in another direction. Nothing but the two of them and the breeze stirred in the night. It all seemed innocent and impossible that someone had thrown a rock through their window. Their lives had seemed so calm and peaceful, other than Mrs. Cardew's illness, before she came along.

Perhaps she, not the loss of the brooch, took ill tidings wherever she went.

The thought distracted Fiona, and she stumbled in a rut, flung out her hand to catch herself. It struck the side of an unlit lantern. Metal clanged against wood. She lost her knife and dropped to the ground to find it, to hide.

Ahead of her, Owain froze, a dark silhouette against the bright night sky. Then he tilted his head, sniffed, and pivoted toward her. "Fiona?"

She gulped, couldn't speak. Her groping fingers found the knife. She snatched it up, rose, and fled back toward the Cardew house.

Owain caught her in a second. His arms closed around her. Gently, but firmly, he turned her to face him. "What do you think you are doing, merch?"

Girl. He'd just called her nothing more than a girl. Tears stung her eyes. "I was looking out for you. I need to take care of someone I—" She snapped her teeth together and started to raise her hand to her lips.

It was the hand that held the knife.

"What are you doing with this?" Owain snatched it away. "Fiona, you could have gotten hurt. Someone here does not like us, and you are a part of our family. You should not have been so foolish as to follow me."

"Faither would not let me follow my brothers either." Tears flowed down her cheeks. "And they did not come home. Murdag would not bring me to America with her. And she did not come home. God takes everyone and everything away from me." Aching all the way through her chest to her soul, she yanked away from Owain and raced the rest of the way home. She heard Mr. Cardew in the print shop, so she remained in the kitchen, washing her face in icy water from the bucket, then building up the fire to make tea—in earnest this time.

Owain entered behind her, set the knife on the table, then stood gazing at her, his eyes as soft as a velvet cloak. "I have brought trouble on my family and you with my actions. As soon as we find your sister or cousin, I will free you from your indenture."

The notion set an ache in her middle as though he'd plunged the knife there instead of laying it on the table.

"Perhaps I should go to Wilmington myself," Owain continued. "With me gone, no one will wish to harm any of you."

"But I—" Fiona began.

Mr. Cardew entered. "Go back to bed, Fiona," he directed.

"But clean the mud off of your shoes first," Owain added, his voice so low, so tender, she wondered if she dared stay with the Cardews for the sake of her heart. Bad things happened to those she loved, and she knew she loved Owain Cardew.

She determined to avoid him, but that proved impossible, for, after his faither told him he would not be leaving for Wilmington or anywhere else because someone wanted trouble. Owain seemed resolved to need her assistance in the shop, to join him on errands, or accompany him to the kirk along with the rest of the family, including Mrs. Cardew—for with the frosty air of November, her health seemed to improve. She came downstairs more often, even chose to sew by the kitchen fire instead of in her bedchamber. She coughed less and read to Fiona as she worked.

"It's your good food," Bronwen said. "Owain always said mine would kill someone one day, which likely means Jamie will never ask me to wed him."

"Unless he can afford a cook," Fiona suggested.

Perhaps she could serve out her indenture with the MacLaughlins. But no, Mrs. Cardew would need her more than ever without Bronwen. And running away was out of the question. The more deeply Fiona fell in love with Owain, the more she thought about slipping away during the night. She would take her bad luck away with her, and she wouldn't be hurt by losing someone else she loved. She could do it. The Cardews trusted her. Mrs. Cardew began to send her on errands alone, buying thread from the dry goods store, or tallow and wax from the chandlery. One day, Fiona stood at the riverside and watched the boats heading down the river toward Wilmington. She could start her search again there, trade her Sunday shawl Bronwen had given her for passage, or perhaps the Bible Mr. Cardew insisted she accept, would keep her in food and shelter until she found work.

Give away the gifts these kind people had given her? Break their trust? No, she couldn't do it. If God was stronger than the good or bad fortunes the old ladies of the village spoke of, then He would have to protect the Cardews indeed.

She started to turn away from the water, and a hand as rough as the hemp ropes that had bound her for her whipping clamped around her wrist. "Miss MacGill," said Constable MacFarlane, "ye are not considering running off from your indenture, are ye now?"

"Nay, sir." She wouldn't look at him. "I am faithful to the Cardews. They are good people."

"Not all that good, I understand." MacFarlane's grip

tightened until Fiona nearly cried out. "Indeed, I understand their son may be involved in sedition."

"You understand incorrectly, sir." Fiona spoke through clenched teeth.

"I want proof of that."

"I beg your pardon?" She glanced at him.

He smiled, showing missing teeth. "I want to be more than constable here in the hills. If I can deliver the printer of seditious pamphlets to the governor, I will be rewarded."

"I cannot help you, sir."

"You can if I can tell you where your sister is."

Fiona swung toward him, eyes wide. "You know? You know? Where?"

"I have her and that precious brooch. Deliver me proof that Owain Cardew is printing seditious news sheets, and I will free your sister."

Chapter 7

Owain once again examined the pamphlet that had been thrown through the window. Besides the poor quality of the printing itself, the grammar was poor, not the careful wording his former schoolteacher mother insisted they all use. Regardless of the wording, the message came through loud and clear—MacFarlane was an unacceptable constable and needed to be gotten rid of no matter how it happened. Fiona wasn't the first young woman he had tried to force into servitude by enforcing the new law—servitude with his household. The man wasn't married, so wanting a female servant to cook wasn't uncommon; however, all the females had been young and pretty.

"But it's not true." Owain showed the pamphlet to Mam.

"Didn't he admit it with Fiona?" she asked.

"Aye." Owain bit his lip. "But she is uncommon pretty and has no relations here that we can find so far and. . ."

Mam's glowing gaze dried up Owain's words.

"You care for her, do you not, my son?"

Owain ducked his head far enough for his queue to

slide over his shoulder. He tossed the twisted hair back and suddenly recalled an image of feather tendrils of Fiona's golden locks caressing her cheeks—how he wished to do so with his fingertips. That led him to think how badly he wanted to kiss her the night he caught her following him and held her in his arms. A man shouldn't feel that way for a maiden without wishing to wed her.

"She will not trust in the Lord," he muttered.

"And neither will you." Mam set down her needle and the shirt she was sewing for him or Tad, and held out a hand to him. "You take on dangerous work to have money to take me to a doctor in Wilmington or even farther afield if necessary. Yet look at how much better I am. Still you take the risks. Do you not think the Lord will provide without you taking so many chances with our safety?"

Owain took her hand, finding it fragile, yet no longer trembling like that of a palsied old woman. "Is there aught wrong with wanting to make extra money for my family's future security?"

"No, but do you feel peace?"

"I feel peace about nothing." He might as well be honest with Mam. "Especially since Fiona came have I felt no peace. She cuts it up like meat in a stew. After the way she was treated—Mam, one day, I do want to write things that may be seditious, to have the freedom to do this, to say what I like about how people are treated without fear of retribution. I want to make a pamphlet about this law about beating vagrants. It can't be enforced. She tried to find work and no one would help her. She's trying to find her family and—"

"If she sees the anger in your heart and not the peace that what you are doing is of the Lord, she will continue to trust in this brooch and the luck it brought her family, not the Lord."

Owain stared at Mam. "Are you saying I should cease the work?"

"I'm saying that with this, as with how you feel about Fiona, examine your heart and ensure it is being directed by the Lord and not your own desires." She glanced around the kitchen. "And now that we talk of Fiona, she has been gone overly long for the errand I sent her on. I'm wondering—"

Footfalls pounded toward the back door. A moment later, Fiona burst in, windblown and breathless, her cheeks ruddy from cold or exertion or both.

"'Tis so very sorry I am." She dropped a parcel into Mam's basket. "Here is your thread. The stew has not burned, has it?" Without removing her shawl, she reached for the spoon to stir that day's dinner.

And Owain saw the ring of bruising around her wrists.

He touched her arm. "What happened to you?"

"Naught that matters." She tugged down her sleeve. "Would you like the bannocks or the leavened bread with dinner, Mrs. Cardew?"

"Bannocks will do well with the stew." Mam began to gather up her sewing materials. "And I think you can make us a batch of those meat pies with anything left over."

"Aye, they will be fine for Mr. Cardew the younger here to eat while he works late." Fiona's voice held a note of tension.

Owain frowned, but he would wait until they were alone

to ask her what was wrong, who had hurt her. She wasn't going to tell him now, that was for certain.

"I need to get back to my printing. Bronwen is not so good at setting the type. She forgets to put the letters in backward." He strode across the kitchen to the shop, thinking of Mam's question, peace, why he worked late, why he'd kept his extra work secret.

As he gathered up the sheets for shipment, he considered the question with care. He wanted no one to think the Cardews possessed little beyond their small house and printing press.

What if all this work was about pride and greed?

Still uneasy in his middle later that night, though Fiona's dinner had been as flavorful and nourishing as ever, Owain wrapped the bundle of news sheets in oiled cloth, headed for the kitchen door, and came face-to-face with Fiona.

"I am going with you, you ken," she announced.

"No, Fiona, you are not. It is not safe."

"Then you will be safer with me along." She displayed the same sharp knife she'd carried the night he'd caught her following him.

"Fiona—" He stopped. "All right. I'd rather have you at my side then following me. I can keep you safe if I know where you are."

In silence, they slipped into the night. This one proved black with thick clouds covering the moon and stars. An occasional home or shop sported a lantern hanging in front of a doorway, sending a dim pool of light into the blackness. Mostly they found their way by the feel of the road beneath their feet, rough from the autumn rains. Once Fiona stumbled, and Owain grasped her elbow to steady her, then didn't let go. The impulse to slip his arm around her waist sent tension twisting through him like a wire in the wind. He wanted her close at his side, now, forever.

No, he couldn't love her. He must not. She didn't trust in the Lord to live in her life. And perhaps neither did he. She trusted in a brooch to save her village thousands of miles away. He trusted in money to save his mam. What was the difference simply because he was less honest about it by reading his Bible and praying?

Unable to talk to her for fear of being overheard in the night, he simply drew her arm through his and walked with her close to his side and the bundle of pamphlets tucked under his arm. They were printings regarding a private person's desire to lay claim that a fellow shopkeeper was dishonest in his dealings with customers, giving short measure and poor quality, which was why his goods cost less. The writer had collected testimonies from people to prove the claims, since it would, no doubt, give rise to a lawsuit. How the people in the bigger cities loved to sue one another over the smallest slights. But it was none of his business. The businessmen would work through matters on their own. Owain was simply the man making the words possible to spread around. Fiona need not protect him. No one in Cross Creek would take offense at his actions. He'd simply let her come because he wanted her close as much as possible. All the time. Which probably did mean he loved her, foolish heart. And possibly hers was just as foolish, if she wanted to come with him.

The sharp tang of river mud rose against the backdrop of fires, animals, and pine trees scenting the night. Fiona slowed as though reluctant to go near the river.

"I am needing the better shoes for walking in mud," she whispered. "I am ruining the cork on these."

"We will get you some pattens. That will keep your skirts clean, too."

"Pattens?" She paused near a dark building used for storage of goods for shipping. "Won't those be expensive here?"

With their iron rings that fastened to the bottoms of shoes fitting over a lady's delicate slippers to keep their skirts high from the dirt, pattens might be expensive. But Owain wanted to spend the money on her, buy her all the fine things denied her in her destitute upbringing.

"Mam and Bronwen have them," he told her.

Ahead of them, a lantern's light danced off the black water. The boat was there, the man waiting for him to make his delivery and pay him the rest of the money.

"You can wait here," he suggested.

"And watch while they throw you aboard a boat?" Fiona's shook her head hard enough to send her hair tumbling around her shoulders. The breeze lifted soft strands and caressed them against Owain's face. He released her arm and kissed a handful of the tresses before smoothing them back behind her ear, a wrong action, perhaps, yet he didn't regret it.

Nor did she object. She simply gazed up at him with her big eyes and lips parted. He would not, would not, would not kiss her.

He bent his head toward her, his face less than a hand's breadth from hers.

"Who's there?"

They both jumped. Owain's bundle slipped and landed on the ground with a thud. The oiled cloth parted, spilling a few pamphlets onto the mud.

"I will help." Fiona stooped and gathered up the fallen papers.

Owain faced the man who had stopped him from doing something silly like kissing Fiona MacGill, bondswoman, against all morality and probably legalities, too. "Martin, is that you?"

"Aye. Cardew?" The man stepped forward, a short, stocky Welshman who had once been a coal miner before the coal played out and the mine closed back in Wales. Now he ran boats up and down the river making whatever deliveries he could to support his family. "Did not expect you to be coming with a merch."

"Mph." Owain gave a noncommittal sound for response. "Redemptioner."

Identifying her as an indentured servant meant nothing, but under the circumstances, it would do.

"I have your papers, now." Fiona straightened and held out the bundle.

"Good." Martin exchanged the bundle from Fiona for coins with Owain, then trotted off toward his boat.

Owain watched him until he was safely aboard with his family, then returned his attention to Fiona and took her arm to start them home. "I apologize, Miss MacGill."

"For what?"

"For touching your hair, for nearly kissing you. It was wrong of me. We cannot even court."

"I ken we cannot because I am a servant. But I did not think you would like a poor thing like me with all the pretty lasses in Cross Creek. You scarce look my way."

"I dare not. Mam sees too much. It is more than your prettiness." Owain sighed and took her hand in his. He didn't care if anyone heard them talking in the lane now the delivery was made. Home was too close to wait to speak. "I want to be around you all the time, with your scent and your voice and the things you say."

"Except when I talk of the brooch."

"Aye, except when you talk of the brooch. God is our strength and our hope, not ancient metal and stones from royalty."

"And you risk your family by printing for the trust of the Lord?" They reached the Cardew back door and she turned to face him beneath the lantern burning there, her face pale. "'Tis love you I do, Owain Cardew, bold as 'tis for me to say so. But I say it because I cannot bear to see you risk your safety, your very life, and your family for the sil'er."

"Mam—"

"Is healing, and I am thinking 'tis the prayers and fresher air, not potions you will buy from some physician. So where is your trust in the Lord when you risk the lives of everyone you love, including me, whether 'tis love me you do or no." And she yanked one of the pamphlets out from beneath her shawl.

Owain snatched it from her. "You stole this? How could you? How dare—" He snapped his teeth together. "I trusted you. I saved your life and brought you into our house. How could you betray my trust like this?"

"To save you. Or are you thinking that rock got through your window all alone?" She spun away from him.

He rested one hand on her shoulder to stop her before she could open the door. "Fiona, that sheet speaking against MacFarlane had nothing to do with us. We did not create it."

She glanced back at him. "He thinks you did."

Owain felt punched in the belly, not because he didn't already guess that MacFarlane wouldn't think he had been the printer responsible, but because she spoke with such confidence of knowledge. "How do you know what he thinks?" he asked in a low voice.

She stood motionless and as taut as a mast for several seconds, then raised her arm and pulled back the sleeve to her chemise. "He did this the other day when I went for your mither's thread. He said. . ." Her mouth worked, and tears filled her eyes. "Owain, I cannot choose. I ken not how to choose the right way. My heart is torn in two."

"Fiona, what are you saying?" Owain turned her fully toward him and took her hands in his. "What did MacFarlane do to you?"

"Nothing." She pulled her hands free and folded her arms across her middle as though holding in her heart. "Everything. If I tell you. . . But I cannot do this alone. 'Tis the printing. MacFarlane wants to prove you are being seditious in what you print so he can buy his way to a higher office or something. He's trying to force me to give him proof."

"But he won't find it here." Owain brushed the tears from her cheeks with his fingertips and spoke in low, soothing tones. "My dear lady, my love, I have done nothing wrong."

"'Twill not stop him, you ken? He will find a way. He did not like you taking me into your service. He wanted to give me a public beating to show those people he is doing his work well. And you took that from him. So now. . ." She grasped his hands and stared at him like a panicked fawn. "Owain, he has my sister. And if I do not deliver proof of you printing illegal materials by tomorrow, he says he will kill her."

"What?" He could not have understood her, as they murmured to not awaken the household. "He cannot possibly."

"But he does. He gave me proof." She freed one hand, then, from inside her bodice, she removed a small, shining object, a brooch reminiscent of a lion's head, delicate and ancient silverwork and semiprecious stones. "Murdag would ne'er let anyone outside the family have this."

Chapter 8

Owain considered running up the steps and waking Tad. He always had answers. No matter what trouble in which Owain found himself, Tad got him out of it, from saving Fiona to not being overly angry regarding the secret press and hoarded money.

The press that had caused so much trouble for Fiona, might cost her sister her life.

"For eighteen years," Fiona said, her gaze fixed on the trinket, "I have thought naught mattered so much if I could only find this. It was a gift for trying to save a queen. But 'tis no more than metal and stone. 'Tis as dead as the queen who granted it to us."

"It is quite valuable, I think."

"Aye, perhaps where people have the sil'er to buy it. If I had a fortnight, I could sell it in a city and buy Murdag's freedom." She ducked her head, then lifted it again and met his gaze. "Or I had a night to make up something MacFarlane could use against you. Betray you, the man I love, for the sister I have wanted naught but to see again for most of my life."

Betray him. The man she loved. Betray him. Love him.

The words echoed in his head, warred with one another like outraged fencers in a duel gone out of control. His heart raced out of control. Should he pick her up and carry her to the river in the hope of catching Martin before he left, force her aboard so she could do him no harm, or draw her to him and declare his love?

Owain held out his hand. "Let me see it." He needed a way to delay the moment of decision, a few precious seconds to think what was best.

Fiona laid the brooch on his palm.

The silver winked at him in the lantern light, teasing him with its reminder of his own hoarded silver. But that was money for Mam, a dowry for Bronwen, his own ability to wed. He had risked so much to save that money, to hoard it, hide it away. His work had done good in other cities, and no harm in Cross Creek. He shouldn't have to give it all up because one man was greedy for power.

But money bought power.

If he did not give up his money, then his heart was as cold as the stones in the pin. If he did not give up his money, then he didn't love Fiona. He didn't deserve to even think of a future with her, let alone have one.

"'Tis naught but metal and stone." Fiona opened the kitchen door, not even trying to take the brooch back. "The old ladies were wrong. It holds no power for good or ill. I have carried it next to my heart for this day and naught good has happened. I ken not how to help Murdag. I ken not how to help you."

"But God does." Owain set the brooch on the mantel and took Fiona's hands in his. "We need to place our trust in Him, do we not?"

"I ken you would say that. But He has ne'er helped me before."

"Have you ever asked Him and given your whole heart to Him?"

"Nay. Have you?"

Owain glanced toward the storage room. "No. I thought I had, but now I see I have not. I have risked too much to build wealth, have money set aside no one knew about. Tad and Mam knew of some, but not all until the other night. Perhaps it is enough to pay MacFarlane to leave us alone and buy his way to power, if that is what he wants."

"But 'tis Bronwen's dowry."

"If Jamie does not want her poor, then he does not deserve her. And Mam does not want a physician from the city. And if I am a man who trusts more in money than the Lord, I do not deserve the bride of my heart." He took a step toward the storage room, then swung back and bent his head to kiss her—the bride he wanted of his heart, Lord willing—then turned back toward his secret stash.

Beneath the stack of crates that hid the press, then beneath the press, he lifted a floorboard and removed a tin box. It weighed heavy in his hands for all its small size. Coins rattled and rang together like tiny bells.

"Lord, this money is Yours, not mine," he said aloud.

Fiona watched him from the doorway, her fingers to her

lips as though she held his kiss there for a moment, then she dropped her hand to her side. "You cannot do this for me. 'Tis my sister."

"It is my disobedience and greed." They looked at one another and smiled. His heart aching with love for her, he replaced the floorboard, then began to slide the press back into place, but stopped.

He would leave it out for everyone to see. No more secrets. No more deceptions.

"Lord willing, one day I will use this for good, but not until I know it is what He wants."

Money box in hand, he turned his back on the press that had made the wealth in the box possible. He wanted to rush out the door and confront MacFarlane, offer the silver to ransom Fiona's sister. But action without thought of the consequences had gotten him and the lady he loved into this difficulty. This time he would think and pray and trust in the Lord.

He set the box on the kitchen table. "That should be enough, I hope."

"Perhaps with this it will be?" Fiona lifted the brooch from the mantel and laid it atop the little tin chest.

Chapter 9

The instant she set the brooch atop Owain's money box, Fiona experienced a calmness, an easing of pain inside her heart she never recalled being gone from her before. Like the ropes that had bound her wrists in preparation for her whipping, her belief that the brooch was all important to her happiness and prosperity, her security and love, had bound her spirit. Now she had given it up in the hope it would save Murdag from Constable MacFarlane.

"Nay, not hope," she said aloud, "trust that God will see us through this. I want to rush out right now and find MacFarlane and see if he will take the money to leave you alone."

"I would like to do the same." Owain smiled. "But I think I need to think before I act for once."

"At last," Mr. Cardew spoke from the kitchen doorway.

Fiona and Owain jumped and swung toward him.

He smiled at them. "Did you not think I would be watching out when two young people were alone together? I did not expect this." He gestured toward the box and brooch.

"Or the ill will of a man in whom we have placed our trust in this village. I would gather all the men I can and have him bodily removed if he were not holding your sister captive. A man willing to go that far may not stop at abduction to gain a means to power."

"I know, sir." Owain's mouth set as grim as his faither's. "I cannot think how we can work a bargain."

"I—" Fiona licked her suddenly dry lips and swallowed against an equally dry throat. "I wish to trust in God to keep Murdag safe and show us the right way. I believe God is not so far away after all, and I have been foolish for not seeing the truth since He brought me to you all."

The two Cardew men she loved so well, the elder like the faither she had lost to illness, the younger the sweetheart she thought she would never find, exchanged glances then held out their hands.

"Come upstairs, daughter," Mr. Cardew said. "My other ladies will wish to be in the praying with us, I'm thinking."

His other ladies, like she was part of the family, not a bondservant. If only Murdag were free, Fiona would know complete joy.

"Lord, if You can—" She cleared her throat. "Nay, Lord, I ken You can bring this mon to justice and free my sister."

And in the morning, He did.

Fiona barely finished lacing up her bodice when pounding sounded on the kitchen door. Heart racing ahead of her, she sped down the steps, slipping on the smooth treads, colliding with Owain coming from the shop.

"It cannot be MacFarlane, no?" Her words came out

between puffs for breath. "He said tonight."

The money and brooch still lay on the table though.

Owain squeezed her hand then strode past her to draw back the bolt and open the door. "Who—"

Six adults and what seemed like twice as many children crowded into the kitchen gabbling in a blend of English and Gaelic. They looked familiar, though red hair had faded a little and silver streaked the blond. But a pair of bright blue eyes met Fiona's from over the broad shoulder of a middle-aged man, and she knew.

"Murdag. And Rory?" Fiona's throat closed. "Seona?"

Her sister and brother-in-law, and her cousin. They were there, alive and free and looking well.

Fiona's head spun. "How? MacFarlane said he had you. He gave me the brooch. He—"

"Will get his just justice." A fine-looking middle-aged man strode forward and shook Owain's hand. "Colin Campbell."

"My husband," Seona added, as she and Murdag vied for who would hug Fiona first. "And here are two men who were naught but boys when you last saw them."

Fiona stared and stared at the two men, tall, broad, and handsome and in their early thirties perhaps. "Duncan? Dougal?" She hadn't dared say the names of her two lost brothers in so long she found them odd to her tongue. "You did not die."

"Our wives said we would if we did not bring you home." They embraced her, explaining their wives were absent due to babies too young for travel.

The children, Seona's and Murdag's, were introduced, too many names for Fiona to remember. The Cardews arrived and, for the first time since her arrival in Cross Creek, the parlor came into use. Bronwen took over care of the younger children while Murdag and Fiona made tea. Seona began to talk to Mrs. Cardew about her illness and make recommendations. The men gathered to discuss what to do with MacFarlane and tell of how they had simply swarmed his house to find Murdag when she did not return with Fiona.

"We simply went there because he was the constable," Rory said. "But now you can come home."

"Nay, I cannot." Fiona stood in the parlor doorway, her hands burdened with a tray of bannocks. "I am a bondservant to the Cardews. I still have ten months to serve."

Her family grew quiet, even the children.

"We did not ken 'twas so bad for you, lass." Rory rested his hand on her shoulder. "But do not fash yourself over it. The Lord has been good to us. We can buy your freedom."

"There is no need for that." From the far side of the room, where he had been engaged in conversation with Seona's husband, Owain strode forward. "We will release her from her indenture. She never should have been forced into it to begin with. The law is wrong and should be ch—"

"Owain," Mr. Cardew cautioned from behind Fiona.

"Aye, sir." Owain bowed his head, sending his queue sliding over his shoulder.

Fiona wanted to grab the end of the twist of hair and yank him to her, demand to know if all he'd said the night before was true. So easily he was letting her go. Much of the joy in seeing her family—most of it anyway—dimmed. A cold lump formed in her middle.

"You all have been more than kind." She managed credible steadiness to her voice. "You paid my fine. You should get repaid."

"We will find a way to get coin," Rory began. "'Tis scarce enough, though we have the means to get it if necessary."

"It is not," Owain reiterated.

"We have the brooch." Murdag retrieved it from the table. "Getting Fiona back is more than worth giving it up."

"But you are the eldest," Fiona said. "'Tis yours."

"I give it to you to buy your freedom." Murdag pressed it into Fiona's hand.

She had wanted it there for so long, she started to close her fingers around it. She had always known it would buy her freedom from poverty, from loneliness, from losing one family member after another. Now, with a simple gesture, she could have the love and laughter and plenty she saw in her family.

And lose what she wanted most—Owain's love and their own family together; a future with him and the continuing certainty that God cared about her every need.

"Lord, I am trusting You to make this right," she murmured.

Then she strode forward and stood nearly toe to toe with Owain. "Is this what you wish for?" She held out the brooch. "'Tis yours if so. 'Twill make a fine gift for a bride."

"So it will." His musical voice sang in her ears. His dark eyes glowed down at her. "But I will need a bride to give it to, will I not?"

A hush fell over the room so profoundly Fiona thought everyone could hear the pounding of her heart.

"Indeed," Owain continued, "I thought I had found one."

"Aye, and you were quick enough to let her go," Fiona shot back.

"I cannot wed a bondswoman." He took the brooch from her hand. "But now you are free to choose to wed me if you will." He grinned. "And perhaps with permission—"

Everyone started to laugh and talk at once.

Owain took Fiona's hands in his and drew her into a corner. "Are you certain? You may not see your family all that often."

"Nay, but I ken they are here and alive and well. And I want to be your wife."

"Ah, Fiona, but I love you." Owain leaned toward her. The end of his queue brushed her cheek.

She caught hold of it and brushed it across her cheek, finding it as soft as it looked. "I love you, Owain Cardew."

He kissed her, in front of his family and hers, then pressed the brooch into her hand. "For our daughter."

Award-winning author Laurie Alice Eakes has always loved books. When she ran out of available stories to entertain and encourage her, she began creating her own tales of love and adventure. In 2006 she celebrated the publication of her first hardcover novel. Much to her astonishment and delight, it won the National Readers Choice Award. Besides writing, she teaches classes to other writers, mainly on research, something she enjoys nearly as much as creating characters and their exploits. A graduate of Asbury College and Seton Hill University, she lives in Texas with her husband and sundry animals.

SUGARPLUM HEARTS

by Gina Welborn

Dedication

To Laurie Alice Eakes for being a mentor,
critique partner, and (most of all) dear friend. . .
despite her love of pets of the feline variety.

To Jeremy for being a man of grace. Always.

But the God of all grace, who hath called us unto his eternal glory by Christ Jesus, after that ye have suffered a while, make you perfect, stablish, strengthen, settle you.
1 PETER 5:10

Chapter 1

Fayetteville, North Carolina
June 1789

"You, Finley Sinclair, have a way with words," Mrs. MacDubh announced with a wee bit of flirtation in her tone while the gray tabby in her lap stared intently at him.

Finley smiled at the couple sitting across from him, both he guessed to be in their midtwenties, near his age. "A way with felines, too," he boasted. Yet he nervously hoped the mother cat didn't take his words as an invitation to befriend him. He had never actually coddled a cat before. Not that he disliked them.

He had merely never owned a pet of the feline or canine or even equine variety.

While Mrs. MacDubh fanned her face in the humid upstairs sitting room, three mewing kittens continued to climb over her husband who sat next to her on the blue velvet settee. Their home above their shop held only the basics of furniture and decorations. Still, Angus MacDubh likely earned more in a month making ropes than Finley had ever made in two.

The young rope maker pried a kitten off his chest. Again. "Mr. Sinclair, did the cat you climbed the ship's mast to rescue appreciate your *way* with felines?" he asked while a second furry barnacle attached to the shoulders of his plaid shirt. Like his wife's, his voice held the barest hint of Scottish burr.

"Aye. Enough to use my body as a scratching post on her way down." Finley patted his buckskinned legs. "Still bear the scars."

Mr. MacDubh held the two white kittens under his left arm and reached for the gray kitten behind his neck. "Would you like a cat, Mr. Sinclair?"

While Finley was tempted to rescue the rope maker, he shook his head. Last thing he wanted was to make a furry friend. At least, not when he had no home to give it.

"You sure?" Mr. MacDubh said, while his expression begged Finley to reconsider.

The kittens were rather cute.

Their short hair was far longer than the black bristles on Finley's scalp—the latter a consequence of the lice outbreak on the ship. An outbreak limited to the wig-wearing captain. Yet the captain had ordered that every marine be "shaved bare-headed as the day he was born," which had made Finley laugh because for generations Sinclairs had been born with dark hair long enough to braid.

Finley felt a smile tug at the corners of his mouth.

He could imagine sitting at home by the fire. Cat in lap. Feet propped up. His wife would be in a chair next to his, darning clothes as they discussed the passage of scripture they'd read that night. Or maybe they would be listening to their sons take turns reading from God's Word. One of his sons would become a doctor, the other a minister. They would heal body and soul.

"Perhaps someday," he answered and finished the apple cider in his tin cup. The sweet tartness of Mary MacDubh's secret family recipe made up for the narrowness of the wooden rocker he sat in. After three years of surviving on one meal a day in order to save as much he could, the hearty meals during his work passage to America had added muscular bulk.

Finley leaned forward, rested his elbows on his knees, and held his empty cup with both hands. Time to focus on the task at hand.

"Well now, Mrs. MacDubh," he said cheerfully, "seeing how I have been in Carolina for two weeks and my thirst has been mercifully sated with this lovely cider of yers, I can say the good Lord had brought us together for a purpose."

Her soft smile added a glow to her pudgy cheeks. "You're a dear."

Finley looked at her husband. "Mr. MacDubh, I would like to broker yer ropes for ye."

A crease deepened between the rope maker's brows.

"Angus, we should hire him."

With an exaggerated groan, the rope maker finally handed the mewing kittens, one at a time, to his wife. "I like you, Mr. Sinclair. I would be honored to work with you, especially since you're from the same part of Scotland that my grandparents emigrated, but I contracted with a new broker last fall. He's earned me a fair profit." With an apologetic furrow to his brow, Angus MacDubh stood and motioned his russet head to the staircase. "I know you have other possible clients to attend. I need to reopen the shop, so I'll walk you out."

Despite the sinking feeling in his gut, Finley handed Mrs. MacDubh his empty cup, quickly muttered his thanks, and then followed the third-generation North Carolinian outside onto Person Street. The dying afternoon sun still brought warmth to the air. He had visited longer with the MacDubhs than he had with any other potential clients. 'Course, none of them had served him cranberry tea biscuits and three cups of cider.

As they stood under the MACDUBH ROPES sign, Finley wiped his damp brow with the rolled-up sleeve of his white linen shirt. "I will be brokering for Overton Shipwares from now on"—*if I can find enough clients to secure the position*—"so I will stop in when I am here next, in case ye changed yer mind."

Mr. MacDubh shook Finley's hand. "Thank you, Mr. Sinclair."

"'Twill be my honor if ye called me Finley."

"Then you must call me Angus." He smiled. "When you're in Fayetteville again, be sure to stop by earlier in the day, Finley. Mary fries her haggis to perfection."

"Will do, Angus," Finley answered heartily. He paused. While the couple was one he would like to consider friends, he feared appearing too presumptuous, but the sweetness of the cider lingered in his mouth. Cinnamon he knew for certain. Maybe ginger. "Might I have another wee cup or two of cider when I return?"

Angus glanced over his shoulder at the closed shop door. Then he leaned closer to Finley. "I'll give you Mary's secret recipe if you'd sell those felines of hers. I woke yesterday to find a kitten's tail in my mouth. A man doesn't need to breathe or eat cat hair."

Finley nodded, even though he knew nothing of a cat's blessings or curses. Still, if he could make money selling felines, he would. At this point, he would sell anything. Not that he was having any luck finding anything to sell.

"Godspeed," Angus said with another pat to Finley's arm.

He nodded and waited until Angus re-entered the shop.

Even if he sold all three kittens and the mother cat, he would not have the clients needed to secure a permanent position with Overton Shipwares.

After having spoken to every tar boiler, pitch man, pine resin harvester, and rope maker in the area, he had not a single client. Somehow he would have to find someone with a product needing to be sold to merchants in Wilmington. Even better would be a product he could sell in Charleston and in Norfolk. If only he could pray clients into existence.

But the day was not yet over.

Nor would his optimism die.

Whistling a hymn that was drowned out by the *clickety-clack* of the numerous horse-drawn buggies rolling down the dirt-hardened street, Finley strolled west down the equally busy pavement as he headed to the Maysion Hotel where he had tied his horse. He dodged people as he strolled past the Cape Fear Bank, a cobbler shop, wig maker storefront, and the two-story whitewashed brick building housing the *Fayetteville Gazette*. He could have picked a good dozen pockets, if he had wanted. That, though, would be the wrong response to his quandary.

As he crossed Town House Square, where east-west Person Street turned into Hay and north-south Gillespie turned into Green, he smiled and nodded at the affable residents who exchanged greetings. The good Lord had not rescued him from his past and seen him safely to America, only to desert him in this hour of failure. Tomorrow, Finley would find a client.

And if not tomorrow then the day after or the day after.

Eventually he would succeed.

He would never quit trying. Or working hard.

If he did, he would not deserve to own his own farmland. He needed that land so he could have the financial means to support the education needed for his sons' futures. Granted, he knew no potential Mrs. Finley Sinclair, so he was presuming much for children he had yet to have. Nevertheless, before the new century arrived, he would have a farm, a wife, two sons, a daughter, and a cat to sit on his lap every evening as he rested from the day's work in the field.

The good Lord gave him more than a new life.

He gave Finley joy and peace and hope for a brighter tomorrow.

At the next intersection, Finley stopped walking and whistling. Across the street, the three-story box-shaped inn towered over the other buildings. Black shutters framed the opened casement windows on each level. Like many of the other bricked buildings in Fayetteville, the Maysion Hotel had a steep gable roof and—unlike what he was used to in soot-covered Glasgow—looked new. Everything in America had freshness about it. Even the breeze.

He breathed deep.

The air smelled of roasted pork. Not a portion of a pig in the oven, but he could imagine the entire thing hung over a pit until the juicy meat fell off the bone. Which made his mouth water. Add some fried potatoes and a slice of pie, like he'd had this morning. He released a weary breath. Considering the dent in his savings after buying a reliable draft horse, what he needed more than food was a client.

Three clients minimum, to be exact. From here in Fayetteville, where he kept finding friendly residents not needing a broker.

I need help. Father, Spirit, Good Shepherd, lead me to where I need to go.

"Then hear me now, Mr. Lamb," the female voice said with just enough force to add crispness to her girlish tone. "You have my answer."

How did—

Finley glanced heavenward.

God had never been so direct before.

Still, who was Finley to doubt heavenly intervention, even though the voice was female and had an odd accent. Scottish yet not. He looked to the building on the other side of the intersection. The owner of the voice gave a linen-covered pewter plate to the lithe man standing under the grapevine-covered archway. Ivy grew from the front of the one-story building to the arch's lattice top. An ebony-haired lass in a pink floral gown stepped outside, closing the door behind her, and what sounded like a lock clicked.

"Miss Cardew, I beseech you for *another* answer."

"You ask for one I cannot give."

"You must reconsider." The man shifted the plate to his left hand, causing the embroidered covering to shift. "Your father agreed a marriage between our families would be beneficial to both."

Was there anything worse than hearing a grown man whine?

She reclaimed her tray. "Then in twelve years, you may propose to my niece." Her response carried enough glee that Finley suspected she was smiling, unlike the brown-suited man standing in front of her. "Good day, sir."

She took a step to the left, and Mr. Lamb grabbed her elbow, just above the lace on her three-quarter-length sleeve.

"Miss Cardew—Seren, may I call you Seren? For my love for you has been seared into my heart. A woman like you shouldn't be working in trade."

"Release me."

He did not. "You must marry me," he ordered, stepping closer.

Between the large gaps in the ivy-covered archway, Finley could see the lass back up until the white cap covering her hair was pressed against the door. Surprisingly, she kept her plate held out away from them, perfectly balanced, although the handkerchief was perched precariously to the side, hanging about halfway off. Best guess was she had some type of pastry on the tray. He would have to move closer to know for sure.

"Step away," she warned.

Mr. Lamb leaned forward, as if to kiss her.

"Miss Cardew," Finley called out. In four strides, he crossed to where the couple stood. Ignoring the more boney-than-lithe man, Finley admired the lass's oval face and heavily lashed eyes. Pale blue. Endless. Like the sky he had admired for weeks as he worked his way across the Atlantic. "Miss Seren Cardew?"

Though looking at him warily, she nodded. "Yes?"

"I have been looking for ye." As the words fell from his lips, he almost believed they were true. "Will ye walk with me to. . . ?" He motioned to nowhere in particular. Really, coming up with a creative response was a bit much to ask a man conflicted between the exquisite lass standing before him and the candied violets peeking out from underneath her tray's embroidered cloth.

Miss Seren Cardew said naught to him.

Mr. Lamb looked equally unimpressed.

So Finley added—this time completely truthful—"I think my Father suggested we speak."

Chapter 2

He was handsome, Seren would grant him that much.

In a rugged, Scottish sort of way. If one found that earthy manliness attractive compared to Mr. Lamb's genteel appearance. However, the stranger's melodic brogue reminded her of Aunt Murdag and of her mother when she lost her temper, although a rare occurrence. Still to this day, though, her mother could coax Seren to sleep with a Gaelic lullaby.

Not that she wanted this man to sing to her.

Carefully readjusting the linen covering her tray of comfits she'd made for her mother's birthday, Seren evaluated the Scotsman standing with his left leg slightly blocking Mr. Lamb from reaching her. He was considerate, she would grant him that, too. Based on the simplicity of his V-necked white shirt, well-worn buckskins and boots, tanned skin, and thick Scottish accent, she guessed he was a new immigrant. The last letter from her oldest brother had said several ships from Scotland had unloaded recently in Wilmington, with a couple more due soon.

Since he wasn't leaving, she ought to say something.

"You *think* your father wishes us to speak?" she questioned, while ignoring Mr. Lamb's lovesick gaze.

"Know, Miss Cardew. I *know*," he said with more confidence in his melodic tone yet his dark brown eyes held uncertainty. "I was speaking to Him, and then ye—Lamb—the answer. . ." His words trailed off, likely because he realized how anomalous his explanation sounded.

Mr. Lamb cleared his throat. "Sir, how is it you know my fiancée?"

"I'm not his fiancée," Seren corrected while not glancing away from the chiseled-cheeked Scotsman.

"You will be," Mr. Lamb bragged.

She glared at the vexing lawyer-assemblyman. "I am not *your* fiancée. Unlike you, I clearly remember saying no. All six times this month already." Praise the Lord, her brothers weren't as daft-minded as this man. To think he represented the interests of Fayetteville residents in the General Assembly.

Though they were less than a handful of inches apart in height, the muscular Scotsman seemed to tower over Mr. Lamb, who wasn't unattractive in his own right.

The Adam's apple in Mr. Lamb's throat bobbed. "I, ahhh. . ."

Since neither man seemed to have a coherent response, Seren muttered a "good day" and stepped around them to walk to the edge of the bricked pavement.

She waited for two buggies to roll past before holding the

linen over her comfits and hurrying across the street. After passing Scott Mercantile, she paused to inhale the fragrance of the herb garden behind it then headed north. In the quietness of the tree-lined lane, she could only hear her heels click against the bricks and a few birds chirping. This town—this perfect ambiance—was something she could enjoy every day for the rest of her life.

Fayetteville was home.

And she couldn't help but smile.

Home.

The sound of the word sated with the same sweetness as her candied violets. No matter what, she wasn't moving again.

She passed the Morgans' stately bricked house, turned left onto Maiden Lane, and then, slowing her pace, waved at Miss Keen who was still working in the garden in front of her small one-story stone home. In the time since Seren had passed Miss Keen's home this morning, her garden looked unchanged.

Besides embroidering linen handkerchiefs, circling all the errors on each edition of the *Fayetteville Gazette*, and waiting for Seren to walk past every day, what did the thirty-eight-year-old spinster do with her time? Clearly the former governess wasn't gardening. Neither her apron nor her mustard-yellow homespun gown had a dirt or grass stain. Although, the dogwoods to the left of her garden had strings tied to the lower branches. Now that Seren noticed them, she also saw strings tied on several of the shrubs framing the pavement to the front door.

Should she ask?

No, she didn't want to know.

Using her hoe as a cane—not that she needed a cane—Miss Charity Keen approached the whitewashed fence. For someone with minimal gray strands in her auburn hair and even fewer wrinkles on her plain face, the petite woman behaved as if she were three times Seren's age.

"What have you there?" she ordered more than asked. As her steely-eyed gaze focused on Seren's scalloped pewter tray, she removed the gardening gloves Seren's parents had given her for Christmas. "Get over here, Miss Cardew. I'm practically blind. Might be deaf in one ear, too."

Seren doubted that.

She met Miss Keen beside the latched front gate, near where a fragrant rosebush grew horizontally along the fence, and removed the linen covering. "Candied violets and a few marzipan figurines," she said dutifully, as if she were standing in front of the classroom reciting a Jonathan Edwards sermon. "Each is a member of the family. They're for Mama's fifty-seventh birthday."

Shaking her head, Miss Keen let out a loud *humph.* "Fiona didn't look ill when she brought me a copy of your father's paper this morning. I should have suspected something when she insisted on sharing a pot of noodle soup overly seasoned with basil. What sickness has she contracted?"

Seren held back her exasperated sigh. Her comfits weren't disguising any medication. How many times did she have to explain that to Miss Keen and the other Fayetteville residents? Listening to the apothecary's chastisement of her this morning in front of the mayor for selling candy-coated pharmaceuticals that she—a female—hadn't been trained to dispense. . .

This time Seren gave in to her sigh.

Why couldn't anyone believe her sugarplums weren't much more than dried fruit, honey, and spices?

She lifted the ivory linen cloth Miss Keen had embroidered with red and pink flowers. "Miss Keen, my candies contain no pharmaceuticals."

Miss Keen's eyes narrowed. "You expect good folks to pay good money for comfits that won't do a lick of good for their constipation and coughs?" She leaned forward and lowered her voice. "They contain poison, don't they?"

"They're nothing but sugar to tickle the tongue. Try a candied violet. My mother loves them." She held the sweets closer for Miss Keen to reach. Only Miss Keen didn't move.

"Do your parents know you're selling poison?"

"They're not poison," Seren ground out.

"So you say."

"Try one."

"Thank you kindly," Miss Keen responded so cheerfully Seren couldn't be offended, "but I'll eat my own non-poisoned violets."

Seren could easily make a list of at least six suitable, though rather sarcastic, retorts. She wisely settled on: "Mine have a sugar coating."

"Thus said the stepmother to fair Margarete von Waldeck."

"For decades, the French have eaten comfits and no one—"

"Miss Cardew!" the Scotsman called out.

Seren jerked her gaze to the left. What had possessed him to follow her? Though his pace was casual, the Scotsman clearly was headed her way with his draft horse trailing. With its white face and legs and brown coat, she had to admit the huge animal was an impressive piece of horseflesh. Her oldest brother would greatly approve.

Still, she allowed a little growl in her throat to linger and die slowly. What could they possibly have to talk about? The man couldn't even form an explicable sentence, and she had no ability to read minds.

"Someone lit a fire on his tail," Miss Keen muttered. "Think he fancies you?"

"I doubt it," Seren insisted.

"Looks like he does," Miss Keen countered.

Seren released a pent-up breath. "Upon my word, I don't know him."

"Is he one of those Frogs you know from Charleston?"

"I told you, I don't know him."

Miss Keen didn't even pretend to look convinced. "We'll see, Lady Macbeth. Where's your maid?"

"Jane is my apprentice, and she went home early today with a stomach ailment."

"You poison her?"

This time Seren didn't respond. She felt her lips tighten and nose twitch.

Almighty Lord, fill me with the patience that passes all understanding because, at this moment, I need it more than I need peace.

The Scotsman stopped a respectable distance from them yet close enough for Seren to touch him if she were so inclined.

She wasn't.

His gaze focused intently on hers. "Miss Cardew—I do not, umm, ye left before—aye, 'twas the good Lord who directed me—I—ye. . ."

Miss Keen whacked the fence with her hoe. "Spit it out, lad. Miss Cardew and I aren't getting any younger standing here."

He ran a hand across the bristled black hair on his scalp. Probably had—

"Lice infection?" Miss Keen blurted.

Somehow the Scotsman's tanned skin took on a reddish hue from his cheeks down to his throat. "Nay, ma'am. 'Twas a precaution. The ship's captain—"

"Was at fault." Miss Keen gave a dismissive wave. "Yes, yes, yes. Every man needs someone else to blame for his woes, which is why I refused every suitor's proposal. Are you looking to court Miss Cardew? I never met a girl more in need of marriage to cure her."

Seren's mouth gaped as she stared at the petulant spinster. Of all the—

She turned to the Scotsman, expecting him to look vaguely ill since that's rather how she felt.

Instead he grinned. His brown eyes twinkled; she thought—no, knew—*twinkled* was the most ridiculous word she could use. Yet she couldn't think of anything else to describe what his eyes were doing. Nor could she stop staring. Or stop feeling as if her world was spinning—or wasn't spinning at all like it should. He transfixed, confused, and annoyed her at the same time.

The man had good teeth, she'd grant him that, too.

Then he shifted his horse's reins to his left hand, leaned against the fence, and gave Miss Keen his full attention. "I thought the good Lord wished me to speak to Miss Cardew, but methinks He wanted me to follow the lass to ye." He reached for her hand and brushed a kiss along the back. "Finley Sinclair, at yer service, ma'am."

One moment Miss Keen's plain face was a reproachful mask. Then something in her blue eyes changed, and she smiled. Smiled!

In the last eight months of living in Fayetteville, Seren had never seen her mother's younger friend look pleased with anything. Now she was beaming. Like a star radiating from the heavens. That could mean nothing good.

They spoke directly to each other, without a care or concern for Seren. He was from Glasgow. Miss Keen's parents had been from Glasgow, too. He thought North Carolina was lovely. She did, too. He was a broker. She broke something that very morning. Somewhere between their numerous commonalities, Seren heard one of them say that love was in the air. Naturally the other agreed.

Naturally.

With a roll of her eyes, Seren turned from the doting pair and headed down the walk to her parents' home. She was one and twenty with her whole life before her. That Miss Keen, a woman ten, twelve, maybe fifteen years older than the man whose name Seren probably couldn't remember, had an admirer—well, Seren would be happy for her. She certainly wasn't interested in hearing of Finley Sinclair's life in Glasgow or what brought him to America or what the good Lord told him about anything, especially in relation to talking to her.

She spared a quick glance over her shoulder.

Whatever the Scotsman had said made Miss Keen laugh.

With a grumble, Seren refocused on the tree-canopied path before her. She had no time to waste thinking about a man she didn't know and whose name she could barely remember. She had far more important things to do, like decorating Mama's cake and planning what conserves she'd prepare tomorrow *and* not sparing another thought on a man who was a bit more than moderately attractive. Even with Miss Keen wearing fancy heels, the top of Miss Keen's head would only reach his midchest. Imagine them at a cotillion. Wasn't there a rule about spinsters not dancing?

There should be.

Especially with rakes.

A man needed to be far more than handsome and considerate to capture Seren's interest. At home in her Bible, she had a list of a dozen items she was looking for in a mate. Doubtful Finley Sinclair would meet more than one—all right, three—qualifications.

Love was in the air.

Seren released a most unladylike snort.

"Mr. Sinclair, you have a way with words," Miss Keen cooed,

with her hand resting on his forearm.

Finley could not cease grinning at the petite woman. She reminded him of Aunt Ailis, his lone kin who supported his decision to leave for America. Why Miss Keen had never married was beyond him. She was a grand lady.

"Aye, ma'am. Have a way with lovely women, too," he boasted, while doing everything in his power not to glance Miss Cardew's way. He would not have minded tasting one of the sweets he had seen her offer Miss Keen.

"You? A way with women?" Miss Keen laughed. Loud. Her gaze shifted from him to the retreating Miss Cardew. "Then why is she leaving?" Before he could respond, she fisted the front of his shirt. "That girl is the least marriage-minded female this side of the Atlantic."

He had a feeling, if she so desired, Miss Keen could tar and feather his hide.

"That has to do with me how?"

She released her hold then smoothed the front of his shirt. "I suppose, laddie, I can't expect you to be smart and pretty."

This time Finley laughed. "I'm here to find clients, not a wife." *Yet.*

Humph sounded from Miss Keen's throat. "Help Miss Cardew sell her comfits, and clients will seek you out for achieving the impossible."

Finley felt his eyes widen. "Broker candy? I know ship wares and farming. I do not sell candied violets and sugar-plums." Still he needed something to broker so he could earn the remaining funds he needed to buy farmland in the Ohio Valley.

He paused and thought for a moment. Sugar did make most medicines more palatable.

"What illnesses do her confections cure?"

Miss Keen shook her head in clear disappointment. "None. They're nothing but sugar. I told her no self-respecting Carolinian has the frivolity to spend hard-earned money on something as pointless as candy, not like those lazy Frogs living in Charleston do. The French. . ." Whatever insult she would have given died off.

They both stared at Miss Cardew. With her linen-covered tray in one hand, she opened an iron gate, walked inside, then latched it closed without sparing another glance his direction. The clever lass had spirit.

How difficult could it be for him to sell candied violets? Unless—

"Are her confections palatable?" he asked, looking at the spinster.

Miss Keen shrugged. "Her maid is at home with a stomach ailment. In twenty-one years, I've never known Jane Wilcox to be ill."

"She could have eaten too much."

"I suspect poison," Miss Keen said grimly. "Miss Cardew apprenticed with a French confectioner when her family lived in Charleston. The girl may be too naive to realize the added ingredients are toxic. Can't trust a Frog to be an upstanding citizen no matter how long they've been naturalized."

Finley held his response. He imagined men good and bad could be found among any nationality.

"What brought the Cardews to Fayetteville?" he wondered aloud.

"Her father is the part owner and editor-in-chief of the *Gazette*." After a quick glance around the empty-but-for-them lane, Miss Keen leaned forward. "Owain Cardew was a pamphleteer during the Revolution. He had a bounty on his head until the British finally left Charleston back in '82. 'Course, once a revolutionist, always a revolutionist. I check his paper every day for secret codes. Haven't found one yet." She sounded oddly dejected.

As the afternoon sun continued to sink down the horizon, Finley tapped his right hand against his thigh. Brokering confections that were not anything but confections? Could he? Should he? Overton Shipwares would not sell them, but Overton Mercantile might.

The more he thought about the idea, the more it seemed possible.

'Twas merely the matter of finding the right buyers.

Aye, he could do this. *If* he could convince Miss Cardew that working together was the solution to both their quandaries. Maybe if she did not gaze at him so intently with those distracting pale blue eyes of hers, he would manage to form a cohesive sentence.

"Miss Keen, will ye—"

"Spare me the marriage proposal, Mr. Sinclair. I rejected enough suitors in my life. I don't need the guilt from rejecting another." The corner of her mouth indented slightly. From the pocket of her apron, she withdrew a folded white linen handkerchief and gave it to Finley. "Here's an excuse for you to follow Miss Cardew to her home. I meant to give it to her earlier, but then you came sauntering down the lane and I forgot."

He found that strangely untruthful. She struck him as having a pinpoint mind. Finley brushed his thumb across the pink roses embroidered along the scalloped edge. He looked at the stitching underneath—as expertly sewn as the top.

"Is this yer handiwork?" he asked, awed.

She nodded yet didn't look the least bit prideful.

"Seren uses them in her shop. The girl, unlike her parents, lives with the simplicity of a Quaker. I think. . ." Her gaze fell to the rosebush beside the front gate. And her voice took on a distant—almost melancholy—sound. "When a person has to be ready to flee at a moment's notice, she must learn to survive only on necessities. She learns to protect her heart against attachments."

Finley said naught, just nodded in understanding. He had a feeling Miss Keen was not solely referring to Miss Cardew.

She smacked the side of his arm. "Stop dawdling, lad. The Cardews will be eating supper soon, and you need to get over there in time to join them."

Finley took a step then stopped. With the edge of his fingers, he lifted Miss Keen's dainty hand to his lips, noticed how threadbare the hem of her sleeve was, and placed a kiss on her knuckles. "I am in your debt."

She muttered another little *humph*.

Instead of arguing with her, Finley took off down the lane with his draft horse following. If supper included those candied violets Miss Cardew had been carrying, he was more than happy to deliver the handkerchief. That he would have another chance to admire the lovely lass's fine eyes never even crossed his mind.

Chapter 3

While their cook and her youthful granddaughter finished preparing the supper meal, Seren stood at the other end of the pine table in the center of the warm one-room kitchen behind her parents' house. A breeze from the opened window on her left fluttered through to the opened window on the opposite wall, cooling her slightly. Seren held the final marzipan figurine over the glazed pound cake. Where should she put this last one?

Her tiny "mother and father" sat on a blanket looking at her mother's drawing, while Seren's minuscule "brothers" were playing catch with a rag ball.

In Seren's memory of that day on the North Carolina upper coast, she'd entertained herself with a book because her brothers had forbidden her from playing with them. Her mother had been drawing a picture of the seagulls soaring above the ocean while her father unabashedly admired his wife's profile. It had been a grand day—despite her brothers being their normal inconsiderate selves. That had been the day Seren began praying for a sister.

Mama's life-size drawing now hung in a frame in the parlor.

Yet Seren had remained the tormented only girl.

That her parents doted on her atoned for much. And she had to admit her brothers weren't all that horrid, especially when they had taken her fishing, taught her to swim, and allowed her to help them pass out Papa's pro-liberty pamphlets.

Yet her family's love for one another didn't change the reality of having no permanent home for most of her childhood and youth. Norfolk, Richmond, and Petersburg. Then south to New Bern and the Outer Banks. From there, to several towns in South Carolina, including Charleston before the British occupied it after the war. Back to Wilmington and New Bern before returning to South Carolina. The year and a half they'd spent in Charleston before moving back to Fayetteville eight months ago had been the longest they'd stayed anywhere.

Twelve moves.

That she remembered.

With a sigh, Seren placed the figurine of herself to the left of the one of her parents and out of the way of the one depicting her brothers. She examined the glazed cake with the candied violets sprinkled along the outer edge. Where she stood mattered far less than the fact she was done with moving. Done.

Fayetteville was her home, and nothing—or no one—would convince her to move again.

She looked up as Prudence balanced a bowl of roasted

potatoes and another of boiled beets on one arm and held a bowl of salt-and-vinegar-coated sallet in her other free hand. Prudence walked through the opened kitchen door to head to the main house, and their manservant, Mr. Montgomery, entered.

"Wife, we need another place setting."

"Oh?" Mrs. Montgomery stopped scooping pickles from a jar.

Seren looked to Mr. Montgomery. A broad smile covered his aged face, which was odd considering he rarely looked like he was having an enjoyable time. He smoothed the front of his cream waistcoat that he wore under his blue frocked coat, regardless of the temperature outside. Even Papa removed his suit coat the moment he returned from a day's work at the *Gazette*.

For Mr. Montgomery to be this delighted, Papa must have brought home one of the authors who wrote serial stories for the paper.

So why did Seren feel an immediate unease?

Mr. Montgomery removed another china dinner plate from the cupboard next to the table where Seren stood. "He looked me in the eyes," he announced, "said it was an honor to meet me, and shook my hand. Like I were gentry. Wife, Mr. Owain Cardew will want to serve his finest ale tonight."

Mrs. Montgomery left the pickle tray and walked to the cellar.

"Mama doesn't like ale," Seren put in, yet neither acted as if they heard her.

"The finest, you say?" Mrs. Montgomery said, opening

one of the cellar's doors. "We must have a special guest."

Mr. Montgomery removed a pewter goblet from the cupboard. "Let's slice one of those sourdough loaves you baked yesterday. Rye, too."

"Papa doesn't like sourdough," Seren reminded them. Again, not a single acknowledgment of her words.

As Mrs. Montgomery stepped down into the cellar, Mr. Montgomery left the building and Prudence returned, wearing an equally broad smile. Was Prudence glowing? The girl was too young to glow or even to think about glowing. Yet she was. As if a man had doted—

Seren's unease turned to butterflies of dread in her stomach. She worried her bottom lip. It couldn't possibly be the Scotsman, could it?

"Oh, Grandmother," Prudence said wistfully, "he said I should thank the good Lord for blessing me with hair as glorious as the flames of an angel's sword." She touched one of the carrot-colored curls that had escaped the white cap covering most of her hair. "I'm smitten."

Like Miss Keen had been. Seren forced herself to stand perfectly still as she stared past the black interior kitchen door, a stark contrast to the white-painted walls, to the short distance between the kitchen and the house. The Scotsman had been infatuated with Miss Keen; he had no reason to follow Seren home. Did he? Yet Prudence's smile looked much like the one Miss Keen had been wearing.

Seren felt sick. . .apprehensive. . .and fluttery.

Mrs. Montgomery climbed out of the cellar carrying a jug of ale and looking quite skeptical. "You do remember you're only three and ten?"

Prudence picked up the divided platter with pickles on one side and pickled radishes and onions on another. "In three years I'll be old enough to marry."

"We'll see, dearest."

Suddenly, Seren didn't feel fluttery at all. Something strange and cold began to rise in her, something quite unpleasant and unfamiliar. Finley Sinclair likely had female admirers from here all the way down from Cape Fear to Wilmington. He didn't seem the type to wait three years to marry the woman he desired, even if she had hair the color of a flaming sword.

"But, Grandmother—"

"Enough," she ordered. "The Cardews and their guest are ready to eat."

Good thing the dining room's walls were painted green because Seren felt greenish from the top of her head down to the tips of her toes. She'd blend in enough so Finley Sinclair wouldn't notice her. She didn't even like green. Shades of pink were her passion.

She nervously smoothed her chemise's white ruffles that stood up along the edge of her bodice. She could possibly feign weariness or a headache. Spend the evening in her room—away from the Scotsman's flutter-inducing presence.

As Seren waited for a headache to develop, Mr. Montgomery and Prudence took turns delivering the food and ale to the main house.

Mrs. Montgomery finally picked up the tiered glass platter holding the lemon-glazed pound cake. "Do you want this brought in now or at the end of the meal?"

"I wanted Mama to see it first, but—umm, perhaps. . ." Seren groaned. She sounded as incoherent as the Scotsman.

"Child, this is no time for indecision."

With her other hand, Mrs. Montgomery nudged Seren outside. They passed the wood-framed well and entered the main house's back door. In the well-lit dining room was the square linen-covered table where Papa and Mr. Sinclair stood beside their chairs while Mama sat.

Papa looked handsome as always in his white shirt and gold waistcoat.

Mr. Sinclair looked—

Well, he looked at the floor instead of at her. Not only were he and Papa about the same height, they had the same coffee-brown eyes and dark hair, although Papa's had as many gray strands as black. Their similarities ended there. Everything about Papa bespoke refined elegance. Nothing about Mr. Sinclair did.

"Serenade," Papa said smiling as he used her childhood nickname, "we invited Mr. Sinclair to dine with us. He said he met you and Mr. Lamb earlier."

Mrs. Montgomery placed the marzipan-decorated cake in the center of the platters and bowls on the table.

Mama gasped and covered her mouth. "Oh, Seren, it's beautiful." She got up from her chair and gave Seren a hug and a kiss. The strands of silvery blond hair escaping from her white cap tickled Seren's cheek.

"I spent all day making the figurines for you." *Since I didn't have any customers.*

"Someday people will ride for miles to buy your comfits."

Feeling Mr. Sinclair's gaze upon her, Seren blinked away the watery warmth in her eyes. Later, when they were alone, she'd tell her parents about the allegation the apothecary had hurled against her. If anyone could understand false accusations, her mother could. Though people thought Mama's delicate features and quietness of character made her weak, Mama was the strongest woman Seren knew.

Mama hugged her again, and Seren held on tight. Some days being like Jesus seemed too great a task so she focused on trying to be like her mother. Mama had unwavering faith. Mama had never failed at anything she tried. Neither would Seren.

"It will work out, sweetie," Mama whispered as if she knew Seren's fears. "Look for God's opportunities."

Seren nodded.

Mama sat.

As Papa led them in prayer for the meal, Seren tilted her head and peeked through her lashes at the Scotsman. His jaw bore a strong curve, and his lips whispered agreements to Papa's prayer with an ease too natural and too humble to be contrived piety. Maybe he was more than what she thought him to be.

"Amen," he said in unison with her parents.

The moment he raised his head, Seren immediately cast her gaze to her folded hands and waited until her heartbeat settled back into a normal rhythm. She felt like a dolt for staring.

If he had seen her—

Despite the warmth in her cheeks, she looked to her parents, who returned Mr. Sinclair's grin. He conveyed his appreciation for the invitation to join the meal. They thanked him for agreeing. As the food was passed around the table, her parents took turns questioning Mr. Sinclair while answering his questions, too. Her parents obviously liked the man.

Seren focused on eating.

She didn't have anything to add to the conversation other than *Mr. Lamb proposed again*, *Jane has a stomach ailment*, *the apothecary wants my shop closed*, and *Mr. Sinclair isn't the good Christian man he's claiming to be.* True, she had no evidence for the latter other than feeling all-out-of-sorts in his presence. She didn't trust him. Or, perhaps, she didn't want to trust him. Now that was an odd thought. Why wouldn't she want to trust him?

Because he looked everyone in the eyes except her?

While she wasn't as pretty as her apprentice, Jane, she'd often been complimented on the contrast of her black hair and blue eyes. She groaned inwardly and kept eating food that seemed unusually bland. Last thing she wanted was for Finley Sinclair to notice her. Once her shop was well established, say in three or four years, she would consider entertaining a man's affections. Mama was five and twenty before she married Papa. At one and twenty, Seren was in no rush to settle with the first man who proposed.

Mr. Sinclair laughed at something Papa said.

Her parents laughed, too.

Mr. and Mrs. Montgomery and Prudence kept finding excuses to return to the dining room.

Seren forked the last bread-and-butter pickle on her plate and ate it. Was there anyone who didn't fall under Finley Sinclair's charm?

As Mrs. Montgomery served slices of cake, Seren noticed Mr. Sinclair's slice seemed—no, was—larger than the others, and had more candied violets on the side. Thankfully, the figurines were laid to the edge of the tiered glass platter. Now that she thought about it, what was the point of making figurines of people, only to dread the thought of actually eating the head off one?

Mr. Sinclair ate the candied violets first. His brown eyes rolled heavenward and he groaned. "Aye, Miss Cardew, ye have a way with sugar."

Papa accepted a mug of coffee dutifully delivered by Mr. Montgomery. "That she does," he said proudly. "Seren inherits her sweetness from her beautiful mother."

A soft blush brightened Mama's cheeks. She reached out and squeezed Papa's hand.

Mr. Sinclair's gaze shifted from her parents to the unlit hearth, but not before Seren caught the look of yearning in his eyes. Had he not grown up with parents who treasured each other? Did he want a love like her parents had?

"Mr. Sinclair, why are you here?" she queried as casually as she could.

Mr. Montgomery returned with a second mug of coffee.

With a nod of thanks, Mr. Sinclair accepted the mug. He sipped the coffee then announced: "To make a new life in America."

"No, here—in my parents' home."

He finally turned her way but his gaze never rose higher than on the slice of cake before her. "Miss Cardew, I believe the good Lord brought us together for a reason."

"How so?"

"Hire me to broker your candies." He took another leisurely sip of his coffee. His gaze shifted to her parents. "I can sell them in Wilmington for triple the selling price here."

Papa's brow furrowed like it did when he was deep thinking. "Seren, I think you should take Mr. Sinclair up on his offer."

Mama nodded in agreement.

"He seems an honorable fellow," Papa added.

Seren slowly shook her head. How could her parents trust so easily? They barely knew the man. Yet when had she known her parents to be duped by anyone? They both had good instincts, were good judges of character. Unless she established a clientele soon and began selling her comfits, she had only enough supplies to last the summer. When those were gone, she would have nothing left of her brooch inheritance from Aunt Murdag except foolish dreams and the shame of knowing she had sold something her mother treasured. Yet Mama had given her approval for the sale.

Aye, daughter, this brooch will to bring you to your heart's greatest desire, as it brought me to mine, as it brought Cousin Seona's to hers.

To this day, Mama would say Papa was that desire.

A successful confectionary was Seren's. Or she always thought it was. Now she felt less sure, less satisfied. For what—for whom—was she looking and wanting?

Nothing. No one. The yearning she felt merely stemmed from the lack of success she was having with her confectionary. When her shop succeeded, she would feel content. Why did that, though, not bring any relief from the wistfulness?

She stood and walked across the wood-planked floor to the window. The sun had finished setting, and she could see a few distant stars. She reached inside her apron pocket to grip the key to her shop—the very building her brothers and father had built. Yet she owned every board, shingle, and glass pane.

If Cardew Confectionary failed, she would have no choice but to marry.

Mr. Lamb, Esquire?

She inwardly cringed.

In all reality, marriage wasn't necessarily her only option. She could become a governess or nanny or gain employment as a chef or laundress at one of the local inns or taverns. Why do anything else when her heart's desire was making sugared sweets? Her dreams were filled with sugarplums. Literally.

She turned and faced her parents, who were looking at her intently while Mr. Sinclair seemed to find the hem of her petticoat most fascinating.

"I need to pray on it," she answered.

As the Montgomeries cleared the dining table, Mama left the room. She promptly returned carrying a feather pillow and a quilted blanket.

"Mr. Sinclair," Mama said walking to him, "we have a loft in the carriage house. There's a cot you can use for the night."

He stood, shook Papa's hand, and followed Mama to the

side door leading to the carriage house. Mr. Sinclair opened the door, but Mama stopped him. They spoke too softly for Seren to hear their words.

Papa walked over to Seren. "You were quiet tonight."

"Not any more than normal."

Papa slowly nodded. Since he rarely was without words to share, she knew his silence meant he expected her to speak.

She trailed her fingers along the white chair railing that ran around the room. "What if he runs off with my comfits?"

"He could."

"Yet you are willing to give him the benefit of the doubt."

"I believe the faith he testified to having is real."

"Even true believers take advantage of others," she said and despised the words as soon as they left her mouth. She hated sounding cynical and suspicious. She wanted to be able to trust and to open her heart to others as her parents and brothers did.

Only she couldn't.

"Serenade, what is it you really fear?"

She glanced at Mr. Sinclair still talking to her mother. "I feel like I always did when you called a family meeting to announce we were to move again. I hate not knowing what tomorrow will bring. What if I don't want Mr. Sinclair involved in my future?"

Papa cradled her cheek in his palms. "No matter what tomorrow holds, God will be with you. Do you believe that?"

She nodded.

He kissed her forehead. "Everything will work out. Your responsibility is to look for God's opportunities."

"Mama said the same thing earlier."

She followed Papa's gaze to her mother.

Her parents grinned softly at the same time.

"That's because Fiona MacGill Cardew is my other half." Papa then winked at Seren. "One day you'll find your other half, and you'll understand my words exactly."

Seren nodded because she had no idea how else to respond. She'd never been in love. Twice she'd favored a young man—once in New Bern and the other in Charleston—only to move before any true affection could grow. She wasn't sure she wanted to experience love, although it had made her brothers more tolerable. As far as Mr. Lamb and his proposals—well, she knew confidently though, that when she did marry, she wanted a passion like her parents shared.

Papa walked to Mr. Sinclair. After giving Mama a bold kiss, he took the pillow and blanket from her and escorted Mr. Sinclair outside.

Seren hurried upstairs to her bedroom.

To pray.

To meditate on the scriptures.

To figure out why Finley Sinclair wouldn't look at her.

Chapter 4

Of all the eyes on him as he strapped the small shipping box on the back of his draft horse, Finley was keenly aware of a set of pale blue ones. So much so that he still had not tied the box on properly and had to try a second time. He would not deny the lass made him nervous. The hair on the back of his neck seemed to prickle under her gaze. Aye, she made him jittery.

Likely because she smelled of spices and honey.

He had never met a sweet he did not like.

Wearing a solid pink gown that accentuated the rosiness of her lips, she watched him from her place under the ivy-covered gazebo and said naught. Other than announcing at the breakfast table that she would entrust her comfits to him, Miss Seren Cardew had not said another word. Not even when they had walked with her father to the confectionary shop.

Mr. Cardew had carried the conversation, until he left to start his day at the *Gazette*. Finley would pay to sit at the older man's feet and immerse in all he had to share about

God. In the last two years, Finley had thought he learned much from reading his Bible and anything he could find written by the Reformers, including Martin Luther, John Bunyan, and John Knox. Thirty years from now, he hoped he had at least a fraction of wisdom Mr. Cardew now had.

'Course Mr. Cardew had not waited until he was two and twenty to turn his life over to Christ like Finley had. Nay, Owain Cardew had grown since childhood in the faith.

'Twas because he had had godly parents, not criminal heathen ancestors like Finley.

Finley looped the rope one final time around the box of confections and knotted it off. After shifting the box to insure it was secure atop the blanket on the gelding's brown rump, he checked the items in his saddlebag: a corked mallet bottle of cider that the MacDubhs had brought him this morning, along with food for a meal. Mrs. Cardew, Miss Keen, and several other Fayetteville residents whom he had spoken to yesterday about becoming their broker also brought jerky and dried fruit for the week's travel down to Wilmington. He had never felt more blessed in his life.

Finley worked his way through the dozens of people standing around, shaking hands and accepting hugs from several of the womenfolk. Miss Keen even kissed his cheek. Mr. Lamb stood on the eastern corner of the Hay and Maxwell intersection. About at the same spot where Finley was when he first saw Miss Cardew yesterday. Mr. Lamb's mouth pursed tight, before he tipped his tricorn hat and walked off.

The crowd soon departed, and Finley stood alone with

Miss Cardew on the pavement in front of her shop. Knowing he ought to say something, he looked at her. . .and thought of naught to say, so he immediately dropped his gaze.

"I promise—ye, uhh, ye—"

She sighed. "Godspeed, Mr. Sinclair." She turned and stepped inside her shop.

Finley followed. Unlike the rest of the shops he had visited in town, this one-room building held naught but necessities. Even the counter, the cupboard to the right of the counter, and long bench under the front double window were simplistically constructed. He withdrew the embroidered handkerchief he had tucked between his shirt and buckskin breeches. He had intended to give it to her last night, but her parents and the Montgomeries had been so engaging that he had forgotten.

Miss Cardew stopped at the counter where her confections had been displayed and turned to face him. She gripped the pewter key she wore on a long red ribbon around her neck.

Finley halted his steps before he ran into her.

She looked sad.

Maybe a bit hurt. And lonely. And—

Disheveled.

Long black strands of hair escaping the white cap on her head grazed the narrow shoulders of her gown as if she had been distracted this morning as she attended her hair. Even the apron pinned to her dress was crooked compared to how she had worn it yesterday. Finley empathized with her, although he doubted she shared his plight.

He fell asleep thinking about her.

Woke up thinking about her and about how to stop feeling all out of sorts so he could engage her in a conversation. 'Twas strange to think his tongue was tied around Miss Cardew when he never had a problem talking to anyone before. Which was probably why he was so well liked. He always knew what to say to people to cheer them up, to make them smile.

Miss Cardew was something new.

He liked all from the first to the last inch of her newness. Aye, the lass was lovely, mysterious, and as blue as the sky the good Lord created. Blue? Finley groaned. He was staring like a besotted fop right into those fine eyes of hers.

"Here," he blurted, offering the handkerchief.

"Keep it. You may need it."

He frowned. "Lass, have ye no care for Miss Keen's gift?" She didn't seem the ungrateful type.

The corners of her rosy lips twitched. "No care?" A chuckle burst through her lips, and she immediately covered her mouth. "No, I mean, yes, I mean I do care, but—" She swiveled and walked to the planked pine cupboard with open and empty shelves on top and two doors on bottom. She opened both doors.

Finley's eyes widened.

Both shelves held folded handkerchiefs stacked upon each other.

Best guess: close to a hundred.

"Miss Keen gives me one at least two times a week." She closed the doors and relatched them. "Some are new. Some are ones she's sewn over the years."

"'Tis generous of her."

"Aye, laddie, 'tis more than generous," she said, mimicking his brogue.

If he were the romantic type, he'd think he'd fallen in love right then and there. Instead, he grinned and said, "If ye have enough, why keep accepting more?"

"Because it brings her joy to give, despite her having very little to give." Smiling, she walked back to the counter. "Miss Keen is a dear soul, but given time, you will learn she's a wee bit off her rocker."

Finley slid the linen kerchief back between his shirt and breeches, happy to keep something that reminded him of Miss Cardew. He then leaned on the edge of the counter.

"I take it yer father does not include secret messages in the *Gazette* and ye know naught about poison and medicaments?"

She released a resigned exhale. "My comfits would be in great demand if they were truly coating pharmaceuticals, although the apothecary would then do more than merely insist my shop be closed. Mr. Sinclair, if you don't find a buyer—"

"I will."

"You cannot be certain—"

"I will sell yer confections," he said, standing tall.

"I would like to believe you."

Finley blinked. Amid her words, her tone had said *why should I trust you?*

Her gaze focused on him. There, behind her apprehension, was something he recognized: the fear of trusting another to fulfill his promises. That was why Finley had struggled for months after hearing the gospel of salvation. He had yearned for a new life. But he feared trusting God to forgive all his sins and set him free from his family's criminal trade.

"I *will* sell your confections," he said firmly, "and I *will* return."

She acknowledged him with a tiny nod.

Finley knew, more than anything, he wanted to prove to her that she could trust him. Why that mattered, he was less sure and, really, had no time to ponder.

"I should be going," he said, pointing over his shoulder toward the open door. "Have ye a maid or someone to"—he motioned to the kettle and worktable surrounded by supplies in the back of her shop—"to help ye with all of this?"

"My apprentice, Jane Wilcox."

"So ye will not be alone?" he asked, feeling concerned for her safety.

"I'm never here alone."

"Good."

"Except yesterday. And today." At his frown, she added, "Jane still has stomach pains. Her younger brother delivered a message earlier this morning."

Finley searched his mind for a considerate means to tell her he didn't want her alone in her shop, but he couldn't think of anything that didn't sound possessive or protective or persnickety. He had no claim on her. He had no right to tell her how to spend her day.

Still, had he not intervened yesterday with the persistent Mr. Lamb—

"Oh, not you, too," she muttered.

"Not me what?"

"I have older brothers, Mr. Sinclair. I am quite familiar with your expression." Mumbling to herself, Miss Cardew walked around the counter, grabbed his elbow, and walked him outside to the bricked walk. As they stood under the shaded archway, she turned, removed the ribbon-tied key, and locked her shop. "Since you have my entire stock of comfits, even if a client appeared, I have nothing to sell, and since I have no assistant, there is no need to spend the day making any sugarplums or conserves."

There was a proper response to her words.

Indeed, a man in his right mind would speak them.

Finley, however, suspected only the wrong part of his brain was working because all he could think about was how soft her skin looked. Her neck, right underneath the turn of her jaw, had the perfect curve for a kiss—

Finley stopped his thoughts and wisely back-stepped to his horse tied to the hitching post in front of her shop. He wanted to stay, not leave, but he knew he should go because his thoughts were straying past those of a broker for his client. He also knew he should not ask, but he could not help it since he was still thinking in the wrong part of his brain.

"What will you do today instead?" he said as casually as he could.

She looped the key back around her neck. "Mama asked me to aid Miss Keen in trimming the foliage in her garden."

"The ones tied with string?"

She nodded.

"'Tis generous of you."

Placing her hands on her hips, she grinned. Her eyes glimmered mischievously. "Mr. Sinclair, do you expect my comfits to sell themselves?"

"Nay, I—" Finley fell silent.

He could no more admit he was enjoying the ease of their conversation and the newfound ability to stare openly at her without sounding like the village idiot when he spoke. Since he really needed to leave before he began admiring the curve of her neck again, he untied his horse's reins and readied to mount.

"Miss Cardew," Mr. Lamb called out. "Miss Cardew!"

Finley looked to his left to see Mr. Lamb waving at them as he hurried across the street. Then he immediately swerved around to see Miss Cardew's reaction.

If Miss Cardew was annoyed, she didn't look it.

Finley felt it though.

His bones verily ached with annoyance.

Mr. Lamb stopped beside the archway, wearing a black suit as fancy as the one from yesterday. Even his white hose looked to be of the finest quality. He drew in several deep breaths. Then he removed his hat, bowed, and offered Miss Cardew his arm.

"May I escort you to Miss Keen's house? I spoke to your father. He informed me of your day's agenda."

Miss Cardew wrapped her hand around his elbow. "Do not presume under any circumstances, Mr. Lamb, this means I am agreeing to any proposal."

A tiny grin curved Mr. Lamb's lips. "Certainly." He placed

his hat on his head and gave a little tap on the top.

"Godspeed, Mr. Sinclair." With that, Miss Cardew walked away, not sparing Finley one last glance before she and Mr. Lamb turned the corner.

Finley mounted and rode in the opposite direction.

He was a good ten miles and one lengthy prayer down the road before he stopped being annoyed. Mostly.

On the morning of the fourth day of his journey, a few miles south of Elizabethtown, a riderless horse trotted toward him. Finley dismounted and caught the biscuit-colored mare's reins. Thunder rolled overhead. Though he hadn't felt a raindrop yet, he could smell rain on the breeze. Walking along the travel-hardened ruts in the dirt road, he came across a broad-shouldered blond man sitting on the ground and rubbing his left arm.

"Morning," Finley called out.

"Morning." The man stood and brushed the dirt off his navy waistcoat, white shirt, and gray breeches. Several strands of hair had pulled free of his queue. He looked around. "Notice my hat anywhere?"

Finley pointed to the evergreen behind him. "Seems the tree has a hankering for it."

The man looked over his shoulder and laughed, and then he reclaimed his gray tricorn. "I see you caught Betsy."

"Aye, she came trotting my way." Finley stopped next to the man who was near the same height and, based on the smile lines about his tired, bloodshot eyes, looked to be only a few years older than he. He struck out his hand. "Finley Sinclair."

"Nathaniel Best."

They shook hands.

Nathaniel put his hat on. "The Almighty told me I needed rest. If I had listened instead of riding through the night, I wouldn't have fallen asleep and fallen off ol' Betsy."

"Where you headed?"

"Home. Elizabethtown." He scratched his bristled jaw where the hair was as blond as on his head. "You?"

"Wilmington. I broker for Overton Shipwares. One of my clients lives in Fayetteville." *Only* client, but Nathaniel needed not to know that. Hearing the man's stomach growl, Finley moved to his saddlebag. He removed the half-filled bottle of cider and the remaining tea biscuit from Mary MacDubh. He offered them to Nathaniel. "Here."

"I can't take your food."

"The good Lord blessed me with enough to share," Finley insisted.

Nathaniel took the cider and cloth-wrapped tea biscuit. "Convey my gratitude to your woman."

"God has yet to bless me with a wife." The memory of Miss Cardew mimicking his brogue caused Finley to grin. "Aye, but there is a lassie I am sweet on." As soon as the words escaped his mouth, he realized how true they were.

"You're a fortunate man. There's a lady I know who—" Nathanial growled. "Blight on humanity she is. I'm happier when I don't think about her."

Thunder rolled some more, this time the sound closer.

Nathaniel glanced up at the sky before looking back at Finley. "If you hurry, you can make it to Dove Tavern before the rain hits." He shook Finley's hand again. "If you're ever in Elizabethtown, come to my coffeehouse. I'd like to return the favor."

Finley nodded. "Will do."

He mounted and hurried down the tree-lined road that paralleled Cape Fear. To pass the time, he listed all the things he liked about Miss Cardew while praying that he would make it to the tavern's stables in time.

Chapter 5

Twas a lovely town, Wilmington. The streets bustled with activity. The bright sky shown with happiness and joy, while the hooves of Finley's horse clomped along the paved street as he made his way away from Mr. Overton's office. He would rather the sky be cloudy to fit his mood. After a week of traveling, he ought to be happy he had one more chance to secure a permanent position with Overton Shipwares despite not having secured a single rope-making, tar-boiling client in Fayetteville.

Finley *was* happy for Overton's generosity.

Somewhat.

"Candy? I don't want candy, Sinclair. Marines can't hoist a sail with candy!"

Overton's words were seared into Finley's mind.

He would sacrifice his broker position if doing so enabled him to sell Miss Cardew's sugarplums. Confections did not have to coat medicaments for them to be edible. Here, in Wilmington, he figured the town's wealthiest merchant would have seen the merit in selling elegant candies to the social elites. What was it Mr. Cardew had asked him to promise to pray daily?

Almighty Lord, open my eyes to see opportunities before me.

Finley had not followed through on his promise. Yet he hoped he had learned his lesson because, more than anything, he needed to see opportunities and have boldness to pursue them.

For his own sake, as well as Miss Cardew's.

After spotting a park next to a white-framed church, Finley rode toward it. He dismounted and tied his horse to a shaded post under an oak with a tremendous canopy. At this moment, he needed a quiet place to think. And pray.

Mostly, though, to listen.

He sat on a bench in front of a flowering hedge.

Father, Spirit, Good Shepherd, tell me what to do. Open my eyes to opportunities.

Amid the birds chirping, he heard—sniffles?

Finley stood and peered around the hedge. A lass wearing a shiny blue gown adorned with flounces, ruffles, and ribbons sat on another bench. The wide, flat-brimmed straw hat she wore had the same shades of blue ribbons as those in the basket-weave pattern on the bodice of her gown. She wiped her cheeks with her fingertips and cried some more. Her maid stood off to the side, looking unsure of what to do.

Finley withdrew the embroidered kerchief he carried. He stepped around the hedge yet stayed a respectable distance from her.

"Aye, lass, 'tis a fine day to cry."

She flinched. Then she gazed up at him and frowned.

"You don't look in despair."

"Men wail." He pointed to his chest. "In here, lass, I am sobbing buckets. I have not had a good day either." He handed her the kerchief. "Would you like this?"

She glanced at her immobile maid then reluctantly took his offering. "Who are you?"

"Finley Sinclair. I broker for Overton Shipwares."

"No wonder you're crying. Internally, of course."

Finley raised his brows at that. "Are you related to Mr. Overton?" The tawny-haired lass was too old to be Overton's daughter. Younger sister, possibly.

She dried her eyes and wiped her red-tipped nose that was a wee bit large for her dainty face. "No, Coy Overton is my father's chief competitor and sells the most glorious French fabrics in his mercantile. Papa refuses to allow me to buy yardage from him for my wedding gown. I will *not* look like a peasant when I marry Harold."

Though she was not as lovely as his Miss Cardew, he doubted she would look like a peasant even if she wore burlap.

"Lass, what gown ye wear will not matter to yer groom." He paused and offered a quick prayer that she would not take offense to his next words. "If ye cannot be happy wearing a simple gown of linen, then ye might want to ask if this wedding is about gaining attention for yerself or about marrying the man ye love?"

"Of course I want to look—" She cringed and twisted the handkerchief. Her voice softened. "I have loved Harold since I was five and ten. He finally noticed me during my birthday ball last summer. I've waited seven years to marry him, and I would do so in this very gown if need be."

He smiled. "That passion and sincerity is why Harold loves ye."

Her face glowed.

And her maid sighed.

Finley motioned over his shoulder. "Since yer feeling better, I'll be leav—"

"Are you truly sad?" she interjected.

He shrugged.

"Mr. Sinclair, Harold does the same when he doesn't wish to admit something truly bothers him." Her brown eyes looked at him expectantly.

Finley ran his hand across his smooth jaw that he had taken care to shave this morning so he would look his best when he spoke to Overton.

Sad?

Nay.

Frustrated.

Aye, he was.

"I promised a lady I could sell her confections," he confessed. "Candied flowers, marzipan butterflies, dry comfits, and sugarplums."

"What illnesses do they cure?"

"None. They are to be eaten for pleasure." On a whim he added, "She learned the trade from a French confectioner in Charlestown."

The lass shifted on the bench to face him directly. "Mr. Overton didn't want them?"

He shook his head. Then he had an idea. "Yer father—"

This time she shook her head. "Papa abhors anything French."

Finley shifted his stance. "I was thinking I could sell to someone having a wedding, but that would only be a one-time event. My client needs continual sales. Maybe a ladies' tearoom. Or the governor," he rambled as he considered possibilities. "I need one well-respected matron to buy the confections thereby making Miss Cardew's candy the thing to buy."

He stood—and she sat—in silence for several minutes.

There had to be someone who could use candy. He would stake his life on it.

Then the lass jumped to her feet. "I know who!" She smiled at Finley. "Madame Ventris, the proprietress of Josephine's Boutique. To become one of her clients, you must have a minimum of two aristocratic ancestors and the papers to prove your lineage, which she has investigated before she agrees to take you on. Some of her clients travel as far away as from Baltimore. I've heard refreshments are served as one waits to be measured and fitted." The awe in her tone matched that on her face.

Though her suggestion seemed a possibility, Finley wasn't convinced. "A seamstress?"

"Yes, and you would have to convince her. Oh." She looked at him apologetically. "Madame Ventris is exclusive. Even with men. You would have to look more—respectable to even gain admittance into her boutique. I'm sorry. I mean no offense."

Finley tapped his right hand on his thigh. His mind spun

with all sorts of ideas and strategies.

She took a step forward. "What are you going to do?"

"Pray fervently."

Her look said she wished him well.

He grinned. "Miss, in the last three years, the Lord has taught me the best way to receive is to begin with asking nicely."

Chapter 6

Seren sat on the tall stool staring absently at the new batch of sugarplum ingredients on her worktable. Mr. Sinclair had left Fayetteville seventeen days ago. Plenty of time to ride to Wilmington, sell her comfits, and return.

Hunger likely compelled him to consume her candies and he was too embarrassed to return. But if he managed to resist and sell her comfits, then he had disappeared with her profits. Although, he had to know Papa would speak to the magistrate about him and realize the consequences to thievery were whipping, fines, even hard labor.

Likely, he was delayed.

When he finally returned, he would apologize with one of those lethal smiles of his, which would make her insides go all warm and buttery. Then he'd say something in that melodic brogue of his. . . .

As her mouth curved, she sighed.

"You're doing it again," Jane grumbled behind the latest edition of the *Gazette* she was reading. While her legs stretched out on the long bench underneath the front window, she rested the back of her lace mobcap against the side wall. Midmorning sunlight spread through the double windows, brightening the one-room shop.

"I'm doing what?"

"Thinking about him."

Seren offered her most *I'm confused* expression, although she knew exactly of whom Jane was referring. "Mr. Lamb?"

Jane tilted her head to the left, and a golden curl slid over her forehead. "Don't patronize me. You have set your cap upon this *enchanting* Mr. Sinclair whom everyone in Fayetteville seems to have met except me. Even Ma admires his—umm, him, to my displeasure might I add. I may be two months younger than you, but I know ghastly swooning when I see it."

"Remind me why you're my apprentice? I can't seem to recall you watching me make a single confection."

"Apprentice. Maid. What I'm called makes no difference to me as long as I don't have to stay at home and assist Ma with the town's laundry." Jane's voice lost a bit of its cynical edge. "You help me, Seren, and I help you. That's the essence of friendship."

Seren swallowed the sudden lump in her throat. Friends? She felt a smile tug at her lips. Why had it taken her so long to realize God had blessed her with a friend? A confidante? In her heart, she knew that despite Jane's ribbing about Seren's feelings for Mr. Sinclair, Jane would hold her secret. If she could trust Jane, then she should be able to trust others, too.

She smiled at Jane, who—with a roll of her eyes—shook

her head yet grinned somewhat.

Then as if embarrassed over the moment, Jane returned to reading the paper. "Let me know when you're done swooning, and I'll sweep the floor of the riffraff."

He most wanted to see *her*. Finley, though, graciously spoke to each Fayetteville resident who stopped him as he rode down the street. Since he still had the shipping crate strapped to his saddle, each asked him if he had sold the sweets. He answered with naught but a smile. The one to know first would be Miss Cardew. He had spent so much time thinking about Seren—as he had come to think of her—and praying about his feelings that he felt as if he had known her for months, not weeks. She shared his faith. She was courageous, adventurous, strong, loving, loyal, clever, and a host of other descriptors that invaded his thoughts and dreams.

As much as he was sure she would like cats, children, and knitting, he was sure she would enjoy watching the sun rise over their Ohio Valley farmland.

Aye, he should have kept the wildflowers he had picked for her early this morning. Of course, brokers did not bring their clients flowers, which was why he had given them to a matronly washerwoman two blocks back.

Though his nerves twisted his innards, he turned the corner onto Maxwell Street with a broad grin. Joy and sweetness to his soul, that's what Seren was. Though 'twas nearing midmorning—a warm, serene, sunny day, perfect for picnicking—he gambled she would be in her shop instead of at home.

Or with Mr. Lamb.

That thought killed his smile.

Ignoring the small crowd following him, he dismounted and tied his horse to the hitching post. He dutifully removed a bag of coins and a cokernut from his saddlebag, the husk-covered shell rough against his palm. He rather hoped she would not ask him for all the details of his time in Wilmington. 'Twas humiliating enough remembering it himself. If Miss Keen's prediction was accurate though, once word spread of his success with brokering for Seren, farming and ship wares clients should seek him out, instead of him having to hunt for them.

Then he could return to Wilmington and secure his position with Overton Shipwares. Best guess: A year of brokering would earn him the remaining funds he needed to buy the farmland he had wanted since his youth.

With a final nod to the crowd, he walked under the archway and into Cardew Confectionary.

Seren looked up from where she sat at the worktable in the back of the room. She smiled, and Finley knew what he had gone through to sell her confections had been worth the cost. Her eyes then shifted to something on his left. On the bench, with her legs stretched out before her and crossed, was a ravishing young blond in a green gown holding an open copy of the *Fayetteville Gazette*. Her hazel-eyed gaze started at top of his head and traveled down to his boots.

Her upper lip curled a wee bit. "I don't see what the fuss was about." She raised the paper back up to where he could no longer see her face. "Seren, your—broker has returned."

Your broker.

He rather liked that designation.

Finley met Seren at the counter. She looked as nervous as he felt.

His throat was so dry he almost feared he could not speak. He managed: "I sold them."

Her eyes grew watery. "You did? Oh, of course you did. You have no reason to lie."

There, in her blue eyes behind her tears, was what he had spent the last two weeks praying for—willingness to believe she could count on him. In time, he would earn her complete trust. And love. Somewhere north of Elizabethtown, his mind began to understand what his heart had been trying to tell him: He was falling in love.

"The most influential lady in Wilmington purchased yer entire stock." Finley didn't have to turn around to know the blond had lowered her paper and was watching them. Likely, with her eyes narrowed. "Aye, the proprietress of Josephine's Boutique, Madame—"

"Ventris!" Seren's lovely mouth gaped open.

"Ye know Madame?"

"Not personally." She drew in a deep breath and fanned her face. "Oh dear, *every* female in the Carolinas has heard of Madame Ventris. Did you speak with her personally?"

He nodded. Madame was not what he expected. Starting with her lack of French blood and lack of a husband—dead or alive.

"What did she look like?" Seren asked. "I've heard she

only communicates through her assistants."

Finley debated his response. Part of his contract with Madame was to keep her secret. "I can only say Madame's identity is surreptitious for just cause."

Seren frowned yet seemed accepting of his answer.

He continued, "She felt your confections were ideal to include with the refreshments she serves to her clients during fittings and while they wait." While gripping the cokernut's rough brown husk in his left hand, he rested the bag of coins on the counter. "This is for what she purchased, with extra as a deposit on next week's delivery."

Seren stared at the bag and then squealed. "Jane, we have a client. A client!" she repeated with more force. And then she hugged him. "Oh, Mr. Sinclair, thank you."

Finley held his breath, which only enhanced how loud his heartbeat was between his ears. Aye, he could rest his chin on the top of her head, well, perfectly. Before he could think about returning the hug or breathing deep to memorize how she smelled of spice and honey, she ran over to Jane and pulled her to her feet.

"Did you hear? Madame Ventris's clients are eating our sugarplums."

"There's not much *me* in *our*," Jane interjected without any of Seren's excitement. "Like a good apprentice, I'll take the credit. You'd better start confecting."

"Confecting?" Clearly realizing the significance of what else Finley had said, Seren's eyes widened. The joy on her face paled. "Mr. Sinclair, what do you mean by next week's delivery?"

Finley leaned back against the counter. "Madame is hosting a special showing and fitting for some Virginian gentry. In eleven days."

Seren and Jane exchanged glances.

"Takes seven to travel to Wilmington," Jane stated. "That leaves only three days to work, plus today."

"How—how much did she order?" Seren asked.

Finley withdrew a missive he had carried safely inside his right boot.

Seren walked to him and took it, breaking the red wax seal. Her eyes shifted as she read the list of the confections Madame desired. Since he suspected Seren had no cokernuts in stock, he had searched all of Wilmington for one, delaying his return.

When she looked up from the missive, he handed her the ugly cokernut. He hoped it would convey what the discarded flowers would have. He cared. He cared about her confections, about her hopes and dreams, about how he could make her happy. He cared about her. If this was not love, 'twas certainly the beginning.

A faint blush brightened her cheeks.

She said naught.

He said naught, too, because he sensed she felt the same as he. 'Twas a marvelous feeling, this sameness. This completeness. And the moment could not be more right.

Or crowded.

Jane sighed loudly. "More riffraff to sweep." She walked over and took the missive from the motionless Seren. "To achieve Madame's order by the deadline, we need organization and a plan." Her tone grew impatient. "Mr. Sinclair, find an extra mixing bowl. Seren, stop—doing what you're doing and inventory your supplies. We have work to do, and by we, I mean you two."

Seren spent the remainder of the day trying to focus on her comfits and not on watching Mr. Sinclair. Even when she didn't see him nearby, she felt his presence. Instead of distracting her, it motivated her to perfect each sugarplum. After he shared with the crowd outside her shop about Madame Ventris's purchase and order, instead of accepting invitations to supper, including one from Jane's mother, he became Seren's manservant.

Several times when a Fayettevillian entered her shop—not to buy a comfit but out of curiosity—Mr. Sinclair graciously explained her need to focus on work then invited the person to join him for coffee at the Maysion Hotel just around the corner. He even spoke kindly to Mr. Lamb, who arrived with a bouquet of mixed flowers and who also received a coffee invitation. Unlike the other Fayetteville residents, Mr. Lamb refused. His impertinence only led Jane to insist she would find someone to run against him in the next election.

Jane then left for the *Gazette*, intent on convincing Papa to run for assemblyman.

Mr. Sinclair also disappeared. Likely to manage the consequences of too much coffee.

Smiling, Seren spooned another portion of sugarplum dough and rolled it into a ball. If she continued to work much longer, she would need to light several more candles before the sun finished setting. To her fortune, she had enough candies, sugar-paste flowers, and marzipan figures already made.

But Madame's list—

The various sweetmeats—jams, jellies, marmalades, and preserves—would need to be started first thing tomorrow. Candied carrots and beets? Like with the sweetmeats, Seren had not made them since leaving Charleston and instead had focused on dry comfits and conserves. Before leaving for the shop in the morn, she would collect what she needed from Mama's garden. She would use the candy-stripe and golden beets she had only planted because Papa favored them. They should be small enough for what Madame requested. When she saw Papa, she'd kiss him for buying her the seeds—the oddest Christmas gift she'd ever received. On the last two days, she would make gingerbread and the sugarplum varieties she hadn't made today: raspberry, melon seed, pistachio, caraway, and filbert.

Seren laid a cherry sugarplum on the tray next to the thirteen matching other ones. She then spooned another portion. Barring no unforeseen mishap, she would have the order completed in time. With Jane's (minimal) and Mr. Sinclair's (generous) help, of course. So far today, when she couldn't find the almonds, he found them for her. He had chopped dried fruits, nuts, and firewood for her hearth without complaint. He even looked at home with her mortar and pestle, grinding the spices for each recipe.

She glanced at the beautiful coconut resting in the

middle of her worktable. Tomorrow she would crack it open because she needed the meat for several recipes. But she didn't want to.

Mr. Sinclair cared for her. Oh, he hadn't spoken the words.

She knew he did though.

She felt it. In her heart. In her soul. In the tips of her toes that tingled whenever he smiled at her. She chuckled. So her toes didn't actually tingle. She was so happy that anything seemed possible. If this wasn't the beginning of love, she didn't know what was. Finley, her shop's success, and spending the rest of their lives in Fayetteville—she couldn't help smiling.

The bell on her door jingled. Carrying a basket of jars, Jane walked into the confectionary moments before Mr. Sinclair arrived. He parked a small horse-cart in front of her window.

"Ma said you could use these for your sweetmeats," Jane announced. She sat the basket on the bench. "The mercantile has more if you need them."

"Tomorrow," Mr. Sinclair added, walking inside. "'Tis time to close shop. Mr. Cardew requested I escort ye two home before darkness sets."

Seren nodded.

Within minutes, her remaining sugarplums were rolled and covered. She cleaned her worktable, bowl, and utensils. After grabbing her treasured coconut, she extinguished the candles and locked her shop.

They walked Jane home first.

Jane stepped up to the black-painted door of her widowed

mother's home. Looking over her shoulder, she said, "Mr. Sinclair, you aren't like most. . ." She grimaced. "Good night." And with that, Jane walked inside, closing the door behind her.

Mr. Sinclair wrapped Seren's arm around his. "'Tis a fine day."

As they walked up Burges Street, Seren looked around. Everything—from the green foliage to the warm evening breeze to the golden streaks on the horizon to the juniper smell—was the same as yesterday. Yet everything was more beautiful.

She released a contented sigh. "Tomorrow will be even finer."

They soon turned the corner onto Maiden Lane. Passing the Morgans' house, Seren saw Miss Keen walk to her front gate. The gown she wore was one Seren hadn't seen before, nor the one Miss Keen had been wearing this morning. Underneath the yellow floral cotton was a solid yellow petticoat. Where had it come from?

Seren looked to Mr. Sinclair. He, oddly, wasn't smiling.

They stopped at the gate.

Without uttering a word, Miss Keen removed an embroidered linen kerchief from her apron, handed it to Seren, and touched Mr. Sinclair's hand, then turned and ran back into her home. Even in the dusk light, Seren had noticed the tears in her eyes.

"Mr. Sinclair, did you—"

"Aye."

"Why?"

He nudged her back into walking. "Because she gives despite having little to give."

Seren stayed silent until they reached the front door to her home. Mr. Sinclair reached for the door handle, but she stilled him.

"Is the gown from Madame Ventris?"

"Aye."

"Her creations are costly."

"Not for a member of her staff."

Seren felt her eyes widen. "*You* work for Madame?"

His face reddened. "I do. Now. She occasionally needs a man to fit special orders."

"So you agreed to work for her in exchange for a gown for Miss Keen?"

"*And* so she would buy your confections."

Seren smiled softly. "You, Mr. Sinclair, have a generous heart."

"'Tis a faithful and devoted heart, too." He raised her hand to his lips.

The kiss. . .

The fluttering of her pulse. . .

The tingling down to her toes and loss of breath. . .

Thankfully, Mr. Sinclair opened the door to her awaiting father, and Seren was spared the embarrassment of an honest-to-goodness swoon.

Chapter 7

Rats? How—"

Not giving her time to finish her words, Finley pushed passed Seren and stepped inside the confectionary; the dozen or so vermin scurried off her counter, leaving evidence of their appreciation of her confections. He looked around for how they could have entered. There, in the back of her shop, morning sunlight streamed through a splintered board on the bottom of the back door. He hurried over, knelt down, and examined the hole. His hand balled into a fist.

He hit the door. Someone did this.

Intentionally.

But who?

As he stood, Seren walked to her counter; Finley met her there.

Tears spilled down her cheeks. "Everything is"—her voice broke—"ruined."

He drew her against his chest. "'Tis only a setback. We will remake the candies."

She shook her head. "There isn't enough time."

"Aye, there is."

"You don't understand. Preserving fruit takes all—"

Jane gasped. She walked inside the shop, clearly more stunned at the rat droppings on the floor and counter than with Finley embracing Seren. "What happened?"

Finley reluctantly released Seren. "Someone broke a hole in the back door so the rats could enter." He focused on Seren. "Have ye any idea who would wish ye harm?"

The two women exchanged glances.

"Tell him," Jane demanded.

Finley stood just in the entrance to the large and well-stocked apothecary shop as the young magistrate and Mr. Cardew alternately questioned the obstinate owner, who pushed his spectacles back up his nose, only for them to slide down again.

No, he had no knowledge of damage to the confectionary.

No, he didn't wish Miss Cardew harm.

No, he never said he would do whatever it took to see her shop closed.

No.

No.

No.

Despite the man's denials, Finley knew he was as guilty as sin.

The magistrate turned to Mr. Cardew. "Sir, with no evidence to connect Gibbs to the crime, there is nothing legally I can do."

Finley stepped forward. "Are not his slanderous accusations to Miss Cardew enough?"

"Not without witnesses," the magistrate answered. Yet from the irritation in his tone, Finley could tell he was frustrated.

Mr. Cardew held up his hand to keep Finley from saying more. "Neither does Gibbs have anyone to verify where he was last night."

"I didn't do it," Mr. Gibbs yelled.

The magistrate collected his tricorn from where he had rested it atop the counter. After placing it atop his dark hair, he looked to Mr. Cardew. "Sir, you may want to sue so there would be record of the incident."

"Sue?" The apothecary launched into a diatribe.

As his pulse pounded in his head, Finley counted the numerous jars and bottles lining the walls behind the counter in a desperate attempt to control his anger. He almost couldn't breathe from the pungent musky odor in the room caused by the myriad spices, herbs, and other liquid concoctions. He wanted to break something. Hit someone. Pound the truth—

"Excuse me for a moment," Mr. Cardew said, interrupting the apothecary. Gripping his own tricorn with both hands, he walked to Finley. "Son, step outside with me."

Finley exited the shop first.

The crowd that had followed them from the *Gazette* had grown in size, spilling over the pavement onto Hay Street.

Mr. Cardew gently closed the door. "Go back to the confectionary."

"I want to talk to him."

"No." He gripped Finley's arm. "Let me manage this. Seren needs you by her side." Releasing his hold, he motioned with his head to the confectionary. "Go on."

'Twas not a request but a command.

Finley looked down the street to Seren's shop. On the small wagon outside were several buckets likely filled with water. If he took the barge down to Wilmington, instead of riding, they could spend more days preparing the confections. 'Twas possible to complete most of Madame's order in time and spare the cost of the barge. Even if they could not, he would not desert Seren when she needed him most. She was his to love, his to protect.

Almighty Lord, fill me with Your peace and wisdom.

If only he could find a way to help Seren—

As the germ of an idea grew in his mind, Finley turned back to Mr. Cardew and smiled. "Sir, I see an opportunity."

Sitting on the bench, Seren wiped her damp forehead with the back of her hand then released an exhausted sigh. With help from her mother, Jane, and Miss Keen, they managed to clean the shop and all its contents in a couple of hours. All the comfits she had made during the last two weeks were ruined, including, ironically, the marzipan mice and cheese figures. Fortunately, the rats hadn't chewed into any of her supplies.

While Mama and Miss Keen dried the last of the mixing bowls and wooden spoons, Jane sat next to Seren on the bench. She held Madame's missive in one hand and the cooking plan she had written in the other.

"We need to discuss changes."

Seren nodded. What she wanted was to crawl in bed, pull the covers over her head, and cry, but that was the cowardly response. She might not fulfill Madame's entire order, but she would work her fingers to the bone during the next three days to complete as much as possible.

She took the organizational plan and missive from Jane and looked back and forth between the two. "Mama and Miss Keen could begin the jams while I pare the citron-melons for—"

"'Tis a fine day for receiving gifts," Mr. Sinclair said, walking inside with a crate. He set it down on the counter. And said nothing more.

Discarding what she held, Seren raced Jane to see what he brought.

Mama and Miss Keen walked gracefully.

Mr. Sinclair removed a gray tabby, gave her to Seren, and handed the three kittens to Jane. "They'll help you find any hidden rats." Next he pulled out a jar. "This pineapple marmalade is from Mrs. McPherson. Also, orange and apple marmalades from Miss Colfield. Black currant, strawberry, and gooseberry jellies from Mrs. Stuart. Preserved green gages from Mary MacDubh and brandied peaches, pears, and grapes from her mother-in-law. Finally, two jars of Mrs. Morgan's damson jam. Were my crate not full, I would have brought more." Replacing the jar, he looked to Mama. "Mrs. Montgomery said she would set out several for Ser—Miss

Cardew to choose from tonight."

As she cradled the mother cat against her chest, Seren opened her mouth to speak but nothing would come. Her eyes burned with unshed tears. Ladies who wouldn't step foot in her shop, wouldn't taste any of the marzipan animals she'd tried giving away, wouldn't believe her when she'd insisted her comfits weren't coating pharmaceuticals, graciously gave from their pantries to help her. Why? They barely knew her yet, like Mrs. Montgomery, now treated her as if she were family.

Jane, though, clearly wasn't as overwhelmed. "How much did the sweetmeats cost?" she asked, placing the mewing kittens on the floor.

"When I shared what had happened," Mr. Sinclair answered, "they gave freely."

Jane looked skeptical.

Mr. Sinclair grinned. "The best way to receive is to begin with admitting a need and asking nicely for someone to fill it."

A smile teased across Mama's lips. "Well, daughter, it looks like the Lord has provided."

Miss Keen pulled a jar from the crate. "*Two* jars of Mrs. Morgan's prized damson jam? Humph. Laddie, why is it you wish to buy land in the Ohio Valley?" She sat the jar on the counter with a thump. "I say the Lord Almighty has gifted you to be a broker, not a farmer."

"A farmer!" Seren said, having found her voice. She allowed the mama cat to jump to the ground as she sought Mr. Sinclair's gaze. "When do you plan to—to—" *leave?*

Mr. Sinclair awkwardly shifted his stance.

Mama looked to Jane. "Be a dear and go buy several lengths of pink ribbons from the mercantile. Apply it to Seren's account. These jars need color. Miss Keen and I will see what preserves we have at home." She nudged Miss Keen to the door, then grabbed Jane's arm when she didn't immediately follow.

Seren heard the door softly close. "Mr. Sinclair?"

He led her to the bench. "Sit. Please."

They sat facing each other, yet far enough apart that a person or two could wedge between them. Seren listened as he explained about his family losing their land during the Clearances, the life of crime the Sinclairs were known for, the landlady and her family who'd reached out to him to share the gospel, his struggle with trusting God's Word, his repentance, and finally how he'd worked at the docks in Glasgow, saving most of what he made to put toward farm land in America.

Seren twisted her apron's edge around her finger. "Brokering has always been temporary for you?"

"Aye, as had working the docks been. 'Tis a good means to earn the funds I need to buy land. Once I make the farm prosperous, I can provide the opportunities I want for my wife and our children, and I would like," he said softly, almost a bit shy, "to see you in my future."

Seren swallowed to ease the tightness in her throat. "I can't leave Fayetteville." She whispered, "I won't."

"Not even with a man who loves you?"

She didn't even have to think about her answer.

She shook her head. "I am not my mother. Papa was a pamphleteer before and during the war, which meant we didn't stay in one town for very long. With every move, he said we had a new opportunity for adventure." She cleared her throat. "I don't want adventures, Mr. Sinclair. I want a home. I want roots. I want my children to grow up seeing their grandparents every day. And I want a confectionary where people can come and buy my sweets and be happy. I don't want to live in the wilderness on a farm far away from the people I love."

He turned and looked out the front window.

As the mother cat leapt onto Seren's lap, she waited for him to say something.

He didn't.

She didn't expect him to understand. Except for the last three years, he had family. Parents. Grandparents. Siblings. Cousins. Aunts. Uncles. He chose to leave his home and family willingly because he wanted a new life. She didn't want a new life across the ocean or across the mountains.

She wanted life here in Fayetteville.

She wanted familiarity.

She wanted to know that she'd not made a mistake in selling her inheritance—the brooch Mama had promised would bring her to her heart's greatest desire. Which wasn't her confectionary. Why had she not realized her greatest desire was to be settled in one place forevermore?

She stroked the tabby's soft fur. "My mother came to America to reclaim a beautiful silver brooch that had been in her family for generations. That took great courage. Were

I her, I would still be in Scotland. Mama wore the brooch at her wedding." She released a sad little chuckle. "I thought I'd wear it at mine. Foolish dreams."

"Why will you not wear it?" he said barely above a whisper.

When she didn't speak, he turned to face her.

She gave a little shrug.

"Why will you not?" he repeated a little too abruptly for her comfort. His brown eyes focused on her, and she felt his condemnation. No, what she felt was her own guilt and shame and—

"Because I sold it," she blurted. "To a jeweler in Wilmington so I could finance my confectionary." Seren gave Finley the cat then stood. "I know that makes me a hypocrite for saying how much family means to me, and yet I sold something that brought my mother and her sister together after so many years apart. I know I've been selfish and cowardly and. . ." Her voice faltered. She took a backward step away from him and the bench. "No matter how much my heart yearns to sacrifice for love like Mama has, I'm too scared of the unknown to take that risk."

"Ye are more than what ye see yerself as."

She didn't answer. She couldn't because her throat—her heart—hurt.

There, in his eyes, on his face, in his tone was the confidence in her that she wished she had.

He believed.

He saw more.

Maybe she wasn't a coward. Unlike the other women in her family, she owned her own business. She had taken the risk regardless of the cost. She had withstood criticism and suspicion from many in Fayetteville. She made delicious candies and comfits.

The kittens raced across the floor to join their mother sitting contently on Finley's lap.

Seren wanted to reach for him. To—well, to do what, she wasn't sure. She wanted to be so honest and so bold about her feelings for him and about how strong she felt when he was by her side. Until this moment, she never realized she had been waiting for someone.

She had.

She'd been waiting for Finley Sinclair.

But she didn't reach for him despite how intently he watched her. Doing so would require confidence and daring and for her to be like Jane. Nothing frightened Jane. Nothing. Jane said what she thought. Jane did what she wanted.

Seren looked through the front window. Mr. Lamb stood across the street, looking their way, although she doubted he could see inside her shop. When Finley left to buy his farm, Mr. Lamb would resume his courting and proposals. Maybe she would grow weary of refusing and finally agree. He was a good Christian man. Nice-looking. Wealthy. He would never leave Fayetteville.

Mr. and Mrs. Meady Lamb.

Seren Lamb.

If she dared laugh at the absurdity of their names together, she would cry.

Father God, I don't want to be a lamb or a Lamb. I want to be a lion. I want to love extravagantly like Mama and Papa. I want to not fear like Jane. I want—

She stopped.

She could choose to live or to merely want to live.

It was time she faced her fear.

Seren stepped to Finley. A good number of reasons why this was a bad idea resonated in her mind. But when he looked at her with those coffee-brown eyes of his—the hopeful, yearning gaze that pleaded for her to say she would go anywhere with him—she knew he loved her. She felt the torment her admission had caused.

He started to stand, and she stopped him. Placing her shaking hands on either side of his face, she touched her lips softly to his. He held perfectly still. She deepened the kiss.

Seren could feel his heartbeat, her heartbeat. Their heartbeat.

She reluctantly pulled back.

"Mr. Sinclair, think on that while you earn money for your farm." She then turned and walked to her worktable, and didn't look back.

She had an order of comfits to fill and little time to think about the kiss.

Six days later, as the sun was setting, Finley was still thinking on her kiss as rode into Elizabethtown with several crates and shipping boxes loaded onto the small wagon that his draft horse pulled. Since he had traveled all day with only minor stops, he was ahead of schedule, but his horse was tired.

He stopped a couple walking along the shops on Main

Street and inquired where he could find Nathaniel Best's coffeehouse. He graciously thanked them for the information and followed their directions. A warm meal and a feather bed were all he was hoping for.

Having spent each night sleeping on the bench in Seren's shop to ensure the apothecary didn't attempt to destroy her confections again, he was tired, sore, and grumpy. Traveling had only made him grumpier. He had no future with Seren, not as long as she refused to leave Fayetteville and her parents. And because he had spent all four days helping her with Madame's order, he still had no farming or ship wares clients.

This time Mr. Overton would not show grace.

Almighty Lord, open my eyes to see opportunities before me, he prayed for what had to be the forty-third time since leaving Fayetteville with Seren's hopes and dreams all packed carefully in shipping boxes. If he could relive the kiss, he would have pulled her into his lap and kissed her soundly. He knew she loved him. Only love was not enough for her.

He was not too sure it was enough for him either.

Finley pulled up to the white-framed coffeehouse and tied his horse to the hitching post. Black shutters bordered the tall windows on both levels of the building and the smaller single windows on the basement level. He climbed the left side of the A-framed steps and walked inside the almost empty building. A few candles added additional light to what was provided by the dying sunlight.

Nathaniel Best sat at a table near the front window, neatly dressed in a simple suit and no longer sporting a heavily bristled jaw. Closing the leather-bound book he'd been reading, the blond man stood. "Finley Sinclair, God must have told you to come see me. Hungry?"

Finley nodded. "Mind if I impose on your hospitality and stay the night?"

"Not at all." With the book stashed under his arm, Nathaniel motioned to the table. "Have a seat. My manservant will bring you some food and coffee, and then we'll discuss the business proposition I have for you."

As he listened to Nathaniel's offer, Finley added another sliced beet to the mashed potatoes and beef wedged inside the chuck of sourdough bread. Though the food was cold, he would not begrudge eating something that was not dried, cured, preserved, or pickled.

"You want to buy Mary MacDubh's cider?" he asked before taking a hefty bite of his food.

"It's the finest I've tasted." Sitting on the other side of the linen-covered table, Nathaniel gripped the edge of his empty coffee mug. "Think you can convince her to produce larger quantities and go into business with me?"

Finley took his leisure to finish his food. He had never considered selling something other than farm equipment or ship wares, but he *had* managed to sell Seren's confections. Any product could be sold if one found the right buyer. But cider?

Didn't everyone make their own? Not that he imagined anyone else's tasted as good as Mary MacDubh's secret recipe.

Brokering cider could not be any more difficult to sell than candy. And he already had one buyer—Nathaniel Best. Who was to say that he could not sell Mary MacDubh's cider to other coffeehouses, taverns, and hotels in North Carolina? He could sell cider as easily as he could sell comfits, marmalades, and candied carrots. He could even sell Miss Keen's handkerchiefs so she would not have to rely on the charity of others. She could support herself. Just as Seren could now support herself through selling to Madame Ventris. Soon others would travel to Fayetteville for sweets from Cardew Confectionary. All because Finley had found a buyer.

He could probably sell anything if he tried.

Sell anything?

Finley stopped chewing and swallowed. He met Nathaniel's focused gaze. "I could sell anything," he said without any boasting in his tone.

"I'm sure you can." Nathaniel grinned. "'Course I'm only asking you sell me cider."

Finley placed the last bit of his sandwich on the plate. "Nay, I could sell anything, not merely farm equipment and ship wares."

Nathaniel snapped his fingers and motioned for his manservant, who immediately walked over and refilled their coffee mugs.

"This enlightenment means what exactly?" Nathaniel asked.

"Means I—" Finley fell silent. He leaned and sipped his coffee while he thought about what this exactly meant. He had planned his future so accordingly that he had not looked for God's opportunities or direction. Nay, he had been the one in control.

New life. New land. A new path lay before him—the one God had prepared him for, not the one Finley thought he wanted. Miss Keen had been right: God had gifted him to be a broker, not a farmer. The challenge of finding clients and buyers satisfied his soul like nothing else he had done in his life. Aye, he liked dirt and the task of sowing and harvesting a crop, but wasn't brokering the same? Only with products instead of seeds. And he liked people. He liked fellowshipping with friends and meeting new ones. The Cardews owned no land, no farm, no great wealth. Yet their children were rich in what mattered most: parents who loved one another and who loved God.

He wanted to continue that inheritance to his and Seren's children.

Finley rested his elbows on the table and leaned forward. "If ye had a lass ye favored, what would ye do to prove yer love and devotion?"

Nathaniel's fingers drummed on the tabletop for several repetitions. His gaze then shifted to the darkened window, and his voice grew wistful. "If she let me, I would restore what she's lost."

Aye, he would restore what Seren had lost, but she had everything. Her faith was grounded in Christ. All that mattered most to her in the world were her family, her confectionary, and—

Slowly, Finley grinned. He smacked the side of

Nathaniel's arm. "Ye are a wise man."

Nathaniel shrugged. "I have been told I give the best advice."

Chapter 8

As the last of her customers for the day paid Jane, Seren placed two candied carrots atop the other comfits on the sheet of butcher paper and carefully wrapped them. She secured the purchase with a piece of twine. "Tell your wife I wish her a joyful birthnight," she said, handing the package to Mr. Trotman who stood on the other side of the front counter.

The blacksmith placed his order in the leather bag he wore draped across his cream-colored waistcoat. "Last year I gave Millie shoes."

"A man can never go wrong with shoes," Jane said matter-of-factly as she stood next to Seren.

"Or candies," Seren added, smiling.

Jane leaned against the counter and faced Seren. "So you're saying a man shouldn't chose a practical gift for the woman he loves over something that will be enjoyed, mind you, but still consumed in a matter of moments?"

Seren focused on the blacksmith. "Nothing says love like a gift given solely to bring the receiver happiness, especially something the practical woman would not purchase for herself."

Mr. Trotman looked hopeful. "Millie likes surprises."

"Surprises are—"

Seren kicked Jane's shin.

"—a delight." Jane smiled broadly. "Yes, Mrs. Trotman will be delightfully surprised, or I'll be surprised. Obviously not delighted though. Give her my best."

The burly blacksmith inclined his head then walked to the confectionary's opened door, only to stop before exiting. Glancing over his shoulder, he said, "Miss Cardew, you could have sued the apothecary. Especially with the mayor willing to testify of his threats against you."

Seren straightened the ribbon-tied jars of sweetmeats in a triangular pattern in the center of the counter. She could have sued. In fact, Mr. Lamb had prepared a case against the apothecary and would have represented her for free. Only she hadn't wanted to be indebted to Mr. Lamb, any more than she had wanted to seek revenge. Remembering what happened brought to mind her last moments with Finley. And that made her heart hurt.

Finley would be nothing more to her than her broker.

She needed to accept that.

"I know," she said with a sigh, "but the apothecary's actions and words have condemned him more than taking him to court would have. Your support of my business means more to me than proving who damaged my shop and comfits."

Mr. Trotman shrugged. "I still would have sued him. My gratitude for the candies." He stepped outside, closing the door.

Seren handed a bowl of marzipan gray mice and yellow cheese wedges to Jane. "Would you put these in a covered jar and I'll—"

The door opened, and Seren knew—*knew*—who had finally returned to Fayetteville. Her heart was so in tune with his, she felt the awareness of his presence. She focused on Jane, who seemed oddly conflicted over what to do or say.

Stay, Seren mouthed. More than anything she didn't want to be alone with Finley.

Only Jane shook her head. She handed Seren back the bowl. "I'll see you in the morning." Without bothering to say anything to Finley, Jane hurried from the shop.

The door closed again.

Seren watched Finley, waiting for him to say something. Except for his black hair which had grown a little longer than the short bristles he had when they first met, he looked the same: V-necked white shirt, well-worn buckskins and boots, and tanned skin. Altogether handsome, in a rugged Scottish sort of way. She knew how his chiseled cheeks felt under her fingertips, how his lips felt against hers, how his coffee-brown eyes twinkled when he looked at her—and how her heart just ached. Ached. For all the beauty that love was, it hurt. Why hadn't her parents told her it would feel like this? Love truly was worse than dyspepsia.

She thought in the last two weeks since Finley had left Fayetteville, her feelings had subsided. Her mind had been so focused on making comfits that she had rarely thought of him or their kiss. Mostly. She'd also thought her life was content without him.

Wrong.

Wrong.

Wrong.

Now that she could see him with her own eyes, she actually feared she would always love him. Whether she should laugh at that realization or cry, she wasn't sure. So she did neither.

The confectionary's front door reopened.

Jane offered a crooked smile. "Sorry. Since I can't stay, I figured I ought to do what I can to maintain some semblance of propriety. Don't do anything I wouldn't do because I'm watching. Not really, but appease me by pretending I am." Then she was gone.

Finley stepped forward.

Seren opened her mouth, tried to speak, but said nothing.

"I love ye," he said softly.

She set the bowl of mice down and nodded.

He took another series of steps until he reached the counter. A waist-high wooden cabinet and a plate of sugarplums were all that stood between them. Well, that and his determination to buy a farm in the Ohio Valley.

His steady gaze focused on hers. "I love ye," he said with greater strength.

She blinked at the water in her eyes.

"Do ye hear me, Seren? I love ye more than dirt. More than crops." He set a small cloth-wrapped package on the counter. "More than knowing the land under my feet is mine."

Tears trickled down her cheeks.

With the pads of his thumbs, he wiped them away. "I

love ye more than what I thought I wanted." He unwrapped the package. "If ye let me, I want to restore what ye lost."

Seren squeaked. With joy, with shock. With hope. Then she covered her mouth and allowed another round of tears to fall. Her brooch! The amber jewels of the lion's eyes glinted in the late afternoon sunlight streaming through the front window.

He had found and purchased her brooch.

"Why?" she managed to ask.

"Because I want you to wear it when you marry"—he grinned—"me."

"But—your farm?"

This time he was the one who didn't speak. He just watched her, and she knew he was waiting patiently for the significance of everything he had said to register. And she knew—in that moment—she wanted to trust him with her future and with her heart, and she wanted him to know he could trust her, too.

She took the brooch from him. The metal was surprisingly warm considering how cold she remembered it always being when she'd held it before.

She met his gaze again. "You used your savings to buy my brooch?"

He nodded.

"Do you have any funds left?"

He shook his head and didn't look the least bothered by the admission.

Seren didn't know how to respond. She placed the brooch on the counter, next to the sugarplums she'd spent the last few days making. Thanks to Finley, her business was growing.

"Why did you do this?" she asked softly.

He reached for her left hand and cradled it in his. "Because where I live and what I do matters little if ye are not by my side. Fayetteville is where I will die, Seren. On this hill. By this river." A twinkle grew in his eyes. "Aye, but I would like to spend sixty, nay seventy years living here with ye as my bride."

"Seren," Jane called in a tight voice from somewhere outside the confectionary, "stop doing what you are doing and put the man out of his misery. Kiss him so I can go home."

Finley's brows rose as he smiled at her. "Ye have a wise friend."

"I can think of a few more appropriate descriptors for her." Seren stepped around the counter. Placing her right hand in the center of Finley's chest, she stood on her tiptoes. "Mr. Sinclair, should I kiss you before or after I accept your proposal?"

"Both, Miss Cardew, both."

"Has anyone told you that you have a way with words?"

A tiny smirk eased across Finley's lips. He drew her up against him, lifting her off her feet.

"'Tis possible," he muttered.

Whether he kissed her first, or she him, Seren wasn't sure. But as she wrapped her arms around his neck, she was fairly certain Finley was right when he said the best way to receive something was to begin first with asking nicely.

His nicely was quite nice indeed.

Years—okay, eons—ago, Gina Welborn worked in news radio scripting copy until she realized how depressing human tragedy was, so she took up writing romances. This Oklahoma-raised girl now lives in Virginia with her youth-pastor husband and their five Okie-Hokie children. Gina likes to put a spiritual spin on her ramblings at www.inkwellinspirations.com, a team blog with eleven other inspirational authors.

HEART'S INHERITANCE

by Jennifer Hudson Taylor

Dedication

I would like to dedicate this story to the memory of our ancestors who fought for our right to worship in freedom and to those who have sacrificed their lives preserving the Word of God—our true inheritance. I've always thought of the Bible as HIStory. Remember to share it with your children and your children's children. It's the greatest history book ever written.

A good man leaveth an inheritance to his children's children: and the wealth of the sinner is laid up for the just.
PROVERBS 13:22

Chapter 1

Pardon me, but if ye're headin' north may I travel with ye?"

Brynna Sinclair stilled at the man's deep Scottish burr, an unexpected shiver racing through her. She had always loved the romantic sound of her ancestors' native tongue, but that alone couldn't be reason enough to invite a stranger to travel with the three of them. She glanced at her friend Jean, who met her gaze with a shy smile, her cheeks darkening to crimson.

"What's your name?" her brother, Rob, stood to his full height of six-two, meeting the stranger eye-to-eye.

"My name's Niall Cameron of Argyll, Scotland." He extended his hand. Rob shook it. A whiff of the salty sea still clung to his garments. "We docked this morn in Charleston. No one aboard was heading to Fayetteville, and I believe there's safety in numbers." His green-eyed gaze drifted to Brynna and to her friend Jean standing beside her. "Of course, I'd pay half the fare." He dug into a pocket and produced a change purse, coins jingled.

As Rob considered the offer, Brynna wanted to warn him against it. Other than the fact that they knew naught about him, no acceptable reason of refusal came to mind. He was obviously from Scotland as he said and well spoken. Dressed as a gentleman, he wore brown trousers, a white collared shirt, a tan waistcoat, complete with black Hessian boots and a conical tall hat, which he now twisted in his hands.

"How do we know you aren't a criminal in disguise?" Brynna asked, clasping her hands in front of her.

"Ye'll have to take my word for it, lass." Mr. Cameron grinned, one dark eyebrow arched and his lips curled, revealing a row of healthy teeth. With his auburn hair pulled back at the nape and tied in a ribbon, his mischievous grin induced her to imagine him a handsome rogue—one she feared wasn't to be trusted.

"Brynna!" Rob scolded, turning back to the man. "I must apologize for my sister's rude behavior. She doesn't trust strangers." Rob's eyes widened at her for emphasis. "Allow me to present Miss Brynna Sinclair, my younger sister, and her friend Miss Jean Anderson."

Jean gave a slight curtsy, while Brynna acknowledged him with a mere nod.

"It's a pleasure to meet ye both." He bowed. His smile faded as he glanced from Brynna to Rob and cleared his throat. "I hope ye're jesting, but if not, let me assure ye that I'm harmless."

"I doubt that," Brynna murmured. Her brother admonished her with a reprimanding look. Feeling guilty, she forced a smile. "Never mind my wry humor, Mr. Cameron." She waved a hand, wiping the words away.

"Brynna, why don't you and Miss Anderson settle inside, while I discuss arrangements with Mr. Cameron?"

She pursed her lips and bounded up inside the coach. A few moments later, the men joined them. After a moment of silence, the wheels lurched forward and creaked over the dirt road as it wobbled on uneven ground.

"Judging from yer American accents, I'm assuming all of ye were born here? Do ye live here in Charleston and are ye visiting north?" Mr. Cameron asked.

Brynna could feel his warm gaze upon her, but she ignored him, staring out the window at the rows of green trees and thick underbrush. The June sun shone bright so she shielded her eyes. After a fortnight in Charleston, she longed for home.

"Quite the opposite. We live in Fayetteville," Rob said. "We visited Charleston to tour the historical museum. My sister dreams of opening a museum in Fayetteville. Even though it isn't open to the public yet, as a librarian, Miss Anderson has connections through the Charleston Library Society. She secured us an invitation from the museum director."

Mr. Cameron chuckled. "A strange ambition for a woman. It wasn't so long ago Charleston was a mere colony. What on earth could the museum have of historical value?"

Brynna whipped her head around. "You've been here less than twenty-four hours, and yet you dare to mock us? The colony of Charles Town was established as early as 1670. We have a history of more than 145 years. I daresay there is plenty worth preserving."

"I admire yer passion, Miss Sinclair, but I prefer to leave the past where it belongs and plan for the future—for progress," Mr. Cameron said.

"What brings you to Fayetteville?" Rob asked, no doubt changing the subject before she could further embarrass him.

"My uncle left no heirs and named me in his will. I've inherited a lumber mill, a clothing store, and a fifty-acre farm."

Her stomach soured and settled like a heavy rock as she realized her former boss must have been his uncle. Brynna leaned forward, her mouth dropping open as she stared at the man across from her. "Was—Mr. Edward Cameron your uncle?"

"Indeed." Mr. Cameron nodded, his green eyes sparkling. From where he sat by the window, a myriad of shadows and light crossed his face from the sun filtering through the trees. "Did ye know him?"

Brynna kicked her brother before he could answer. He rubbed his shin as he glared at her.

She turned to Mr. Cameron. "I believe we did. May the Lord rest his soul, your uncle was a prominent gentleman in our town. Everyone knew him and thought well of him. What are your plans? Will you be staying?"

"Aye, Fayetteville will be my home now. I plan to carry on in my uncle's footsteps. Progress is my goal." He shrugged. "I'm sure some change will be necessary. Improvements are hard to make without it."

Change. Why did she have a feeling that he had every

intention of ruining things? She knew she should be nice to him, but something about him irked her in spite of him being a handsome rogue. Her throat constricted like an allergic reaction. She forced her fists to unclench in her lap.

"Necessary change benefits everyone. Unnecessary change usually benefits only one," Brynna said.

Niall raised a glass of water to his lips and drank like a parched man dying of thirst. The stale water aboard the ship over the past few months had dulled his taste buds and led him to question if it wasn't the source ailing some of the poor souls who had languished in the lower decks.

He glanced around the tavern where they had stopped for the night. Only three tables were occupied of the available ten, most patrons having retired for the night, including Miss Sinclair and Miss Anderson.

"Yer sister doesn't seem to care for my presence on this trip. Do ye have any advice before I suffer another tongue-lashing on the morrow?" Niall asked.

Rob grinned and rubbed his reddening nose. "Brynna has a passionate nature that lies hidden beneath a vast knowledge of history. Our parents would love to channel her interests in more prosperous areas to secure her future, but Brynna seems quite against the idea."

"Ye mean marriage?"

"I do." Rob nodded.

"That's strange," Niall said, scratching his ear. "Where I'm from, a lass had better catch herself a man as soon as possible. A good match is a woman's only hope."

Rob leaned forward and propped his elbows on the wood table, his grin broadening. "My friend, here in the States things are much different. Not only do men have more choices being free from a dictating monarch and the confines of titles and nobility, but in a sense so do women. Some have set up shops and reputable boardinghouses, while others are working as librarians, clerks, and in post offices. My sister doesn't see marriage as her only hope. For her to marry, a man will have to endeavor to capture her affections."

"Well I seemed to have incurred her wrath." Niall flattened his palm against the tabletop and shook his head. "I've no idea what I might have done. Since we'll all be living in Fayetteville, I'd like to at least have her friendship."

Niall rubbed his chin as images of Miss Sinclair came to mind. Her eyes were the color of coffee and matched her temperament, strong and potent. She only spared him an occasional glare, but he had finally witnessed her joyous expression when a toddler escaped her mother and staggered into Miss Sinclair's legs. Miss Sinclair bent down and swept the babe into her arms, laughing and abandoning her reserve. Her smooth complexion carried a rosy glow as the child pulled the combs from Miss Sinclair's hair and chestnut waves tumbled over her shoulders and down her back. She left it down all evening, mesmerizing Niall like a sea wench casting a spell.

"If you want to get along with my sister, you only have to do two things." Rob held up an index finger. "One, don't change anything." He released another finger. "Two, gain an appreciation for history and antiques. Learn about it so you can carry on a conversation. Otherwise, you may never have anything to discuss."

"Goodness, mon, ye make her sound like a complete bore." Niall wrinkled his nose in distaste, dismissing Rob's advice as nonsense.

"My sister is anything but boring. Did she not entertain you with her fascinating version of *The Highwayman*?"

"Absolutely." Niall nodded in eager agreement. Truth be told, the woman was a complete enchantress, but he wasn't so sure her brother would appreciate such stark honesty, so he dropped the subject, certain he would have vivid dreams of a chestnut-haired angel throughout the night.

"Enough about Brynna. I'd like to know more about Scotland. Our ancestors came over from Argyll back in 1739. What's it like?"

Niall studied his new friend, taking in the excitement burning in his blazing blue eyes. His eagerness for adventure reminded Niall of his younger brother, Kyle. He shifted in his seat, determined to block out the painful memories.

"There isn't much to tell. The land is still the same—beautiful lochs, majestic moors with purple heather in the spring, peat moss in abundance, and peaks touching the skyline. The people still suffer from hard labor, high taxes, and unaffordable rents. Their hard lives make them even harder. But new laws have made some things more bearable. The monarch has less power and parliament more. At least through parliament, the common man now has a voice he didn't have before."

"Do the Scots still speak Gaelic?" Rob asked.

"Some, but just as many speak English. The old language is dying out at home as much as it is here."

"What about the kilts and plaids? Do they wear them every day?" Rob shoved his empty mug to the side.

"Not so much on a daily basis. They have them and save them for special occasions. We dress for work and travel in English attire as I'm dressed." Niall glanced down at himself and lifted the opening of his jacket for emphasis. "Yer sister may not like it, but sooner or later change comes. It's inevitable. My uncle's death is proof enough of that."

Chapter 2

Brynna woke to voices downstairs, mingled with sounds of silverware brushing against plates, footsteps, and chairs scraping the floor. The familiar fragrance of bacon and pancakes drifted through the closed door. She rolled on her side, thankful to be back home and upon her new cotton mattress.

Laughter erupted from the dining room below her chamber. A male voice she had come to know well floated above the others—Mr. Niall Cameron and his Scottish accent.

She frowned, staring up at the white ceiling, and sighed. A strand of hair blew to the side of her face. Since Rob had invited Mr. Cameron to stay the night in their home, she would have to go down and face the man at some point.

They had arrived home in the middle of the night. She supposed it would have been rude to send him to the inn at such an hour when they had plenty of space to accommodate him. If only he wasn't the sort of man to value future progress over preserving history. She imagined he couldn't wait to get his hands upon his uncle's businesses, change everything in the name of progress, and make her life miserable in the process.

Her stomach rumbled. She should hurry or there might not be a morsel left. Brynna threw back the covers and swung her bare feet to the hardwood floor. She tiptoed to the basin and washed her face, then strode to her oak wardrobe.

Brynna selected a dark green linen bodice with a low neckline and a cotton plaid skirt of matching green and blue squares with red lines. Once donned, she grabbed a white sheer handkerchief and tucked it in the neckline. Holding her arms out, she was satisfied with how the sleeves ended just below the elbow in white trim.

Next, she brushed through her long hair and swept it up, winding it upon her crown and securing it with two combs on each side. A few curls hung by her ears. She left her room and made her way down the stairs. The boards creaked with each step.

"There you are. I was beginning to wonder if you'd sleep the whole morning away. It isn't like you." Her mother set her coffee down with a worried frown. "Are you feeling all right?"

"Yes, I'm fine. Just a little tired is all. The coach was too uncomfortable to sleep, and we could only find one inn to rest between Charleston and here."

"Upon my word, there is indeed more wild country than I'd realized. When I first arrived in Charleston, the place was so busy and booming with life, I had no idea such a vast wilderness lay beyond," said Mr. Cameron.

When no kind response came to mind, Brynna turned toward the kitchen.

"Brynna, aren't you going to greet our guest this morning?" her mother asked.

All eyes focused on her as she forced a thin smile. She hated to be on display, even if only in front of her family. Her father sat across from her mother, wearing a curious expression. Rob shook his head as if he couldn't believe her rude behavior, while Jean stared up at her with wide eyes.

Mr. Cameron cleared his throat. "It's all right, Mrs. Sinclair. I believe she's still waking up and needs a cup of coffee and a wee bite to eat." He winked at Brynna.

She lifted her chin and stifled a surprised gasp at his audacity. Brynna gripped the back of an empty chair and met his gaze. "Good morning, Mr. Cameron. I hope you slept well?"

His wavy hair was combed to one side with bangs brushing his forehead. Crisp green eyes stared back at her like a blade of grass sparkling in the sun. Today he wore a wine-colored shirt that complemented his auburn hair and accentuated his muscular shoulders. She took a deep breath, determined not to be fazed by his distracting presence, but it was hard the way he grinned at her. No one had affected her like this since—Dean. Even she was wise enough to know when to let some histories go.

"Aye, I did, but I won't be taking advantage of yer family. I'll move to my uncle's place this afternoon as soon as I figure out where it is and meet with Mr. Isaac Anderson."

"Oh, you have a meeting with my brother?" Jean asked.

"He's the town's attorney."

"Then I suppose I do." Mr. Cameron's gaze slid from Brynna to her friend.

"That reminds me, Brynna," Rob said. "I've spent too much time away from the candy store. Dad has some chores he needs to attend to here on the farm, so will you escort Niall to see Isaac and take Jean home?"

"You can take the carriage," her father said.

Shocked, Brynna groped for a reason to deny them, but she couldn't think of one. The only thing she had to do was open the clothing store and since Mr. Cameron owned it, she was really at his service—or his disposal.

"I'd be honored to have Miss Sinclair show me around town. Who better than the highly acclaimed town historian?" He raised an auburn eyebrow.

She started to protest, but he held up a hand. "Don't deny it. They've already told me all about ye. It takes a lot of dedication to visit all the elderly members of a community, interview them, and record their memories. I'm impressed."

Brynna could feel her lips thin in anger. She hadn't done it to impress anyone—least of all him! Brynna glared at Rob and her parents as she pressed her lips together.

"We're proud of you, Brynna." Her mother shrugged and beamed with pride. "I know you dislike attention, but everyone is thankful for what you're doing for the town."

"And I'm especially grateful for yer assistance today." Mr. Cameron's Scottish burr reclaimed her concentration.

"I'm happy to do my part." Brynna gave a tight smile. The sooner she took him to Mr. Anderson, she'd be rid of him. "Rob, would you and Mr. Cameron hitch the horses to the carriage and load his luggage? As soon as I have my breakfast we'll leave."

Niall tried to relax against the hard seat as Miss Sinclair took the reins and guided the horses down the dirt street. Miss Anderson was squeezed between them. It felt awkward riding in a carriage beside two women and not driving. He folded his empty hands across his chest.

When he had offered his hand to assist Miss Sinclair up into the carriage, she had lifted her chin and forged by him as if he didn't exist. Miss Anderson had offered him a hesitant smile, almost as if in apology. Niall assisted her instead.

As bonny and fascinating as Miss Sinclair was, her coldhearted attitude began to annoy him. Granted, at home he had made plenty of mistakes, but here no one knew about them. He had a chance at a fresh new start, and the last thing he wanted was some spoiled, pride-filled lass using her homegrown influence to persuade people against him.

Back in Scotland everyone knew about his failure to please his father, his being fired for defending a tardy co-worker, his years of loyal service at the furniture company only to be overlooked for promotion. As a result, he certainly hadn't been a favored bachelor among the women and their disapproving mammas.

Niall had hoped he'd find God's favor here in Fayetteville. Now as a businessman and landowner, people would respect him, not overlook him as a nobody. His new financial security would lend him as a prospective husband, not a rejected failure. Only one person stood in his way—Miss Brynna Sinclair, an intelligent woman who had the community's ear and possessed the worst opinion of him. He could either win her approval or prove her wrong. Niall smiled. Perhaps he could achieve one by accomplishing the other.

"What are you smiling at?" Miss Sinclair's curious voice lifted above the rolling wheels and the rhythmic *clip-clop* of the horses' hooves. Her bottom lip protruded as if insulted by his good mood.

"Lass, if I'd known a simple smile could gain yer notice of me, I would have gladly done so sooner. However, please forgive me if I keep my thoughts to myself."

"Fine, but I wish you wouldn't call me lass." Her lips twisted and her eyebrows furrowed, creasing lines upon her smooth forehead. "It sounds so—so—improper."

"Brynna," Miss Anderson gasped. "It is not. I think you're being overly hard on Mr. Cameron. It's common knowledge that the Scots use the term, especially for unmarried women."

They pulled up beside a blue two-story house with white trim. Miss Sinclair steadied the horses and set the brake. She turned to her friend with a haughty look of annoyance. "Then he may call you a lass instead of me."

Niall grinned as he bounced down from the carriage and reached up to help Miss Anderson. Miss Sinclair jumped to the ground on the other side, stirring up enough dust that she sneezed.

"God bless ye!" Niall said as she came around the carriage.

"Thank you—lad." Her coffee-colored eyes blazed as her

tone emphasized the last word.

"If ye please." Niall chuckled and motioned ahead of him, gesturing to the house. "I'll follow with the luggage."

As Miss Sinclair brushed passed him, he leaned toward her. "Ye may call me lad all ye like." He lowered his voice.

"Humph!" Miss Sinclair lifted her nose and glided up the steps and into the house. He hoped she wouldn't miss a step and trip.

Niall grabbed Miss Anderson's trunk and satchel. An older woman in a gray gown held the door open for him. She wore an apron around her middle so he assumed she was the maid.

"You can set them down there." Miss Anderson pointed to the corner in the foyer. "I'd like you to meet my brother, Isaac."

A man of average height with black hair and graying temples strode toward Niall. His mustache moved with his greeting smile as he held out his hand. Niall shook it in a firm grip, noticing Isaac's black trousers and boots, a white shirt and cravat beneath a gold vest and brown jacket.

"I'm Niall Cameron of Argyll, Scotland. I received yer letter about my uncle's demise."

"Yes, I'm sorry. Do you have any papers on you to prove your identity since there is an inheritance?"

"I do, the ones I used on the ship." Niall produced a thin stack of folded papers from the inside of his vest pocket.

"Good." He motioned for Niall to follow him down the hall. "Let's go to my office. Brynna, would you come as well? I'd like you to be a witness for the reading of the will since

Jean must get to work at the library and my assistant is out on an errand."

Niall ignored her drooping shoulders and sudden frown. He much preferred to see her bonny face all cheerful and bright. It didn't help that he was the cause of her distress.

He followed Isaac. Miss Sinclair entered the dusty office and took a seat beside Niall facing Isaac who sat behind an oak desk littered with papers, books, ink, and quills. The walls were of dark wood paneling, and a framed fox hunting scene hung behind Isaac. A side window afforded some natural light.

Isaac read the short will. It contained no surprises as the letter Isaac had sent was very detailed.

"Do you have any questions?" Isaac peered over the paper at Niall.

"No." Niall shook his head. "I suppose I need access to the house and businesses and their location."

"Yes, here you are." Isaac opened a drawer and pulled out a set of keys. They jingled as he handed them over. "I must be in court in less than half an hour." He glanced at Miss Sinclair. "Would you mind showing Mr. Cameron the way to his house and then to the lumber mill and store if he so desires?"

Her dark gaze widened and then she cut her gaze at Niall. Her lips thinned. "Yes, whatever the lad desires."

Isaac blinked at her and opened his mouth. Fearing she was about to be chastised, Niall cleared his throat. "Lass, it doesn't appear ye're quite rid of me, yet." He stood, and extended his hand. "Mr. Anderson, thank ye."

Miss Sinclair slipped from the room like a silent star.

Chapter 3

Brynna snapped the reins and they headed south of town toward the Cameron place. With Jean's absence, she was acutely aware of Mr. Cameron's presence beside her. He had closed the distance between them by spreading his long legs out and relaxing.

His strange silence unnerved her. Why wasn't he talking? Or provoking her? After a few more moments of silence she risked a glance up at his profile. He stared out at the countryside, the white sandy road and the tall pines on each side of them. A pensive expression deepened his dark green eyes as he shoved a piece of hair to the side.

She longed to know his thoughts. A man like Mr. Cameron never had an idle mind. His gaze shifted to hers and this time no smile tugged at the corners of his lips. His rugged complexion and sharp features sent a wave of heat through her system, but the intensity of his eyes chipped at her heart.

"Please—tell me—did my uncle die peacefully? Was he alone?" He looked away, but not before she caught a glimpse of moisture in his eyes. Or had she imagined it?

Guilt ripped through Brynna. How could she have been so insensitive? It never occurred to her that he might be mourning his uncle's loss. She had assumed that he didn't know his uncle—or at least not very well since they were separated by a whole ocean.

"He was surrounded by friends. He had a heart attack, but lingered for three days afterward. The pastor and two widows took turns attending him, as well as the doctor. I attended the funeral as did most of the town. Your uncle was well liked. I can assure you of that."

"Thank ye." He released a deep breath. "That relieves some of my guilt for not being here."

"You mean you would have come had you known?" She concentrated on the road, trying to find the right words to ask what she wanted to know without sounding heartless. "Even without—"

"The inheritance?" His voice hardened. "Ye must think me a monster, Miss Sinclair. And I confess, I know not why." He scratched his ear, a habit she was beginning to recognize. "Aye, had I known, I would have come regardless. When my brother died, Uncle Edward arrived and was the only one who defended me. Kyle was eight and I was twelve. As the elder, my parents blamed me when he fell through an icy loch." He sighed and kicked the floorboard. "I don't know why I'm telling ye this, except to say that Uncle Edward was the only one who recognized my grief, who told me it wasn't my fault. He wrote me often and came to visit one summer when I was sixteen. I thought a lot of him."

Stunned into chastisement, Brynna swallowed the sick feeling rising to her throat. He had only been a boy—of course his brother's death wasn't his fault. As cold as she had been to him this past week, she didn't expect him to take consolation from her now.

"I'm sorry. Please forgive me." The words tumbled from her tongue, not nearly adequate enough for the remorse she felt.

He didn't respond as they passed a white two-story house with a barn, stables, a chicken coop, and pastureland.

"Whose farm is that?" He pointed, changing the subject.

"The McDuffs. My sister, Bonnie, lives there with her husband, Doug, and their new baby girl. They're your neighbors."

A while later they rolled to a stop in front of a modest house painted gray with black trim and window shutters. It even looked like a bachelor's home with dull colors and a lack of flowers and shrubbery in front. She thought it would suit him very well.

Once inside, he dropped his luggage and took a deep breath, surveying the small foyer. "I should have come sooner."

His resigned voice pinched Brynna's heart. She hung back as his boots clicked against the hardwood floor in need of a deep cleaning. He walked from room to room running a finger along the empty furniture. A few times he scratched or tugged on his ear. Very few paintings or decorations lined the walls.

A small living room to the right led into a dining room. A kitchen was located in the back, while the master bedroom lay in the front left side of the house. Two small bedrooms were upstairs.

After Mr. Cameron remained silent for quite some time, Brynna backed toward the front door. "I'll give you a moment alone."

"Stay, lass. I prefer yer company to my own." His strained voice floated over her like honey draped on the silver platter of his Scottish burr. For once, she couldn't be angry that he had called her lass.

"Where are the servants who work the farm and maintain the house?"

"I believe the field hands have been tending the crops and caring for the animals as expected, but the house was closed," Brynna said. "No one knew what your preference might be so they left it for you to decide. I'm sure people would be willing to help."

"No need." He shook his head. "I'm ready to go see the lumber mill now." Mr. Cameron's tone turned back to business, and he strode by her toward the front door. "We'd best be on our way."

The abrupt change in his attitude disappointed Brynna. She preferred his sensitive side. Would she have a chance to discover more of the man she had just witnessed, or would Mr. Cameron bury himself under a facade of prideful business etiquette?

Niall stared up at the long rectangular wood building that was Cameron Saw & Lumber Mill. Smoke billowed from two large pipes over the roof on one end, while a powerful waterwheel churned on the other side pumping water from a dam. It sounded like a waterfall. The idea that he could own something so magnificent overwhelmed him. If only the people back home could see him now.

Fear of inadequacy seized him, but pride masked it as he set his chin in determination. He must show his new employees that he was now in charge. If there was one thing he had learned from his past failures, it was that respect had to be earned.

Miss Sinclair joined him and his heart swelled at having her by his side. She had a comforting assurance that he admired and appreciated—when she wasn't debating him.

He held out his elbow offering his arm. She stared at it as if considering her options. Niall held his breath, hoping she wouldn't reject him again, not now when he needed her strength of support.

"Shall we?" She slipped her delicate hand on his arm and smiled with encouragement. He covered it, resisting the urge to bring her long fingers to his lips.

"Aye." He nodded.

Together they climbed the five steps leading to a porch landing where barrels were stacked on each side of the oak double doors. Inside, the scent of pine and sawdust thickened the air in wee clouds that burned fresh tears to one's eyes. They blinked. Miss Sinclair burst into a fit of coughing, drowned out by the numerous sounds of sawing.

Niall leaned over her in concern, pressing his palm against the middle of her back, ready to steady her if needed.

Two nearby sawmen paused, having noticed their entrance.

"We should get ye out o' here," Niall said.

"No, no." Miss Sinclair shook her head, gripping his arm with one hand and touching her throat with the other. "It's just that I've never been in here before. I've passed by the place on a number of occasions, but never had a reason to explore inside—until now. I only need a moment to adjust."

"Are ye sure?" Niall bent to survey her expression, but she nodded and then turned to clear her throat and gulped, wiping at her eyes.

"This place needs more light." Niall surveyed the long windows spaced ten feet apart along the walls. "That shall be the first change I make around here."

The sounds of grinding wood and saws pierced the air from every direction as one by one the workers noticed their presence, and the noise dissipated, except the huge saw in back, which Niall assumed was being operated by power from the waterwheel outside.

A tall man who had been talking to one of the saw operators strode toward them. His blond hair tapered down his neck in layers, but the front was combed over to the side. He wore black trousers, black boots, and a white shirt with sleeves rolled up to his elbows. A sheen of sweat glistened on his brow as he stopped before them.

"I'm Andrew Henderson, the mill manager. How can I help you?" Before Niall could answer, Mr. Henderson's brown gaze slid to Miss Sinclair. "Brynna, I can't recollect ever seeing you in 'ere." He grinned as if enjoying an inside joke with her.

"Drew, meet Mr. Niall Cameron, the new owner and

your new boss." Miss Sinclair bit her bottom lip as a wee smile invaded her features.

Niall tensed. Was she blushing? He couldn't tell if the color in her cheeks was from the heat, the stuffy, littered air, or this Drew fellow. Disliking his uncomfortable reaction, Niall concentrated on forcing an expression of indifference.

"Well, it sure is good to meet you." Drew held out his hand.

Gripping him in a firm handshake, Niall met his gaze. "Likewise. I'd like to see the running of the mill, the layout of everything, and I'd like to take home the most recent historical records to read at my leisure. Before I can make adequate decisions, I need to learn as much as I can."

"I'm glad to hear you say that, sir." Drew beamed at Niall with approval. "Most new business owners would have come in here and ordered change before taking the time to learn the business. I've seen it 'appen before at other mills I've worked."

"Don't let him surprise you, Drew," said Miss Sinclair. "Mr. Cameron has every intention of making change. He's a huge believer in economical progress."

"What Miss Sinclair means is, I can't promise I won't change anything, but any decisions I make will be for the best interest of the company and the next logical step in progress, not just to be making change as Miss Sinclair would have ye believe."

Drew raised a golden eyebrow in suspicion. "Well, I've grown up with Brynna and known her all my life. She may be a bit prone to exaggerate, but never a liar."

"I'd never be so bold as to suggest that. I meant that she doesn't understand the nature of business the way we do and her uninformed opinions could give her and others the wrong impression."

She gasped. Her eyes narrowed upon him, her lips twisting, as if she'd bitten into a lemon. "I may be uninformed about business matters in a sawmill, but I most certainly am not misinformed about *you*, Mr. Cameron."

"Pray tell, what exactly is that supposed to mean?" Niall stepped closer, leaning down to read her expression. Heated anger emanated from her. He loved the way she challenged him. The woman was never boring, but he wished her efforts didn't always target him.

His towering height didn't faze her. She tilted her head back and pierced him with a smoldering gaze. "In spite of what you say now, I believe you came here with the agenda of making your uncle's businesses prosper in the way you're accustomed to in Scotland. Your unguarded comments on the day we met testify to your original intentions." She gave a sarcastic laugh and shook her head. "Not that my opinion matters. Still, you disappoint me. I'd hoped Mr. Edward Cameron's nephew would have the same peaceful mannerisms and wise countenance that he possessed. I'll pray upon the matter. Perhaps God could touch your heart in a way that I never could. I've found He's the best defender and the most convincing when we are in denial about our behavior and motivations."

Rage ripped through Niall as he stared at her. All amiable thoughts about her beauty and passionate nature flew from his mind. "Ye dare to preach to me? After all the rude behavior ye've bestowed upon me since the day we met—even to the point of yer being chastised by yer own brother and your friend? One could question which of us is in denial about their behavior."

Drew cleared his throat. "Um, perhaps a tour of the mill would be the perfect distraction?" He waved a hand around him.

Both Niall and Miss Sinclair swung their heads toward him. "In a minute!" they said in unison.

Chapter 4

Brynna jumped down from the carriage in front of Cameron's Weaving and Tailor Shop. The tour at the sawmill had taken about thirty minutes, but both she and Mr. Cameron hardly spoke to each other. Brynna wouldn't allow his poor mood to dissuade her from asking questions. The mill's work fascinated her, and she had enjoyed learning about the process of preparing different types of wood for shipbuilding, log homes, furniture, paper, and the pine sap being converted to tar and other products. Their ride to the store continued in tense silence. She smiled, waved, and returned greetings to townspeople as they passed.

She dismounted from the carriage and stood in front of the shop. Mr. Cameron pulled out his keys and unlocked the door. He stepped back, allowing her to enter first. The bell jingled on the door. She blinked at the darkness. Knowing the layout of the shop, Brynna walked over to the front bay window, shifted the drapes to each side, and secured them with a tie cord. Then she flipped the sign around from CLOSED to OPEN.

"That's much better." Mr. Cameron glanced around the shop, his eyes taking in the tables of fabrics and bolts of cloth, the tartan samples hanging on the side wall on display.

In the middle of the shop, Brynna lit an oil lamp on each wall where they were fastened on a brass arm. Mr. Cameron's boots pressed against the wood floor as he walked toward the back of the store where her weaving machine, the spinning wheel, and the tailor's tools were located.

Too warm for a fire, Brynna lit another oil lamp and set it on the mantel. On the other side of the mantel, she leaned up on her tiptoes and opened the belly door of a ticking clock to wind it. The springs rotated until it wouldn't go any further and she adjusted the time by ten minutes as she did each day.

Mr. Cameron walked back toward her, a perplexed expression on his handsome face. "Why wasn't the shop open? Who's supposed to be here running things? Where are my employees?" He gestured to the empty room as if he couldn't believe the sight.

"You are." Brynna smiled, crossing her arms over her chest.

"Me?" His dark brow wrinkled. "There must be some mistake. Mr. Anderson distinctly said I had two shop employees for the shop, a tailor and a weaver. When I find out who they are, there will be serious consequences to pay. It's well into the business day and this shop should be open for business just like the sawmill."

"And pray tell, what do you intend to do? Has it not occurred to you that perhaps your employees weren't sure if they were supposed to be here until you arrived?"

"Nonsense." He waved a hand in the air. "They know their jobs, do they not? They should be doing them. Now I'm concerned about the lost profits and customers I might have suffered since my uncle's death." He scratched his ear. "I need to find the record books. I wonder where they would be in this infernal place."

"There's a small office in the very back where your uncle often conducted business negotiations and does—did his paperwork. He didn't like it in the winter though. It gets extremely cold back there. He complained about it often enough."

"So ye spend that much time here at the shop?" His face relaxed into a grin. "Good. We need loyal patrons like ye."

He grabbed the lantern off the mantel and strode to the back.

Brynna sighed and shook her head. Having him for a boss would no doubt try her patience. She loved weaving and the people in town seemed to enjoy her work, but would she be able to endure working for this man?

She heard a bump then a groan. Brynna smiled to herself. Mr. Cameron looked so out of place here. Once he discovered she was the weaver, would he really dock her pay? After all, it was his fault she hadn't opened the shop this morning.

Footsteps pounded toward her where she stood sorting through the latest tartan pieces she had weaved. Mr. Cameron carried a thick book in one hand and pointed his thumb over his shoulder with the other. A lock of hair had fallen over one eye, reminding her of what he might have looked like as a lad.

"Where does the door in the back lead to?" he asked.

"Outside, to a pile of wood for the fireplace and an outhouse."

"Oh." He opened the book where he stood beside her and flipped to the latest entries. "Well, it looks like someone has been keeping the store open. The handwriting is different compared to where my uncle left off. The figures appear to be accurate. I wonder who has been keeping up everything in my absence?" He slammed the book shut. "Whoever it is, I owe them a debt of gratitude."

"Does that mean you won't dock their pay?" Brynna lifted an eyebrow.

Fluid emotions flowed across his expression as he considered his response. "I suppose not, but I'd like an explanation. I deserve that much at least. I don't want my employees thinking they can get away with anything."

"I wasn't here to open the shop this morning because I've been taking care of business with you. I've been keeping the books. I'm the weaver your uncle hired two years ago and Mrs. Cora Ward is your tailor and seamstress. Today she arrives at noon. We take turns opening the shop and on occasion, your uncle runs the shop if one of us is sick or we need time off."

Mr. Cameron's shocked features shifted from surprise, to perplexity, and then anger. His lips thinned. His green eyes turned a shade darker. He took a menacing step closer. Brynna gulped. Her legs trembled like a lifeline to her now quivering heart.

Shaking with anger, Niall advanced toward Miss Sinclair. At the mill she had expressed disappointment in him. The words had clawed at him, digging deep until uncovering similar statements from his past, like an age-old wound festering in his heart. She had made a mockery of him by letting him believe—believe what?

Niall paused with his finger in her face. She hadn't exactly lied, but she hadn't been truly honest either—especially regarding her involvement in his business. Her behavior bordered on deception and it stung like betrayal. He clenched his jaw. The pulse at his temples pounded.

She leaned back and blinked in vivid fear. Remorse clipped the other half of his heart as he gazed into her eyes. Her long black lashes were like iron bars holding him captive. His temper warped into unexpected desire, washing him in a fresh wave of confusion.

He lowered his hand and the slight movement caused her to flinch. Guilt rose like an unbidden tide, prompting him to do something to ease her fear. He brushed the bottom of her chin with the top of his knuckles. Her soft skin tingled against him as he indulged in her improving countenance, her oval face a delicate carved structure that suited his liking.

"I can only fathom what ye must think of me, lass. No doubt, it must be some inaccurate detestable image that ye've conjured in yer mind." He lowered his voice to a gentle burr. "But let me reassure ye, I'd never sink so low as to strike a woman."

The doorbell jingled and they both took a step back from one another. He ran his hand through his hair, while she laid her palm across her chest, her breath coming in short gasps.

A woman who looked to be in her midforties sauntered in carrying a bag. Her brown hair was pulled tight into a bun with silver highlights stretching from her crown. She lifted a hesitant gaze toward him and then quickly looked at the floor. Her rounded shoulders were wrapped in a plaid shawl of tan and brown squares with red lines. Her brown linen dress was made of simple cut pleats from a high waistband of satin.

"Cora, it's so good to see you!" Brenna strode over to the woman, holding her arms out and embracing her.

"My, is everything all right, dear?" Cora asked, returning Brynna's hug.

Niall realized he had just thought of Miss Sinclair by her first name. He scratched his ear—a habit that had started with his brother's death. What harm could it be to think of her as Brynna so long as he remembered his manners and addressed her properly?

"Of course, but allow me to introduce ye to the new owner, Mr. Niall Cameron." Brynna led the woman toward him. "Mr. Cameron, I'd like to introduce you to Mrs. Cora Ward, your tailor and seamstress."

He bowed. "A pleasure to meet ye, Mrs. Ward." His gaze slid between the two women. He sensed Brynna's protective nature toward the older woman. He wondered if there could be a family connection. Stepping aside, he said, "Never mind me. Just do what ye normally do. I need to go over the record books for the mill. In fact, if the two of ye are comfortable, I'll go home and read over them and get myself settled into my new house. Will ye both be all right here alone?"

Brynna smiled. He couldn't tell if mischief or relief lingered in her gaze. "Mr. Cameron, we've worked here alone on many occasions while your uncle had other pressing business matters to attend. We'll be fine."

Was she eager to be rid of him? The thought deflated his hopes of reconciling whatever she had against him. "Still, I prefer that neither of ye stay overly long on yer own. If one of ye canna make it in for some reason, please send word to me, and I'll make sure someone is here to assist ye for the day."

"That's very kind, Mr. Cameron." Mrs. Ward's voice resembled the high-pitched tone of a bird.

"Ye're verra welcome." He gave Brynna a look of emphasis in spite of her silence on the subject. He turned and strode back to his office to collect the rest of his books and grab his hat. The bell jingled on his way out.

Standing on the dirt street, Niall sighed, realizing he'd have to walk the whole distance home. The aroma of fresh baked cinnamon rolls teased him. He went in and bought a couple since he didn't know what food would be available at his uncle's house. Besides, he needed enough sustenance to make the journey.

He passed more merchant shops, the library, and then came to the smallest courthouse he'd ever seen. It was made of wood and painted a faded white. Based on the size of this town, it was high time they built themselves a bigger one.

Niall rubbed his hands together. The idea certainly had merit. It would serve as a benefit to the town—and his lumber mill. He studied the current structure. Too small for a lucrative business, it would be perfect for a start-up shop. He thought back to the mass furniture company where he had worked in Scotland. His handcrafted custom pieces had been rejected due to the inability to mass-produce them, but here he could provide such craftsmanship. If he offered to purchase the courthouse, it would give the town seed money for a new one, and he wouldn't appear as if he were out for mere personal gain even though he stood to profit.

Pleased with his new idea, Niall walked home with a lighter step. He greeted people as he passed, some on foot, while others rode horseback and in carriages and wagons. When he left town and followed the long road home, he took out the cinnamon buns and bit into the moist, chewy substance.

His thoughts lingered back to Brynna, never straying far from her. The woman exasperated him. He didn't understand her, and worse, he didn't understand this increasing need to gain her approval.

Once he arrived home, he stared at his luggage in the foyer where he had left it. Emptiness greeted him—pure emptiness. He didn't like it. The house had felt so much better when Brynna had been here.

He looked up at the ceiling where a simple iron-framed candle chandelier hung. "Lord, it's just us again. I thought a new world and a fresh start would change things, but now the loneliness seems even worse." An image of Brynna came to mind. Longing squeezed his heart.

Chapter 5

The next Sunday Brynna adjusted her bonnet as she settled on the Sinclair pew in the third row. Her sister Bonnie sat behind them with her husband Douglas McDuff and their daughter Seren—her grandmother's namesake. Seren alternated between whimpering and giggling. Bonnie kept shushing her two-year-old daughter, while Brynna smiled at the innocent distraction. Her niece pulled at Brynna's bonnet. She lifted a hand to hold it in place and leaned toward Rob—out of reach for Seren's wee fingers.

Brynna wondered if the earlier Gaelic service had been quite as long. Even though their ancestors had arrived to the Carolinas back in 1739, the Scots clung to their old ways. They had the only Gaelic printing press in the area, and she was quite fond of the language.

Mr. Cameron came to mind. Would he have attended that one or the current English service? She didn't dare look around to find him. All week she and Cora continued to work at the shop, while he arrived promptly at eight o'clock and by noon he left for the mill. Brynna always breathed a sigh of relief when he was gone. He never ran out of questions concerning the business. The man was thorough and rarely forgot a detail.

The baby sounds from behind faded. Brynna glanced back to see her sister wearing a triumphant gleam. Seren lay sprawled over Bonnie's lap and arms. No longer distracted, Brynna listened as Pastor McNab read from the book of Esther. According to the Bible, God had used a common woman to save a nation. Brynna's heart swelled with yearning—a desire to make such a striking difference one day. Perhaps in her own way that was what she did by working to preserve their heritage for future generations.

They bowed their heads as Pastor McNab said a closing prayer. Afterward, Brynna stood with the congregation and followed her brother into the aisle. She smiled and greeted people as they passed. Her gaze locked with a pair of familiar green eyes and a shiver raced up her spine.

Niall Cameron stood in the back row. The intensity burning in his determined gaze reminded her of how dangerous he could be to her vulnerable heart. The day he had touched her chin, an awareness of his protective nature and warmth awakened dormant feelings she hadn't anticipated, especially after her recovery of a broken engagement to Dean Maxwell. She had known Dean all her life, but naught prepared her for the change in him after he left for college in New York.

By the time she reached the back, Mr. Cameron was talking to Mr. Ward, the baker. Brynna marched by without looking in their direction. The bright sun shone through the open door, beckoning her. She rushed past her brother, slipped out the door, and hurried down the wooden steps to their carriage.

"Brynna!"

Bonnie headed toward her, carrying Seren in her arms. Her sister's golden curls framed her smooth forehead and rosy cheeks. Clear blue eyes glistened like brilliant jewels. Five years her senior, Bonnie was the beautiful one. Next to her, Brynna always felt like a chunk of wood.

"Why"—Bonnie breathed heavy as she slowed to a stop—"are you in such a hurry?"

Seren's bright eyes stared up at Brynna as she struggled, reaching for her aunt.

"Come, sweet one." Unable to resist, Brynna held out her hands and took her niece, who wrapped her wee arms around Brynna's neck. Brynna kissed the child's cheek, brushing her hand down Seren's blond locks.

"You didn't answer my question," Bonnie said. "Are you trying to avoid me?"

"No, not at all. Just my new boss." Brynna met her sister's eyes over the child's head.

"But why? Is he dreadful?" Bonnie lifted golden eyebrows, twisted her lips, and glanced behind her.

"No, it's too complicated to explain." Brynna shook her head, wishing she had never mentioned Mr. Cameron. The sooner she distracted her sister, the better. "Do you have news?"

Bonnie's confused expression transformed into delight.

"Indeed I do. I know how you've had your heart set on building a new museum, but someone has proposed a new courthouse building. Doug told me about it just last night."

"I don't understand. What does that have to do with the museum?" Brynna bounced her niece on her hip while Seren played with a strand of Brynna's hair under her bonnet.

"Since he serves on the town council, Doug says he knows there is only enough funds for one building. The courthouse will be considered more of a necessity than the museum. He wanted me to let you know to sort of prepare you for the blow."

"I see." Brynna's dream deflated in an instant. While some people in town helped her advocate to preserve their history, others thought it a waste of time. They saw things as Mr. Cameron did—that funds should go to future progress. She fingered the edge of her sleeve where her arms linked around Seren. "Do you happen to know who made the suggestion?"

Bonnie nodded and leaned toward her as their parents approached. "Your new boss, Mr. Cameron," she whispered.

Brynna's mind reeled like a wheel in motion. Of course, he hoped to gain new business for his lumber mill. Anger burned in the pit of her stomach and spread upward. The back of her neck felt like it was on fire.

"Brynna, are you all right? You look a bit flushed." Bonnie tilted her head in concern.

"I'm fine. Thank you for telling me. And please, thank Doug for me as well. Will you detain Mama and Papa for me? I need to speak to someone before we leave." Brynna handed Seren back to her sister. "I'll be right back." She kissed the top of Seren's head.

Brynna hurried to Mr. Stewart, the town mayor. He stood on the church steps talking to Pastor McNab. Both men paused and gave her their attention as she approached.

"I'm sorry to interrupt, but I just heard some news and wanted to make a suggestion for the progress of our town."

"Of course, Miss Sinclair. I'm always of an open mind. Tell me about it." Mayor Stewart offered a smile, his black mustache moving with his upper lip. As a man in his midforties, he had yet to show a sign of gray in his black hair.

She glanced at Pastor McNab, who wore a kind expression as his blue eyes peered through small round spectacles.

"I heard about the idea of a new courthouse. If you decide in favor of one, I thought a building of stone would benefit the town better than wood. After visiting Charleston and admiring some of their significant buildings of historic value, stone will last and isn't as easy to burn. Wouldn't you both agree?"

Both men nodded in unison.

"Your suggestion has merit. I'll mention it to the town council when it goes to a vote. Thank you for your input, Miss Sinclair," Mayor Stewart said.

"I might add," Pastor McNab said, "that it's very humble of you to make such a suggestion knowing you have your heart set on the museum you've proposed."

"Thank you. As much as I value the preservation of our town's history, I care more about what best benefits our citizens," Brynna said. She gave a slight curtsy. "I'd best be getting to the carriage. I don't want to hold up my parents too long."

Monday morning Niall lit the oil lamp on the mantel as the shop doorbell jingled. He looked up. Brynna stepped over the threshold. She wore a dark blue gown with a plaid shawl and white bonnet.

Her dark eyes shone brilliant, warming his heart. Smiling, Brynna untied her bonnet and pulled it off. "No matter how early I arrive, Mr. Cameron, it seems you're already here. And I thought no one else in this town could be more punctual than myself, but I believe you've proven me wrong."

"Please, we see each other every day. I give ye leave to call me by my given name, Niall."

"Thank you, but that is impossible." She hung her bonnet up on a peg.

"Why?" He walked toward her. "I've heard ye call other men in town by their first names."

"But I've known them all my life. I've only known you for nearly three weeks." She strode to the loom on the other side of the unlit fireplace and sat down, examining the strings and patterns before beginning.

"Aye, and ye don't spend near as much time in their company as mine these days," he said.

"That's different. We work together."

"Is it?" Niall's teasing lingered as he strode toward the back. "Speaking of which, I've been studying some of the books and have a few things I'd like to discuss with ye."

Grabbing a black book and some papers off his desk, Niall hurried to where Brynna wound thread through a spool.

"I noticed ye ordered some wool from a South Carolina plantation right before my arrival. Why? I thought we provided our own wool. The additional charges for delivery were quite exorbitant." He tapped a finger on the page of an open book.

"Normally, we do, but some of your uncle's sheep did not survive the winter," she said. "We had a short freezing spell, haven't had such a blizzard in years. I'm sorry you disapprove of my decision, but you were not here to consult, and we had orders to fulfill."

"I do disapprove. Not only are we paying more for wool and fabric, but am I now to understand that I must purchase more sheep?" He scratched his ear and paced in front of her loom. His booted heels clicked against the hardwood floor. How could he make her understand the magnitude of such simple decisions? They might be turning a wee profit at the moment, but it could tip to the negative with only one bad season. "Until I can purchase more sheep, ye must not order more fabric from them. We'll need to find a place that is less expensive."

"You mean sacrifice quality?" Brynna's lips thinned and turned white as she stood. Her dark eyes blazed. "This company is not destitute, Mr. Cameron. You can certainly afford some decent wool for the patrons who have been loyal to your uncle all these years."

"Ye mistake me. I only meant that we can find an inexpensive supplier while I finance the purchase of more sheep. The balance in our budget will deplete quickly with such significant expenses." He reached inside his jacket pocket and pulled out a wool patch and tossed it at her. "Here, I found this. It isn't quite as smooth, but it should do nicely until our situation improves."

She caught the material and rubbed it between her fingers and thumb. A frown of disbelief forced her lower lip down and wrinkled her eyebrows. "Our situation is fine!" She tossed it back at him. "Especially if this is what you're proposing as a replacement. I'll not have it. Our customers deserve better. Pray tell, do you plan to lower the price of what they should pay as compensation?"

"Of course not." Niall crumpled the fabric in his fist. "Do ye intend to see me in the poorhouse, lass?"

"Don't call me that!" Brynna stomped toward him, her finger pointing at his chest. "I knew you'd do this as soon as you got the opportunity."

"Do what?"

"Change everything. Cheat people. Ruin the quality for which we're known. You'll destroy everything I've worked so hard for."

"Ye talk as if ye built this business rather than my uncle." He gestured around them, his heart hammering at the unwanted controversy. As her boss, he had to make her see reason, didn't he?

"I take great pride in my work." She pulled at her sleeve near her elbow. "I'd think a business owner would want such an employee, but I suppose you're only interested in your personal profit and gain."

"That's enough." Niall's voice sliced between them like an ax severing their only connection. He succeeded in gaining her attention, but he didn't care for her stricken expression. She stared at him with wide eyes as her mouth dropped open in blessed silence.

"I must dispel ye of the notion that there's a choice in the matter," he said. "Ye're an employee, while I'm the owner. I value yer opinion, but the final decisions are mine as are the successes and failures, as well as the expenses required to keep it running."

"I understand your meaning very well." She lifted her chin in defiance.

"Good, I'm glad we understand each other." He lowered his voice.

Her shoulders stiffened as she returned to her seat.

Niall feared he had just sacrificed any hope of a deeper relationship with Brynna.

Chapter 6

For the next week, Brynna did her best to tell the truth to her friends and family about the quality of the wool and fabrics.

The tension between her and Mr. Cameron had grown even colder than before. She only spoke to him when forced and didn't bother to offer opinions or suggestions. When patrons were in the shop, she struggled not to show her disrespect or contempt for him.

During the past few days Mr. Cameron had taken to staying at the shop past noon rather than heading over to the mill as was his usual habit. She wondered if he remained to watch over her and Cora as if they were schoolgirls intent on disobeying his new rules. The temptation to break her silence and encourage him to visit the mill burdened her. She found herself clenching her jaw on several occasions, not trusting her tone of voice.

In the mornings, Mr. Cameron brought her something from the bakery. She saved it for Cora. He offered to give her rides home. She refused, preferring to walk. He brought her a book from the library that Jean suggested. She confessed that she'd already read it. If he thought these little gestures made up for his other behaviors, he was wrong.

The doorbell jingled and in walked Jimmy Clark, Mr. Anderson's assistant. Taking his hat off, he nodded at Cora. "Afternoon, Mrs. Ward."

"Good afternoon, young Jimmy."

He strode toward Brynna and lifted a sheathed sword. "I didn't come for any of your fine wool today, but I was in town and thought I'd get your opinion on this sword I found in my grandfather's attic."

Brynna cut her gaze up at Mr. Cameron who stood on a ladder, hanging a tapestry he had discovered she'd weaved last year. "You'd better ask my boss if I can look at it while I should be weaving."

Mr. Cameron closed his eyes a moment as if praying for patience. He looked down and met Jimmy's gaze. "Miss Sinclair knows verra well that she may view yer sword, but pray tell, why would ye require a woman's opinion of such a weapon?"

"You may not realize it since you're new to the area, but Miss Sinclair is well known for her self-study on local history and antiques. If anyone could tell what kind it is or how old, it would be her."

Mr. Cameron's gaze shifted to Brynna, and she wanted to hide from his scrutiny. Ignoring him, she smiled at Jimmy, a childhood school friend. "You exaggerate my knowledge, Jimmy." She held out her hand. "But let me see."

"Nonsense, Brynna. Rob takes you to Charleston

twice a year to meet with historians and view their latest acquirements," Jimmy said, handing the sword to her.

She carried the heavy blade over to a table by the lantern and moved a few tartans to the side. Jimmy helped her slide it from its sheath as the steel blade glistened.

"Oh, this is magnificent!" She couldn't hide the wonder from her voice as she examined the handle with a cross-hilt in a downward slant. "*Claidhermh-mor.*"

"Pardon me?" Jimmy leaned forward. "I don't remember the Gaelic my grandpa used to speak."

"It's a Scottish Claymore. See the way the handle is straight? It can be used in either the right or left hand. This is a double-edged blade." She pointed along the steel, careful not to touch it. "No rust and only a bit of discoloration. Your family kept it in excellent condition."

"How old is it?" Jimmy asked.

Both Cora and Mr. Cameron leaned over Jimmy's shoulders to see.

"Cora, will you get the ruler?" Brynna asked.

"Of course." Cora rushed over to her materials and shuffled back, handing out the long stick.

"The blade is about forty-one inches long." Brynna held it up to the lantern light and squinted.

"Why don't ye take it to the window? It would provide better light," Mr. Cameron said.

As much as she hated to admit it, he was right. She glanced up at him. "That's a good idea. Thank you."

She walked to the bay window and they followed her like a flock of birds. "The handle is made of brown leather with a twisted design and the cross-hilt is of brass." She held it up in both hands, judging its weight. "It's at least five pounds. I'd say this sword was made sometime between 1680 and 1700."

"Really?" Jimmy asked in excitement.

"That's my best guess. Your grandfather may have gotten it from his grandfather or great-grandfather. Have you searched the attic thoroughly for letters, notes in the Bible? There might be something to indicate the sword's history."

"We found a chest with some old handwritten journals, but it was in Gaelic. My grandfather was the last in our family who could read and understand it. Could you interpret any of it?"

"I'll try." Brynna nodded. "I'm not as good at reading it as I'd like to be, but I'll do my best."

"Perhaps I could help," Mr. Cameron said. "My family still reads and speaks Gaelic, including me."

Brynna closed her eyes in exasperation. Spending more time in his company was not an option.

That afternoon a wagon loaded with new logs came in from the south lot. Niall carried his logbook over and nodded to the driver who tipped his hat. He counted forty logs and wrote down the number.

"Where you want these to go, boss?" Drew walked up beside him.

"Do we have any special orders for poplar?" Niall glanced at him.

"What about the wagon maker? Looks like enough wood

to cover his order. He didn't specify a specific kind." Drew tilted his blond head and placed his hands on his sides.

"Sounds perfect. Send it to Team Four," Niall said.

"Will do, boss." Drew walked over to the driver to give him directions.

Niall finished his log sheet and turned to see Horace Stewart walking toward him.

"Good morning, Mayor!" Niall extended his hand and the mayor gripped him in a firm handshake.

"Niall, I wanted to personally stop by and thank you for offering your lumber for the new courthouse," Mayor Stewart said.

"So it's been approved?" Niall asked, keeping an even tone.

"Yes, but we've decided to build it out of stone. Your offer was quite generous, but the suggestion of stone was made and the town council voted on it. We've had a couple of small fires in the past decade and they thought a foundation of stone would be less risky."

"Well, ye still have to use lumber for the inside walls and that burns just as easy and it happens to be where the records are located," Niall said.

"True." The mayor nodded, stroking his black mustache. "But we talked about building a special room with stone walls to keep the most important records."

"I see." Niall scraped his teeth across his bottom lip.

"I wanted to ask if your offer still stands to buy the old courthouse building?" The mayor gave him a direct stare.

Niall scratched his ear. If he backed out now, it would

make him look insincere, as if he were only after the profits. "Ye know, I'd planned to use the lumber profits to buy it as a means of helping the town, but without taking a loss."

"I realize that and I'm truly sorry. But the town council wanted me to ask. If not, we need to advertise quickly to raise more funds for the stone. Depending on what you plan to do with it, the old courthouse could be turned into a small profit. You could consider it a business investment and rent it out."

Niall rubbed the back of his head. "Tell ye what, I'll send over a proposal in the morning."

Mayor Stewart relaxed into a grin, his eyes shining. "I knew you'd come through for us." He slapped Niall on the shoulder.

"Out of curiosity, who suggested stone?" Niall asked.

"The smartest little lady in town, Miss Brynna Sinclair."

Niall went numb. After a moment his head began to tingle. Somehow he managed to respond coherently as the mayor said good-bye. Niall took deep breaths, trying to clear his head, but the smell of fresh-cut wood filled his lungs and made him cough.

Anger ripped through him. He'd confront her and demand to know if she had suggested stone to spite him. Why did she hate him so much, especially when he thought so highly of her? A bitter ache throbbed in his chest. Just the aroma of her heather scent and coffee in the mornings had become a welcome fixture in his life. Keeping to the old ways of her ancestors, she grew heather in the backyard. When she walked by, she reminded him of home, the good thoughts he loved about Scotland—and lately of her.

He stormed through the lumber mill yard, grabbed his horse, and mounted. Pulling the reins around, he urged his horse into a gallop. She'd explain herself.

As he flew by the library, a man called his name. Recognizing Rob Sinclair, Niall slowed his horse with reluctance. Rob caught up to him. "I was hoping to catch you before you reached the shop, but you were going so fast I wasn't sure if I could stop you."

"Aye, I'm in a wee bit of a hurry," Niall said, not wanting to be rude, but hoping to move on.

"What have you done to upset Brynna?" Rob asked. "She's not acting like herself and all she does is talk nonsense about how bad you're ruining the quality of the wool and fabric in the store. Even my own mother decided not to place her usual spring order. Is it true you've weakened the quality of the wool you're selling?"

Niall sighed as he glanced up at the sky. "Some of my uncle's flock didn't survive the winter and we must place orders outside the district. Brynna's upset that I requested her to conserve our expenses and save on delivery costs. She doesn't understand business."

"True. Brynna won't accept your reasons for change. I thought perhaps I could talk to you, get a better understanding and see if I could reason with her. Sometimes she'll accept things better from me than from others."

"I appreciate yer help, Rob. Really I do. But I've got to handle this and reason with her myself."

"You don't know Brynna like I do," Rob said. "Give me a

chance to talk to her."

"I'm sorry, Rob, but she's done more than merely meddle in my shop business. She's now going after my lumber mill as well. Today, she'll deal with me."

Chapter 7

The shop door slammed open, hitting a table. The bell jingled, slid off its hook, and flew to the floor, rolling to a stop against Cora's foot where she sat at the spinning wheel. Her hand flew to her chest as she gasped in fright.

Brynna stood from the seat at her wooden weaving machine. Anger spiraled through her that the man would dare frighten Cora. She stomped toward the shadow silhouetted by the bright sunlight behind him.

"What is the meaning of this?" Brynna demanded. "You nearly frightened poor Cora to death." She tried to shield her eyes to see the man's face.

"I'm the one who should be asking that question, lass."

Mr. Cameron. A steel edge rang in his tone and an eerie foreboding crept up her spine, crawling over her skin and raising tiny bumps.

"Oh, it's you. I couldn't see your face since the sun is so bright," Brynna said. "Are you trying to tear down the door? I would think you'd take better care of your things than that.

It's a wonder you didn't break the hinges."

"Brynna, be quiet and for once in yer life listen before I lose what wee patience I've left," Mr. Cameron said.

He kicked the door closed. It rattled in the frame, causing Brynna to jump and Cora to rub her upper arms in fear. Brynna gulped, forgetting to chastise him for calling her by her given name without permission.

"Sit down and listen, and ye'd better listen well." He pointed to the wooden chair she had vacated.

He turned to Cora. "And I want ye to be my witness to the fact that I'm not strangling her and be able to later recite what I say to her should it be necessary."

"Y–yes, sir." Cora bobbed her silver-brown head, swallowing hard. "Whatever Brynna has done, please don't hurt her."

Without answering, he pulled his hat off and tossed it onto the hat and coatrack in the corner. He took an intimidating step toward Brynna, who moved back. Mr. Cameron stalked her like this until her knees hit the edge of her chair, and she plopped down as bidden, though she wanted to stand and defy him for the brutish way he behaved.

"I've discovered your wee plot to convince the town council to build the new courthouse out of stone instead of lumber. Do ye deny it?" He raised a dark brow.

"I do not." She lifted her chin and met his gaze with a glare of her own. Brynna hoped her trembling knees didn't betray her.

"Was yer motivation to prevent my lumber company from benefiting because ye really believe that stone is the best option?"

"Both. I think you're a greedy man determined to profit at the misfortune of others," Brynna said. "Do you know how long Rob and I've been working on the plans for the museum? And this time I believe we could have gotten their consent, but not now that you've put the grand idea of a new courthouse into their heads. They'd never approve both projects at the same time. In one day, you've managed to ruin everything I've worked so hard to achieve."

"Now who's being greedy? Did ye not take it upon yourself to tell half the town that the quality of our wool and fabric isn't the same?"

"Yes, and I'm glad of it since you're cheating people. You don't deserve their hard-earned money if you refuse to lower the price for less quality."

"And *ye* don't deserve to be paid." He leaned forward, resting his hands on the arm of her loom. "If I don't make a profit, there won't be enough to pay ye or Cora. Did ye think of that before ye tried sabotaging my businesses? My profits pay yer salaries, among many other people who need to feed, clothe, and house their families. Ye call it greed, lass, but I call it being responsible."

Brynna glanced at Cora who held trembling fingers to her mouth and worried a nail. Guilt sliced her heart as she realized how devastating no salary would be to her friend. "Mr. Cameron, if you must forgo our salaries, please, give Cora hers. I'll work for no pay for a whole month—two if necessary, but don't punish her for what I did."

Before he could respond, the door opened and a thin man who was partially bald on top with graying brown hair on the sides rushed to Mr. Cameron. His worn clothes were disheveled and full of grime. He pulled off his cap and crinkled it in his hands as he hunched his shoulders in a humble manner.

"Please—Mr. Cameron. My name is Frank Murray and—and I need to beg your forgiveness."

"What for, man?" Mr. Cameron scratched his ear. "I've never even met ye before, have I?"

"Naw, sir." The man shook his head and shifted his weight from one foot to the other. "But I rent a house and some acreage from you and I'm four months behind. I promised your uncle I'd have it caught up by now, but I wasn't expectin' my wife to stay ill so long. My crop didn't yield as much as I'd hoped, and it barely carried us through the harsh winter. My wife—she needs a doctor real bad, and I can't pay for it. I came to beg ye not to turn us out. Please—we got nowhere to go."

Mr. Cameron rubbed the back of his neck. "How would ye like a job at the lumber mill? I could have one of my men train ye. It would be decent pay and ye could catch up on yer debts in a few months' time."

The man's face lit into a smile, revealing crooked, stained teeth. "Oh, thank you, Mr. Cameron. You're a generous man."

"I'm glad we have a deal," Mr. Cameron said. "I'm always in need of good hardworking men. Show up at the mill in the morning at seven. Ask for Mr. Drew Henderson."

They shook hands, Mr. Murray eager and happy, while Mr. Cameron was sure and firm in his grip. "And, Mr. Murray, take the doctor to see yer wife. Tell him I'll take care of the bill."

By the time the man left, he floated out of the shop with a taller countenance and improved posture. Brynna could hardly understand Mr. Cameron's generosity. She'd never witnessed this side of him.

Remorse and confusion consumed her busy mind. She would have never guessed that such compassion dwelled within his heart. What other accusations could she have misjudged him on?

"Now where were we?" He whirled.

"About to fire me, no doubt," Brynna said, rising to her feet.

"Wait, Brynna." He touched her arm in an attempt to stop her. "I've said no such thing." His voice softened into a husky whisper, melting her resolve into a flood of confusion.

A tidal wave of emotion assailed her. Brynna's lower lip trembled. With brimming tears, she gazed up at him, memorizing his handsome features and the sound of his Scottish burr. "Why can you not make it easy for me to hate you?"

Brynna's lovely face flushed, and Niall wondered if he'd heard her correctly. "Why would ye want to hate me?"

"Because it's better than liking you now and being thoroughly disappointed later." She waved a hand in the air and blinked. "Never mind. I'm too distraught to make any sense. Please go ahead and fire me and be done with it."

"I'm quite tempted." Niall folded his arms over his chest

and lifted a hand to his chin as he studied her. "Brynna, ye puzzle and vex me, and yet, you've impressed me when I least expected it. Yer work ethic is to be admired, and so is yer passion. Lass, ye take on a cause and defend it until the end." He raised a fist for emphasis. "I've never known anyone quite like ye. I've spent my life trying to win the approval of people who would never give it. I came here to start fresh, among people who don't know my past, but all I can think about is *ye*, a woman who wants to hate me." He scoffed and shook his head in disbelief.

"I'm sorry." Brynna twisted the edge of her sleeve, a habit of her own. "I don't want to hate you. It's just that I don't want to repeat the same mistake I made with Dean. I trusted him. Thought I knew him. But I was wrong—so wrong."

She dropped her gaze, but not before he witnessed the startling tears that surfaced. "I'll save you the trouble of firing me." She brushed past him.

Niall stood there trying to process her words, but he couldn't figure out who Dean was and what he had to do with Brynna and himself. The front door opened, drawing his attention. Glancing over his shoulder, he saw Brynna slip out.

"Brynna, come back!" He hurried after her.

"Sir, imagine the scene it'll cause if you chase her down the street." Cora stopped him, tugging on his arm. "Think of her reputation."

Niall knew she was right. He paused, staring into the older woman's brown eyes. "Please—tell me what just happened. Who is Dean?"

"Dean Maxwell was Brynna's fiancé two years ago—at least he was until he decided to stay in New York." She sighed and shook her head. "They grew up together. He was Rob's best friend, and they went off to college. Rob came back home, but he didn't."

"Was another woman involved?" Niall asked, not understanding how someone could voluntarily give up Brynna.

"Not to my knowledge." She shook her head. "Dean tried to convince Brynna to marry him and settle up there where he had gotten a nice, fancy job. Brynna said that wasn't what they had planned, but she agreed to visit. Rob took her to New York. They stayed for about a month. Brynna came home saying Dean had changed, and she hated New York."

Niall could now see where Brynna had gotten her aversion to change. And him arriving from Scotland to take his uncle's place had set her at unease, but for her to want to hate him? Wasn't that a wee bit much, even for Brynna?

"Some of her behavior is starting to make sense to me, but I still don't understand why she would compare me to Dean. I'm nothing like him, am I?"

Mrs. Ward patted his arm. "Maybe not in looks and you definitely don't sound the same. But in some aspects you're alike. You both have a keen ambition to be successful in business. By coming so far you've proven you don't have a problem uprooting yourself and starting over someplace else—much like Dean. Both your decisions have shattered Brynna's dreams."

Tugging on his ear, Niall drifted over to the chair by

Brynna's weaving machine and lowered himself. His gut felt like a cannonball weighing him down. If only he'd known all this before. He wouldn't have suggested the new courthouse building. Niall closed his eyes searching his mind on how he could make it up to her. *Lord, please help me think of something.*

The clock on the mantel chimed the hour of three. He didn't move, too absorbed in his broken thoughts.

"Sir, didn't you say you had a meeting with the mayor near three?" Cora asked.

He sat up, realizing he'd forgotten about his purchase of the old courthouse. Then an idea came to mind. He'd have a free building to do as he pleased. Instead of starting a furniture business, he could donate the building to Brynna for her museum.

"Thank Ye, Lord," he whispered.

"What did you say?" Cora leaned forward.

"I'm going to make things right." He walked over to the wooden stand in the corner and grabbed his hat. A plaid shawl of red and blue squares with black and white stripes caught his eye. He touched the soft wool material between his finger and thumb. *Lord, please help her to forgive me.*

Chapter 8

Brynna stepped out of the carriage in front of the white courthouse building. She breathed a sigh of relief that Rob and Bonnie hadn't tried to drag her to the shop. She fidgeted with her sleeve as Bonnie descended the carriage behind her and Rob took her elbow on the right.

Their parents' candy store stood across the street and smells of sugarplums drifted in the air, making her mouth water. The morning sun cast slanted rays through the town buildings, heating the remainder of the night dew. Sounds of wagon wheels and distant conversations carried through the air as patrons crossed the street.

Bonnie took her other arm, her brother and sister flanking her like mother hens. They tugged her forward, but Brynna dug in her heels.

"I don't know why Mama and Papa would deed us a chunk of their land now. Neither of them have said anything, and you know how they always discuss big decisions with us first," Brynna said. She glanced up at their profiles, but their firm expressions gave no further information. Insecurity shifted inside her like a heavy board.

"Come, Brynna. You dally long enough," Bonnie said.

"Yes, I'll have to get back to the store directly," Rob motioned to the candy store. "Besides, who said Mama and Papa are giving us land today?"

"Well, why else would we be here?" Brynna gave him a skeptical glare as he opened the courthouse door and ushered her inside. She blinked, allowing her eyes to adjust in the dimness. She smiled, recognizing her mother and father standing at the counter where a large deed book lay open with an ink bottle and quill.

"I had wondered where the two of you were heading off to so early this morning after breakfast," Brynna said, striding toward her mother. She paused as someone stepped out of the corner shadow, his black boots clicking against the hardwood floor.

Niall wore brown breeches, a white shirt and cravat under a gold vest, and a tan short-waist jacket. Her breath hitched in her throat, betraying her heartfelt thoughts of how handsome he was, but quite contrary to her stinging thoughts of his behavior yesterday. The scent of leather and musk drifted to her nose, evoking more betraying emotions.

"You!" She pointed an accusing finger. "What are you doing here?" She glanced at her mother's guilty expression. Her father looked down at his feet. The knowledge of their piercing treachery wounded her soul as she backed up shaking her head in disbelief. "Wasn't it enough that I apologized for what I've done? How have you managed to coerce my whole family against me to further my shame?" Tears threatened as the back of her throat burned and her eyes stung. Her nose filled until she couldn't breathe and she forced out a long breath.

"It isn't like that, lass." Niall stepped forward. "Please, just hear me out. I've something I want to give ye, and I knew you'd never come as a favor to me so I asked yer family for help."

She couldn't hear this—an explanation of why her family had betrayed her. True, what she'd done was wrong and she'd pray for forgiveness, but this? Brynna turned, but both Rob and Bonnie blocked her exit. In surrender, she raised her hands. "Why are you all doing this?"

"Brynna, I think you should hear what the lad has to say." Her father's stern tone rang through the room.

"It appears I've no choice." She ran a finger under her eye to wipe away the moisture now crawling onto her skin. Straightening her shoulders and meeting Niall's green gaze, Brynna waited.

He gulped and tugged on his earlobe. She wondered when he had started the endearing habit. Even now as angry as she was, tenderness for him warmed her aching heart. What a contrary idiot she'd become. First, Dean Maxwell, and now Niall Cameron. Would she never learn?

"I've already told ye how much my uncle meant to me, but what I haven't told ye is how much of a failure I was in Scotland. Naught I did ever succeeded, at least not in anyone's eyes. I saw my inheritance as a new chance to start over. I wanted to make an honorable name for myself here in Fayetteville—to be approved, admired, and respected."

He paused and cleared his throat. "Then I met ye, Brynna. And ye changed everything. I no longer sought the town's approval—only yers. Somehow yer opinion is the one I care most about, even to the point of praying for yer affection or the ability to not crave it so deeply."

Confusion swirled in Brynna's mind like the approach of a huge storm, but her heart began to thaw. Would a man risk his reputation in front of her, the whole Sinclair family, and the clerk whom she now realized stood on the other side of the counter, if he wasn't sincere?

"I don't understand. What are you saying?" Brynna asked, afraid to hope for what she thought he might be saying.

"Only this," he stepped forward. "Before yesterday, I had no idea how my suggestion of a new courthouse building would shatter yer dream of building a museum. I want to make things right. I want to tell ye I'm sorry and to ask yer forgiveness."

"Of course, how could I refuse to forgive you?" Brynna swallowed. "I've my own set of faults. I'm sorry about your business and for what I did."

"Lass, don't worry." He waved a hand. "I believe in yer dream of preserving our history, our Celtic culture. Having such a museum will remind me of home, just like the heather scent ye wear."

She blushed, touching her hand over her chest, unsure how to react.

"That's why I'm deeding this building to ye. I purchased it yesterday, and as of today, ye'll now be the proud owner. All ye have to do is sign right there on the line." He pointed to the large open book on the counter. "All the paperwork has been written and everything is in order."

Brynna gasped, covering her hands over her mouth. She blinked back tears for several moments, unable to trust herself to speak.

"Brynna, lass, are ye all right?" Niall leaned over her in concern.

She nodded, regaining her composure and wiping the tears of joy from her eyes. "Do you mean to say that this building is mine to do with as I please?" she asked.

"Aye, ye may even build a museum here, if ye wish. We'll all help." He gestured to her family.

The moment overwhelmed Brynna as she sought his eyes. She leaned up on her tiptoes and kissed his cheek. "Thank you," she whispered in his ear.

"Does this mean I'm forgiven?" he asked.

"Yes, I already told you that."

"Does this mean ye no longer think me a greedy man?"

"I stopped believing that when I saw how generous you were to that poor man who couldn't pay his rent." He offered her his arm, and she took it as he led her to the counter. "Niall, you're a surprising man."

He took her hand in his. "Say my name again, please?"

"Niall."

Over the next few months, the town imported stone and hired a company to build the new courthouse. To Niall's profound relief, Brynna agreed to continue working at the shop. While the cold tension between them had evaporated, Niall didn't want Brynna to feel obligated toward him for what he'd done. Yet his growing attraction to her bordered on pure torture as he struggled to hide it.

Tonight the mayor held a public ball to celebrate the opening of the new courthouse building. When Niall asked Brynna if he could escort her, she hesitated and shook her head, saying she'd arrive with her parents.

Now he hovered near the entrance determined to at least secure a dance with her. He sipped a glass of red wine as he nodded greetings to newcomers. Rob waltzed in looking sharp in a pair of black breeches and a red vest over a crisp white shirt and cravat in an elegant wide tie. He wore black hose and matching pumps in proper evening attire. Niall noticed several of the gentlemen sporting kilts and jackets of their tartan clan colors, which he assumed had been woven by Brynna.

"Don't look so eager, my friend. Women only need a hint of your interest and then they begin playing mind games," Rob said, leaning toward him and lowering his voice to a whisper. "If I were you, I wouldn't give my sister so much power."

"Too late," Niall said, training his eyes upon the entrance where Brynna stood wrapped in a dark green and navy plaid arisaid over a white satin gown with pleats in the front. Her chestnut hair was swept up in curls on the crown of her head and her dark eyes searched the room, landing on him. Her pink lips slid into a welcoming smile as her cheeks darkened.

She floated toward Niall as he left Rob's side to meet her.

They stopped within a foot of each other. "Ye look lovely, lass." The words escaped his tongue before he lost his nerve to say them.

"As do you." She glowed. "I've never seen you wear a kilt before."

He followed her gaze down the length of his green squares on red kilt. She reached out and touched a bronze medal pinned to his black double-breasted jacket.

"It's an award my great-grandfather received from the Clan Cameron Chief when he fought in the Jacobite War against the English Crown."

"So you're as much of a rebel as I am?" Brynna's beautiful eyes widened.

"Aye, but we were forced to swear our loyalty to the Crown or suffer death. So if we had migrated to the colonies before the Revolutionary War, we might have been Tories—for we Camerons always keep our word." He smiled and she returned the sentiment.

"Ah, Miss Sinclair, you've arrived," Mayor Stewart said. He held out his elbow. "Allow me to escort you over here to meet some important individuals who came all the way from Charleston to greet you." He winked at Niall over her head.

Niall grinned, excited to watch her surprised reaction to what she was about to discover. They walked over to a long rectangular table with a red and green checkered tablecloth. A band with ready instruments sat in one corner. Food and beverages were arranged on the counter. The wooden benches had been moved against the walls to open the middle of the new courthouse floor for dancing.

"May I have your attention?" Mayor Stewart's voice rose above the hum of conversations around the large room. Voices faded into silence as all eyes turned straight toward him.

"As you know, tonight is in celebration of Fayetteville's first Celtic Museum, the first of its kind here in America in the old courthouse building, thanks to Miss Brynna Sinclair." He gestured toward Brynna. People around the room clapped.

Brynna blushed as she gripped the edge of her sleeve, a habit Niall had come to love about her. Over the last few months he'd learned how much she disliked being noticed, but tonight she could scarce avoid it.

"Miss Sinclair, this table is dedicated to the items that the townsfolk will be donating to your museum. To make the occasion even more special, we've invited Mr. Eric Sloane, the Director of the Charleston Historical Museum, to assist you in identifying some of the first pieces you'll acquire tonight. He's brought his assistant, Mr. Charles Atkins, and an antiques expert visiting all the way from France, Mr. Louis Napier."

People gasped and clapped in surprise. Brynna covered her hands over her mouth in disbelief as tears gathered in her eyes. Mr. Eric Sloane approached her first. He had black hair, thick sideburns, a mustache, and was thin, but of average height. He looked to be in his midthirties.

The Frenchman was easy to spot with his deep accent and squeaky voice. In his midforties, Mr. Napier had gray hair, a mustache, and goatee. He was a heavy-set man with a round belly. With each sentence he took a deep breath, as if struggling to breathe.

The assistant, Mr. Atkins, hung back and out of the way as he was the youngest of the three. With brown hair pulled back at the nape by a ribbon, he was taller than the other two with no facial hair. At times he wore a bored expression, but greeted everyone amiably.

Pastor McNab brought forward the church's first Gaelic Bible. Jimmy Clark gave her the sword she had identified for him. One man donated his great-grandfather's kilt. After they had gathered about ten items, Bonnie walked up with something small in her hands.

"Brynna, I knew you've always wished you could have been the firstborn female to inherit this brooch passed down through our family, but I believe it belongs with you here in your museum."

"Bonnie, no!" Tears slid down Brynna's smooth cheeks. "I couldn't possibly take this." She wiped her face with her hands and gulped.

Brynna opened her palm revealing a silver brooch in the shape of a lion's head with eyes of topaz gemstones. Niall leaned closer, trying to get a better view. Even from a distance of five or six feet, he could tell it was a magnificent piece, a beautiful heirloom.

"May I see zat, pweaze?" Mr. Napier stepped forward, blocking Niall's vision, as he pulled out a pair of spectacles and slipped them over his nose. "Dis looks just like a painting I saw in Scotland of Mary Queen of Scots, she wore somezing similar. It looks to be of zee Renaizance period. Quite valuable."

Chapter 9

Brynna lifted her face to the morning sun, increasing in warmth. The thought of a long walk appealed to her so she had informed her family that she wouldn't be taking the carriage to work. She wanted to stop at the museum on her way to the shop.

Niall's handsome image came to mind as he had whirled her around the marble floor of the new courthouse building. He was an excellent dancer, but quite unfamiliar with the Virginia reel. She smiled at the memory of his large hands around her waist and upon her back. His green eyes had shone bright as he stared down at her. There were moments when she secretly hoped he'd kiss her, but he played the part of a gentleman—almost too well.

As she reached the front door of the museum, Brynna pulled out the key from her reticule, but the door squeaked, already ajar. Who would have opened it? She glanced down and saw that the lock was broken.

"Hello?" Brynna stepped inside, wondering if she was alone. The room was dark, but she could still distinguish the outline of the counter and the locked trunk where she'd stored the precious items people had donated. She approached in caution, her feet crunching debris. Reaching the trunk, Brynna slid her fingers down to the lock. Her heart pounded.

The lock was shattered. That must have been what she'd stepped on. She stood and fumbled for the lantern on the counter, lighting it. Brynna crouched down, lifted the trunk lid, and searched inside. She felt for all the familiar objects she could remember. Everything was accounted for with the exception of the brooch.

Panic seized her chest, tightening around the air she breathed like a tight corset. Brynna searched through the items and ran her hands along the floor, but found nothing. Mr. Napier had estimated its worth to be around ten thousand dollars. It was the most expensive and significant item they had as he believed it was somehow tied to Mary Queen of Scots.

Pressing her fist against her mouth to stifle a cry, Brynna gathered her skirts and ran outside, up the street, past the bakery, and burst into the shop. Tears slipped past her lashes, but she no longer cared. The brooch had been in her family for centuries. It meant more than the museum, more than anything else she could think of.

"Niall?" The bell on the door jingled. "Please, Niall, I need you! Someone broke into the museum and stole the brooch."

"Are ye sure it was stolen?" He hurried from the back office. Concern wrinkled his brow.

"What else could have happened? The lock is completely broken! They didn't take anything else but the brooch. I should have taken it home with me. I should have never left it there."

"Shh." With the pad of his thumb, he wiped away her tears. "We'll find it. I promise. I know how important that brooch is to ye. I'll do everything in my power to get it back."

"You promise?" She couldn't stop her chin from trembling as her heart ached and her mind ran rampant with possibilities.

"I promise. Let's go." He turned the CLOSED sign around and ushered her out, locking the door. "Who was the last person to see it besides yourself?"

Brynna searched her memory, retracing every move from the night before. "After we carried everything from the new courthouse, you and Rob walked out with Mr. Napier and Mr. Sloane. Mr. Atkins remained behind asking if I was certain everything was safe and secure." She dropped her forehead into her palm. "If only I'd listened to him more closely. He tried to share some safety ideas with me from the Charleston Muesum, but I was so tired." She swallowed with guilt for being so starry-eyed from dancing with Niall.

"Brynna, he may not have been asking ye about the building's safety to give ye any advice, but to use it for his own purposes."

She gasped, lifting her head in shock as she hurried to match his stride. "Mr. Atkins? Why on earth would he do such a thing as that? He works in a place that has ten times more profitable items." She shook her head. "No, I can't believe it."

"I'm not saying he did it, but I don't want ye to rule out

the possibility. He was the last one to see it besides yourself, and he was asking ye questions. I think it may be too much of a coincidence."

After Niall examined the door and the trunk, he cupped her cheek and gazed into her eyes in the lantern light. "I want ye to go across the street and tell Rob what has happened. Ask him to contact the sheriff."

"Where are you going?" Alarm rose inside her.

"It's my understanding that Mr. Napier is touring the country while he's here visiting. They plan to stop in Salem, the Moravian village west of here. That's one of the reasons Rob and I were able to convince them to stop by for last night's celebration—that and the fact that ye made quite an impression on Mr. Sloane when ye last visited Charleston."

"You're going after them? Alone?" She grabbed his arm.

"I thought ye didn't think they could have done it?" He gave her a mischievous grin. "I only want to see if they noticed anything suspicious and if they would mind checking their items. A brooch is small and easy to lose or could have gotten caught on someone's garment."

"Let the sheriff do it," Brynna said, not wanting him to endanger himself.

"No, it could be too late by then. I need to catch them before they get too far." He leaned forward and pressed his lips to the top of her head. "Lass, go to yer brother. I'll be back soon."

Brynna's heart squeezed in fear, and she didn't want to let him go, but neither did she want to lose an opportunity to get her family brooch back.

"Be careful and God be with you," she called after him.

On horseback Niall caught up with the museum historians sooner than he expected. He waved the driver over about thirty miles west of Fayetteville.

Mr. Sloane leaned his black head out the window. "What's the meaning of this? Has something happened?"

"Aye," Niall nodded as he slid down the side of his winded horse. "This morning the lock on Miss Sinclair's museum door was broken and the trunk lock shattered. Everything was there except the brooch. It's gone."

Mr. Sloane stepped out of the private coach and Mr. Atkins followed.

"I'm sorry to hear such devastating news, but what does that have to do with us? We're supposed to be in Salem in a couple of days," Mr. Sloane said, adjusting his hat to shield his eyes from the bright sun.

"I know and I do apologize for the inconvenience, but since ye were the last ones to see the brooch besides Miss Sinclair and myself, I wanted to ask ye a few questions."

"Sounds like you're suspecting us!" Mr. Atkins growled through tight lips. His brown hair was tied by a ribbon at the back of his neck. His fists clenched and unclenched as he stepped forward.

Niall realized the man intended to use his great height against him, but he didn't back down. "The first thing ye need to learn, Mr. Atkins, is that too much defensiveness rouses suspicion. My mother once lost a brooch my father had given her before they married. She later found it clinging to a wool shawl. I wondered if something similar might have happened." Niall shrugged. "If there's naught to hide, ye certainly wouldn't mind checking through yer belongings, right?"

"Except we don't have time for that kind of nonsense." Mr. Atkins narrowed his eyes.

"Mr. Sloane," Niall said, "for a ten-thousand-dollar brooch that belonged to the Charleston Museum, wouldn't ye be asking everyone around to look in the most unlikely places?"

"Indeed, I would." He nodded. "I'll let Mr. Napier know what's going on. He's probably curious about all this." He turned and leaned inside the coach.

"This is all a waste of time." Mr. Atkins folded his arms across his chest and glared at Niall as if he'd like to strangle him.

"Well, it may be," Niall said. "But at least I'll know we tried. Why don't ye start by checking inside yer jacket pockets?" Niall gestured toward him. "Why were ye so curious to ask Miss Sinclair about the safety and locks on the building last night?"

"I was merely concerned." Mr. Atkins shifted his weight to his right leg. "You people must be crazy allowing a woman to have so much responsibility. It's more than she can handle."

"And did ye set out to prove it?" Niall demanded.

"Prove what?" Mr. Sloane rejoined them, looking from Niall to his assistant and back again.

Mr. Napier took it slow and steady as he lowered himself

from the coach to the ground. His heavy bulk reminded Niall of a giant pumpkin as he rested his arms on his belly. "Dis is a disgwace! To zeal somezing so valuable from Mademoiselle!"

"Mr. Atkins, since ye were the last one to leave with Miss Sinclair, would ye mind checking yer clothing first?"

"Yes, I mind. This is ridiculous! Tell him, Mr. Sloane. How could he question your invaluable reputation like this?"

"He's doing no less than he should. Go ahead and satisfy him. Check the garments you're wearing and then pull down your luggage." Mr. Sloane pointed to the secured bags on top of the coach.

Mr. Atkins opened his jacket and pulled out a gun as he backed in an angle, wide enough to see the driver. "I didn't want to do this, but it looks like I've no choice. That ten-thousand-dollar brooch could do a lot for me. I've a buyer in South America who's willing to pay top price. Did you honestly think I'd want to spend the rest of my life playing second fiddle to the perfect Mr. Sloane?" Mr. Atkins slid his gaze from Niall to his boss.

"No, but I thought you were at least honorable," Mr. Sloane said, raising his hands in the air. "You don't want to do this, son. Why don't you put the gun away?"

"That's enough talking down to me like a child!" Mr. Atkins shook his gun at him. "I'm tired of being overlooked and ignored. If you hadn't been so detailed in your inventory and safeguarding everything, I wouldn't have had to wait for the opportunity of Miss Sinclair's brooch, but now I'm glad I did. It's worth a lot more than any of the pieces in my care."

"To Miss Sinclair it's worth more than money. It's a

family heirloom and has a lot of sentimental value," Niall said.

"I'm sorry, but she shouldn't have given it up to a museum."

Niall refrained from pointing out that Brynna wasn't the one who had donated it. He suspected if Brynna had been the firstborn daughter, she would have held on to the brooch and nothing could have made her part with it. That was why he had to do everything in his power to get it back.

"You—" Mr Atkins motioned to Niall. "Send your horse over to me. Nice and slow." He glanced at Mr. Sloane and Mr. Napier. "I'll leave you all tied up here with the coach, while I get away."

Niall took deliberate steps toward his horse, careful not to draw unwanted suspicion. Reaching for the reins, he coaxed the animal forward and around the other two men. When they were safely out of the way, Niall slapped the horse on the side and sent him charging toward Mr. Atkins.

Startled, the younger man lifted his gun, aimed at Niall, but the animal raced between them. Niall ran at Mr. Atkins hoping the animal would serve as his cover, but the horse was too fast, exposing him. Mr. Atkins fired. The driver jumped from the top seat at Mr. Atkins, bringing him down.

Hot iron ripped through Niall's body, rendering his muscles like liquid fire. His legs continued moving from momentum, but his weight crumbled as his knees crashed into the ground and the rest of him followed, his face eating the sandy road.

The echo of the gun continued to ripple in his ears like a foggy dream as he lay willing his body to get up. He gasped for air and the smell of charged gunpowder filled his nostrils. His sight faded to black.

Brynna wrung her hands as she paced back and forth in her parents' candy store. Not even the sweet scent of caramel, sugarplum, and peppermint sticks eased her nerves. The one consolation she had was the fact that Rob had gone for the sheriff. Niall had put himself in danger—for her—after all she had done to jeopardize his success. She had been so wrong about him.

"Brynna, you really ought to find something to do," her mother said as she added a measure of honey in a bowl and stirred with a large wooden spoon.

"Are you not upset that we may have lost the brooch that was passed down from your great-grandmother and her great-grandmother?"

"Of course, but as you very well know, I myself nearly lost the brooch had it not been for your father."

The door opened. Rob walked in with a bloodied shirt, rumpled jacket, and disheveled hair. His grim expression tore at Brynna's heart as she and her mother rushed to him.

"Son, what happened?" Her mother reached him first, touching his arm. "Are you hurt?"

"No, Mama." He glanced at Brynna. "I'm fine, but I'm afraid Niall isn't. By the time I reached them, a quarrel had ensued. Niall was shot."

Brynna gasped and covered her open mouth in shock as she tried to process Rob's words. Niall shot? Fear slithered up her spine like a serpent on a tree. "You must be mistaken."

"I wish I were. He's at Dr. Smith's office in surgery. By the time I got 'im to the doctor, he was unconscious. He's lost a great deal of blood."

"Take me to him. Now!" Brynna started for the door, but Rob grabbed her arm. "Brynna, he was determined to retrieve your brooch. Here." He placed it in her trembling hands, wrapping her fingers around it.

Brynna gripped the silver piece, the hard gemstones pressed into her soft skin. The cold brooch seemed so unimportant now.

"Thank you, Rob, but I'm more interested in seeing Niall. I'll never forgive myself if he doesn't survive," Brynna said.

"What do you mean? Brynna, how in the world could you blame his accident on yourself?" Rob asked, his eyes narrowing in confusion.

"If it wasn't for me and my desire to have my brooch returned, Niall wouldn't have been shot, and he wouldn't now be fighting for his life. Please take me to him. I want to be there when he wakes."

Several hours later Brynna sat by Niall's side in fervent prayer for his recovery. One eye peeked open. He groaned and struggled to open both eyes. Brynna leaned forward and squeezed his hand in emphasis.

"Niall, I'm here. Can you hear me?" she asked.

"Aye, lass. Ye—have yer brooch."

"Indeed, but I'd much rather have you healthy and well. Otherwise, the brooch may become a bittersweet token."

"Careful. Ye might give me the impression ye care for a

greedy Scotsman like me." He grinned then winced.

"I can tell you're going to be just fine if you've enough wits to tease me at a time like this." She wiped at the silent tears dripping from her face. "I do care about you. At the risk of my reputation and your rejection, I'll tell you the truth. When I learned you were shot, naught else mattered. I'm so sorry I've given you such a difficult time. Please forgive me."

"We're beyond that, lass. Stop frettin'. Dr. Smith says I'll be well—soon." He paused, taking a painful breath, his lips twisting in a momentary frown. "I'd like only one thing."

"Tell me." Brynna scooted to the edge of her wooden chair as it creaked. "If it's in my power, I'll do it."

"God saved my life, but I'd be happy to know ye'll be in it."

"Of course, we're dear friends and I'll always be here for you," Brynna leaned close and brushed his hair off his forehead. His green eyes watched her, an intense expression saying more than he had yet confessed.

"Brynna, I want more than that." He swallowed, his eyes blinking. He fought the effects of Dr. Smith's laudanum. "No woman has ever challenged me so thoroughly or occupied my mind so often."

Unexpected hope rose in Brynna. "Shush. Get your rest." She couldn't resist a tender smile as she bent to kiss his forehead. He drifted off to sleep.

For the next few hours, she sat by his side, read the Bible, then drifted into a deep slumber. She woke with his hand gripping her wrist.

"Brynna, ye stayed." Relief filled his voice.

"Of course." She covered his hand.

"I fell asleep before I could finish saying what was on my mind." He grinned. "I've asked yer father for permission to court ye a while back, but he warned me that I'd have my work cut out in convincing ye." He lifted the top of her fingers to his lips. "He was right."

"You succeeded," she whispered as fresh tears stung her eyes. "I'm so glad I was wrong about you. God could not have brought me a more generous man—and He had to bring you all the way from Scotland."

"Aye, a trip more arduous than crossing the Highlands, but well worth it." His voice lowered to a timbre.

With a grateful heart, Brynna leaned over and kissed Niall. His warm lips were tender and endearing. "Now I've sealed the promise of a courtship with a kiss for when you're well." She pressed the heirloom brooch into his hand. "And since I've no lock for our museum, I entrust this treasured gift to the one who risked his life for it."

"No, lass, I only did it for ye, because I thought it meant so much."

Brynna cupped his face in both her hands. "At one time the brooch might have meant that much, but while I was praying for you, God showed me how incomplete I'd be without you. Niall, you mean more—infinitely more. You're my heart's inheritance."

Jennifer Hudson Taylor is an award-winning author of historical Christian fiction set in Europe and the Carolinas and a speaker on topics of faith, writing, and publishing. Her work has appeared in national publications, such as *Guideposts*, *Heritage Quest Magazine*, *Romantic Times Book Reviews*, and *The Military Trader*. She serves as the Publicist at Hartline Literary Agency. Jennifer graduated from Elon University with a BA in Journalism. When she isn't writing, she enjoys spending time with family, long walks, traveling, touring historical sites, hanging out at bookstores with coffee shops, genealogy, and reading. Jennifer's fiction is represented by literary agent Terry Burns with Hartline Literary Agency.

A Letter to Our Readers

Dear Readers:

In order that we might better contribute to your reading enjoyment, we would appreciate you taking a few minutes to respond to the following questions. When completed, please return to the following: Fiction Editor, Barbour Publishing, Inc., P.O. Box 719, Uhrichsville, OH 44683.

1. Did you enjoy reading *Highland Crossings* by Laurie Alice Eakes, Pamela Griffin, Jennifer Hudson Taylor, and Gina Wellborn?
   - ❑ Very much. I would like to see more books like this.
   - ❑ Moderately—I would have enjoyed it more if ________________

____

____

2. What influenced your decision to purchase this book? (Check those that apply.)
   ❑ Cover ❑ Back cover copy ❑ Title ❑ Price
   ❑ Friends ❑ Publicity ❑ Other

3. Which story was your favorite?
   ❑ *Healer of My Heart* ❑ *Sugarplum Hearts*
   ❑ *Printed on My Heart* ❑ *Heart's Inheritance*

4. Please check your age range:
   ❑ Under 18 ❑ 18–24 ❑ 25–34
   ❑ 35–45 ❑ 46–55 ❑ Over 55

5. How many hours per week do you read? ________________

Name ____

Occupation ____________________________________

Address ______________________________________

City________________ State__________ Zip__________

E-mail _______________________________________